KU-428-320

About the author

Catherine Byrne has always wanted to be a writer, and began at the age of eight by drawing comic strips with added dialogue and later as a teenager graduated to poetry. Her professional life however, took a very different path. She first studied Glass engraving with Caithness Glass where she worked for fourteen years. During that time she also worked as a foster parent. After the birth of her youngest child, she changed direction, studying and becoming a Chiropodist with her own private practice. At the same time she did all administration work for her husband's two businesses, and this continued until the death of her husband in 2005. However she still maintained her love of writing, and has had several short stories published in woman's magazines. Her main ambition is to write novels, and has now retired in order to write full time.

She was born on the Island of Stroma, and was brought up hearing stories from her grandparents about the island life of a different generation. An interest in geology, history and her strong ties to island life has influenced her choice of genre for her first novel.

Since first attending the AGM of the Scottish Association of Writers in 1999, she has won several prized, commendations and has been short listed both for short stories and chapters of her novel. In 2009, she won second prize in the general novel category for 'Follow The Dove.' She has attended an Arvon Foundation course and a Hi-Arts writing program, receiving positive feedback on her work from both.

Catherine Byrne lives in Wick, Caithness.

By the same author

Follow the Dove
The Broken Horizon

The
Road
to
Nowhere

Catherine M. Byrne

Copyright © 2015 Catherine M. Byrne

The moral right of the author has been asserted.

Apart from any fair dealing for the purposes of research or private study,
or criticism or review, as permitted under the Copyright, Designs and Patents
Act 1988, this publication may only be reproduced, stored or transmitted, in
any form or by any means, with the prior permission in writing of the
publishers, or in the case of reprographic reproduction in accordance with
the terms of licences issued by the Copyright Licensing Agency. Enquiries
concerning reproduction outside those terms should be sent to the publishers.

This is a work of fiction. Any similarity to persons
who may have existed is merely coincidental

Matador
9 Priory Business Park
Wistow Road
Kibworth Beauchamp
Leicester LE8 0RX, UK
Tel: (+44) 116 279 2299
Fax: (+44) 116 279 2277
Email: books@troubador.co.uk
Web: www.troubador.co.uk/matador

ISBN 978 1784622 114

British Library Cataloguing in Publication Data.
A catalogue record for this book is available from the British Library.

Typeset in 10.5pt Book Antiqua by Troubador Publishing Ltd, Leicester, UK

Matador is an imprint of Troubador Publishing Ltd

Printed and bound in the UK by TJ International, Padstow, Cornwall

I wish to thank the following people for help in getting this book ready for publication.

As always, members of my writer's circle for support and encouragement.

Also those friends willing to pre-read, comment and give editorial and constructive criticism where necessary.

Margaret MacKay, Margaret Wood, Tom Allan, Sheona Campbell, and for supplying cover photograph, Douglas Cowie.

Cover photo by www.cowiephoto.com

Prologue

Sometimes, in the hours when sleep claimed her, Isa's dreams took her back through the years to when her love was new. To the Island of Raumsey.

'Where does that road go?' she had asked of the clay and stone track that stretched across flat moorland and disappeared over a rise in the undulating landscape.

'Nowhere,' replied Davie, but he wasn't looking at the road, he was looking at her with a glint in his eye. The sun slid over his hair, highlighting the blond wisps that lifted in the breeze. She knew he barely listened to a word she said because he was impatient to get her between the haystacks behind Jessie's wee cottage.

She laughed and sprung away from him. 'It must lead somewhere. If I'm to live on this island, I need to know my way around, have I not?' She began to run down the road leading across the gradual slope of heather-covered moorland. The scent of heather-bells and sea-salt lay thick in the sunshine and the bog-cotton danced in the slight breeze. In the sky, seabirds wheeled and cried and from inland came the lonely hoot of a curlew. In the distance, the kittiwakes glided low over the pink sea-thrift and the firth lay flat and blue, reflecting the hills of the neighbouring island, Flotta.

'Aye, that might be an idea and all.' Davie ran after her, his bare feet slapping against the hard-baked clay. He grabbed her arm. 'Go canny. There's quite a drop up front.'

She slowed to a walk. They neared the coastline and angry mother birds, shrieking a warning, swooped at their heads.

The road stopped at the cliff-top. Stone steps which appeared to have been chiselled from the flat layers of the rock-face, led to a sheltered cove. Below, waves sloshed up the shingle, rattling the pebbles.

'Take care.' Davie wrapped his arms around her from behind and his breath warmed her neck. 'Ye'll be over the edge with another step.' He pressed his face against hers and continued. 'Before they built the harbour, the men used to land their catch here. The women carried the fish up to the top.'

'The women?' Isa stared at the narrow, dangerous-looking footholds.

'Aye, for the men did the hard work catching them in the first place.'

'The fish or the women?'

He laughed.

She didn't. Unsure of his meaning, her skin grew hot.

'Want to go there?' He nodded towards the beach.

His warmth bled into her. She stared at her feet, swallowed and nodded, both fear and excitement churning in her belly.

Down the narrow steps they went, Davie leading, one hand inching his way along the cliff face, the other stretched behind to protect her.

Much later when they returned home, Jessie looked at them with her shrewd old-woman eyes. 'Where have ye been, lassie?'

Isa patted her skirt, unsure if she had managed to shake all the sand from her clothes. 'Nowhere,' she said, and Davie caught her glance. Unable to stop herself, a bubble of laughter rose and forced itself from her mouth.

With a start Isa opened her eyes, the giggle still in her throat, and blinked herself into the present. Reaching out, her hand fell on an empty space, flat and hard, in the bed beside her. She sat up. Daylight brightened the cabin window. Only the tick of the clock and the settling of embers broke the silence in the room. She pulled herself out of bed, threw her shawl over her shoulders and padded to the door of the cabin.

Davie sat where she expected, on the front step, cigarette in his hand. The smoke spiralled into the frigid air of a Canadian spring.

'Bad night?' she asked. Nightmares plagued him since an accident which had happened before they'd come here.

He said nothing, but stared at the straight empty road which stretched through the sea of waving prairie grass before disappearing where land and sky became one.

She lowered herself onto the step and put an arm around him. 'I was dreaming too.' She laid her head on his shoulder and the sharpness of bones beneath his jacket pressed against her cheek. 'We were back home on Raumsey. We were on the road to nowhere.'

When he turned to her, there were tears in his eyes.

Part One

Chapter One

1906 Canada

The train carrying Isa and her family hurtled across the Canadian prairies. The days melted into each other, air growing thick with the smell of tobacco, unwashed bodies and a less than pleasant odour from the lavatories. None of those things dampened Isa's spirit, however. With little knowledge of what lay in wait for her in Northern Alberta, she embraced each new experience with enthusiasm.

On the seventh day from when they left Halifax, the train slowed and the guard told them they were approaching Stony Plains. She turned to look at Davie and, although his skin was slack with fatigue, he winked.

'Are ye alright, lass?'

She nodded.

His eyes crinkled at the corners and, seeing the love in them, her heart warmed. They were together, she, her children and her man, what could go wrong? The weariness of the last few days fled and the blood rushed through her veins as if she had too much of it in her body. Tonight she would sleep in a bed with warmth, comfort and a full belly.

'Stay close, Wee Dan.' She grabbed her five-year-old son's hand and hoisted her baby daughter onto one hip. 'We're nearly there.'

'Ye're squeezing, Mam.' The boy tried to pull away.

'Sorry.' She loosened her grip slightly as passengers stood up, pulling boxes and cases from luggage racks.

Few people waited on the small platform; men with cowboy hats and booted feet, women with bonnets and heavy jackets, faces lighting up when they caught sight of their loved ones – but

3

none lit up for Isa. Her folks were a bit late, that was all, she told herself. But patience had never been Isa's strong point,

Clutching their children, Isa and Davie stepped from the carriage. The air was fresh and clean, but cold; the type of cold that seeps through the skin and finds the bones. Their breath condensed in small clouds before them. She gazed around, at first hopeful and finally in despair as the station emptied and a new wave of passengers swept by and boarded the train. The engine pulled away with a clanging bell and clacking wheels. The smoke and steam settled, the train disappeared in the distance, and only the high-pitched wails of a strange bird and the strong scent of pines filled the air.

From the other end of the platform, a solitary figure dressed in grey, leaning sideways with the weight of her bag, came towards them. The girl was pretty in a fragile way, green eyes, cheeks pale but freckled, hair reddish-brown, hanging down her back in a single pleat, the stray wisps tucked under a white bonnet with a frilled edge.

Isa held out a hand. 'We seem to be abandoned. I'm Isa. The man with his arm in a sling is my husband.' Davie had suffered a fishing accident back home in Scotland.

'I'm Sarah. Pleased to make your acquaintance.' The words were measured, as if they had been rehearsed, the voice small, timid. 'Someone was supposed to meet me.'

'Aye, us, too. Who was going to meet ye?' asked Davie.

Sarah shook her head. 'A man. I'm to be his wife, but I've never met him.' Her chin fell to her chest.

Isa, deciding it best to ask no more, squeezed Davie's arm to silence him. Already worried, her mind raced around possible explanations as to where her own family could be. What if they hadn't received the last letter or the telegram she sent from Halifax to confirm the time of her arrival? How would she know where to go? The address was little more than a box number. 'I...I thought my folks would be here too.' She stared at the trees surrounding the station. Trees tall enough to blot out whatever heat the sun had to offer and she fancied she heard the distant creak of wheels. Holding her breath and straining her ears, she waited.

'Someone's coming,' said Davie, relief in his words.

'But who is it?' whispered Isa as a short, broad-set man, grey pleated hair hanging down either side of his head, drove a horse and light cart alongside the platform. He swung down and walked towards them.

Isa was aware of dark skin, a slash of cheek bones, a prominent, narrow nose, and small, black eyes that met and held hers. Nut-brown skin, creased and lined, bore testimony of the many years he had been on this earth. Wearing a Stetson, a red kerchief and a skin jacket with the fur on the inside, he seemed oblivious to the sharp cold. Surely this was not the man Sarah had been sent to marry.

'Isa Reid?' His eyes flitted between the two women.

So he had not come for Sarah, but for them. Isa stepped forward. 'I expected my parents...'

'I have come for you. They call me Pierre Whitewater.' The man's accent was guttural and one Isa did not recognise. He stared at her without smiling, unnerving her. He gave the impression he was looking into her soul and reading what was there. At last, as if satisfied with what he saw, he nodded.

Davie greeted him. 'We're right glad to see ye.'

'Gonna get cold. Your clothes are no good here.' Pierre picked up their kist and threw it into the back of the cart. The horse flattened his ears and shifted position.

Isa didn't tell him it was the warmest clothes they owned. 'Is my father all right?' she asked. Sandy Muirison's heart had been bad since an episode the previous year, but according to his letters, he had recovered well.

'He is tired.' Pierre didn't look at her as he spoke.

She wanted to shake him, knock reassurances out of him, but instead she stepped back. Soon she would see for herself. Angling her head towards Sarah, she said, 'We have to take her with us.' She couldn't imagine leaving the girl here.

'Who is yer man?' asked Davie.

5

Sarah pulled a letter from her pocket and with fumbling fingers, unfolded it. 'Patrick O'Brien,' she read.

Pierre remained expressionless. 'O'Brien's spread is on the way.'

'Have we far to go?' Isa asked.

'We will be there by dark.' Pierre handed her a dusty, red-wool rug smelling of horses. 'There are more blankets in the wagon.'

The trap jolted through the town and out onto rough tracks where mud clung to the wheels and fell off in blobs making smacking sounds. The others dozed, but Isa was too distracted to close her eyes. Simultaneously, excitement about her new life and concern for her father's health fought for supremacy.

Thawing snow had left the ground wet and glistening and water rushed along ditches by the road in front of several narrow, wooden buildings which reached towards the sky. 'What are these?' she asked.

'Grain towers,' Pierre answered. 'Merchants collect the grain here before transporting it east.'

They drove past a batch of wooden cabins with logs lying sideways underneath them, each harnessed to a team of oxen. A group of men followed each house, grabbing a log from behind and running to place it in front. They repeated this action as the house moved forward.

Isa stared. 'What are they doing?'

'Men built the railroad in the wrong place. Now they move the town to the station.'

Isa could not contemplate the possibility of moving one building let alone a whole town. 'Will you look at that,' she said to no one in particular. 'If only we could have moved our wee house on Raumsey to the mainland as easily.'

The chill in the air grew more pronounced. The countryside stretched to either side, flat and desolate with few homesteads along the way. In the distance were trees, their tops ink-drawn shapes against the sky. Once they passed a lake, still as glass with a pale beach around the edges.

Wee Dan and Davie slept. Isa fed Annie, and the child, too, nodded off. Neither Sarah nor Pierre spoke again and there was a silence in the air, a stillness broken only by the whispering wind, the creak of cart wheels and the horse's hooves falling in regular thuds against the ground.

In the distance, a herd of buffalo moved over the plain like a dark sea. Once, a coyote loped across their path. A few shredded clouds moved lazily within an enormous sky. Isa already sensed the infinite loneliness of this place.

About two hours later, they pulled up at the edge of a forest in front of a broken-down shack with a barn in no better condition to the side. A cow with a large belly and prominent hip bones languished in a paddock surrounded by fencing that would not have secured a more active beast. A scraggy hound, tethered to a cart with the remains of night-blue paint clinging in places, ran at them barking, before jerking to a stop when he reached the end of his rope. With one wheel broken, the cart angled drunkenly and grass sprouted from the seams where the planks of wood met. Weeds grew high around the shack itself and one window had been boarded up, the other stared hopelessly without signs of life or light from within. Some effort had been made to paint the outer walls white at one time, but those were now streaked grey. On the side wall, a variety of farm tools and a tin bath hung on stakes hammered between the logs that made up the cabin.

'Here is O'Brien's.' Pierre turned to Sarah who was staring at the shack.

She grabbed her bag, jumped down and fixed sorrowful eyes on Isa. The dog snarled and snapped in a frenzy now. Nothing from inside the house stirred.

Pierre cracked the whip and the horse took off at a trot.

Isa twisted around in her seat. The image of Sarah, standing alone in front of a ramshackle shack in a big, empty space, pulled at her heart.

'We shouldn't leave her,' she said.

Pierre shrugged. 'This is not our business.' He urged the horse on faster.

'I'll come and see you tomorrow,' shouted Isa over her shoulder, but her words were lost on the breeze.

Chapter Two

Sarah

Sarah watched the trap pull away, then looked round the flat miles of grassland verged with thick forests and blue hills, or was it clouds, in the distance. The family had been nice, except the man who came to fetch them. He scared her with his black eyes and dark skin. She wanted to stay with Isa, move on with her to whatever comfortable home she would find that night.

She turned slowly to study the shack. Behind it, pine trees reached into the sky. Sarah shuddered, imagining all sorts of wild animals watching her from the black depths. The blank window stared. The dog ceased his barking and now whined, his ears flat. Kneeling down, Sarah held out her hand, allowing the animal to sniff her fingers and when he wagged his tail she fondled his ears. She had always wanted a pet of her own. Suddenly from somewhere nearby, came a deep baritone voice singing a song she knew, a song she often heard her father deliver while the worse of drink. This voice, however, was note perfect.

Oh Danny Boy, the pipes, the pipes are calling,
From glen to glen, and down the mountain side.

The voice grew in volume and the strains drifted into the still evening. Sarah straightened up and at that moment the low sun caught the glass of the remaining window and turned the panes to fire; a rare streak of beauty amidst the depressed surroundings.

Oh Danny Boy, oh Danny Boy, I love you so.

She picked her way up the path between weeds, broken glass and lumps of wood. A pile of green logs and an axe lay against the wall. At the door she stopped, fear of what might be inside preventing her from raising her hand to knock. Then she noticed it was slightly ajar. She pushed at it with her fingertips and, with a slight groan, it swung open. Before her, on a cracked-leather chair, sat a man with his head drooping forward, black, curly hair hiding his face, broad shoulders, thick arms bent at the elbows and big hands dangling between his knees.

He began to sing again, this time the chords muffled and the voice blurred.

Oh Danny, Oh Danny…

Sarah's bag hit the floor. The man lifted his head. A big, unclean man with a ruddy complexion. His hands shot to the arms of his chair and he pushed himself to his feet. 'By Jaysus, where'd you fall from, girl? Ye made my heart jump like a grasshopper on heat, so ye did.'

Sarah swallowed. 'Are… are you Paddy O'Brien?'

'That I am. How … how'd you get here?' He glanced at the clock. 'Holy Mother o' God, will you look at the time.'

Rays of low sunlight fell across his unshaven face; a broad face, coarse, heavy eyebrows, dark, slitted eyes with deep crinkles running from the corners. His nose had been broken at one time. Below the full lips jutted a deeply-clefted chin and a thick, short neck. The room stank of stale whisky and neglect. Sparse furniture, crude home-made efforts, littered the space as if tossed in by a careless hand.

'A family going west gave me a ride.' It was cold in here, cold enough to make her breath feather before her.

Paddy O'Brien ran his hand over his head. 'Ah, ma coleen, I should have come to meet ye.' He crossed to the table, picked up a lantern and raised the globe. 'We'll get a light and a fire going.' He lumbered around, scratching matches which burned his nicotine-stained fingers and fell to the ground before they reached the wick.

'Let me.' Sarah took the matches from his hand, lit the wick, shook the match to extinguish the flame and replaced the globe.

'Ach – ah. It's a fine girl ye are. Now the stove. I meant to have it all right and proper for ye, so I did.' He dropped to his knees before the pot-bellied range. This time he managed. The flames caught on the scrunched paper and licked up and around the logs.

Paddy stood up, swayed and wiped his hands on his trouser leg. Bloodshot eyes travelled from Sarah's face to her feet and back again making her skin prickle.

'Ye're not like I expected, no not at all. Ye look more like a girl from a convent than one from the streets.' He turned away. 'Ye'll be wanting a bite to eat.'

'Ye...s, please.' Her words sounded thin and dry. She couldn't remember when she last ate or drank anything. Even her stomach cramps had deserted her. 'Could ... could I have a drink of water?'

'Ye can that, ye can that.' Paddy pulled the lid off a wooden bucket and the cover fell from his hands and rattled on the floor. He took a tin mug from the dresser and filled it from the pail. The water splashed over the side as he as thrust it at her. Sarah grabbed it in both hands and swallowed the water in gulps.

'Sit yourself down. Down here.' He pulled out a chair and wiped the seat with the flat of his hand and then his elbow.

Sarah stepped forward, lowered herself onto the seat and fought to remain upright; the legs were of different lengths.

Paddy placed a plate of thickly cut bread and a slice of cheese before her, then took a seat opposite. 'Made them earlier. Since my wife died ain't had a home cooked meal. But things'll be different now, eh?''

The bread was stale, curling at the edges, but to Sarah it was manna.

The hound in the yard howled.

'Best let Ned in.' Paddy made an unsteady exit and returned with the dog. It bounded in, sniffed at Sarah's hands, jumped up, placed his front paws on her knees and began licking her face.

'Settle down, boy,' said Paddy in a rough voice. The hound dropped and slunk to the corner.

'I…I don't mind. I like dogs.' Sarah already missed the warmth of the welcome.

'Can't have that, no, can't have that.' Paddy shook his head. 'Got to keep them in their place, dogs and women, eh?' He gave a laugh.

Sarah wasn't sure if she was supposed to respond, so she forced a smile. Exhaustion hit her like a sledgehammer and she swayed where she sat. Longing for sleep, she glanced at the back wall where a bench covered with a deerskin rug stood. What would be expected of her this night, she wondered, shuddering at the thought of being touched by this great brute of a man, by any man for that matter. The heat from the range warmed her body, her head fell forward and she fought to keep her eyes open.

Paddy's words continued filling the room with meaningless chatter. She was aware of the glug of liquid being poured into a container and of Paddy's voice as if from far away, now singing a song about going *'off to Dublin in the green'* as the room swam and sleep overtook her.

Chapter Three

Isa

As dusk gave way to a black night and a full moon turned the prairie lands into a colourless sea, the darker outlines of buildings rose in the distance. Beside a high barn, the pale glow of light welcomed them to their journey's end. As they drew nearer, Isa saw that it was not just the light from a window, but also from a lantern which hung outside a substantial, log-built cabin.

In sharp contrast to O'Brien's, this cabin had a yard and was in good repair. Two steps led up to a platform running the length of the house, and on which stood a rocking chair. From the rafters of the wooden canopy above, hung a swing seat and the lamp.

Pierre pulled the horse to a standstill. The door of the cabin opened and Isa's mother stood on the step, a yellow glow spilling out behind her, throwing a long, thin shadow over the decking.

Stiff with cold, Isa climbed from the trap. Her throat grew thick. She stepped forward and clasped her mother's hands, felt the tremble, the calluses on the dry skin.

This close, the well-remembered features were clear. Although not yet fifty, the beauty which had once been Martha Muirison's had gone. Lines now mapped her face, hollows outlined her eyes and her skin stretched tightly over cheek-bones. Her hair, almost white, was pulled back and tied in a severe bun.

'Mam,' Isa said at last, her voice dry.

Martha blinked hard as if trying to wring out the tear which quivered on one edge of her eyelash. 'I got your telegram.' She drew in a long breath. 'You'd best come in. Out of the cold.' She turned away, indicating that Isa should follow her.

'We've fixed up the cabin your father and I had when we first came over. It's comfortable enough. When your aunt and uncle died, it made sense for us to move in here. You'll have something to eat first, of course.'

As the baby began to wail, Davie shook his bad arm free of the sling and picked her up.

A welcome wave of heat and the aroma of roasting meat met them as they entered a room almost as big as their wee cottage back on Raumsey in its entirety. A leather armchair was positioned at either side of the largest iron range Isa had ever seen and in the far chair, sat Sandy Muirison. His head rose from the folds of a tartan rug, his face paper-white, the marks of the rug still on his cheek. What was left of his crinkled hair stood on end. He blinked as if surprised. 'You've come at last,' he whispered.

Pushing down with his hands on the arms of the chair, he unfolded himself and emerged from the rug which slid and puddled to the ground. 'Isa, ma lassie.' He stood for a moment, slightly unsteady, and held out thin hands. Skirting around a wolf-skin, with head intact, lying on the floor, she went to him.

She forced saliva past the lump in her throat. Her eyes drank in each line on his skin through a mist of tears. This was not the strong, vital man she carried in her memory, but a wasted shadow, a parody of what he had once been. She wanted to hug him, longed to, but that had never been the island way. He squeezed her hands, but there was little strength in his grip.

'And you, Davie lad.' He looked past her, then extended a hand, grasping and shaking Davie's as if he too was of his blood. 'And the bairns, ah.'

'Say hello to your other granddad.' Davie nudged Wee Dan forward.

The boy lowered his head, stuck a finger in his mouth and chewed on it while keeping his eyes riveted on Sandy.

Sandy opened his arms. 'Come and see me, wee lad.'

As he went to his grandfather's side, Isa scanned the rest of the room. A long white-wood table was set for a meal. The walls were white-washed with a couple of rifles mounted to one side of the fireplace and, on the other, a framed photograph of the family taken back in Orkney when Isa and her sister, Annie, were children. She walked over and touched the glass. 'I remember the day this was taken.'

'Aye.' Sandy gave a deep sigh. 'Little did we think we'd come to this, eh? But you're here now, lass. That's the best I can hope for.'

'Take off your jackets and take a seat. Supper won't be long.' Martha held out her hand for their coats, then looped them onto a stand, smoothing the folds so that they hung neatly.

Sandy caught Isa's eye and winked. Suddenly she was back home in Kirkwall, mother always fussing, always cleaning, father rolling his eyes at the girls as if they shared a secret joke. She sniffed and wiped her cheeks.

'Who is Pierre?' she asked as her mother returned.

Martha raised her eyebrows. 'Pierre's a Metis. He's all we can afford to pay.'

'Metis?' Isa had never heard the word before.

'The early trappers came here with no women. They married into the Cree and the Blackfoot. Pierre's father was a Frenchman. Pierre married a native. Don't know where she is, like enough the Indian village. He stays there sometimes.'

'So he's not an Indian?' said Davie.

'He favours his mother in looks, right enough, but he's been a good servant. He speaks English, French and the language of the Cree. Doesn't say much, but he's very wise.' Martha's voice shook slightly. 'Without Pierre we would have no farm for you to come to. We would have been forced to sell the land and move to town.'

'But now we're here, we can bring it back.' Although Isa had surmised from her mother's letters that all had not been well, Martha's words and work-weary stance painted an even bleaker picture.

'I wish we had more to offer you.'

'Hush, woman,' said Sandy. 'The girl's just arrived. Enough of farm-talk later.'

Without being asked, Davie set Annie on the rug, lowered himself into the second chair and pressed his hand to his forehead.

'Are ye alright?' Isa remembered his injury. 'He's not been well.'

'I thought he looked poorly, what's wrong with him?' asked Martha.

'I'll be fine. Just need a wee rest,' said Davie.

'Come on, get the men a drink.' Sandy held out his arms to Annie, smiling as Isa set the child on his knee.

Wee Dan leant against his leg, still chewing his finger.

Martha opened a cupboard and brought out a beaker from which she poured a measure into two mugs, handing one to Davie and the other to Sandy.

Davie swallowed, made a face, then drank again.

'Moonshine,' said Sandy. 'And the best round here, so it is. But no one can make whisky like the Raumsey men. Isn't that right?'

'Have ye got a still?' Davie's eyes lit marginally.

'Had one once. But I never found the time. We buy our whisky from an Irishman up the road.'

Isa immediately became interested. 'Irishman you say?'

'Aye, Paddy O'Brien. Makes a decent enough moonshine though sometimes when he samples his brew too often he forgets to clean the still and we have to strain the stuff to catch the bugs.' Sandy gave a dry laugh. 'But at least the wee beasties die happy.' His words tumbled over each other before he began to cough.

'He's a rough man. This country makes rough men.' Martha plucked at the material of her skirt as if brushing away dust.

'A lassie travelled with us. Came to marry him.'

'Oh, the poor girl. His first wife was a Metis. Worked her to death. A bairn every year and all of them in the ground.' She bent down and stroked Annie's hair, effectively changing the subject. 'She's a real bonnie bairn. Our family always produced bonny girls. That's one thing I'll say.'

An image of Sarah standing in that yard, her shadow stretching unevenly over the waste of careless human habitation, filled Isa's mind. 'I'll need to call on Sarah, see if she's alright. Tomorrow maybe.'

'Paddy's right enough,' said Sandy. 'Likes the drink a bit, but he doted on the native woman. Your wee friend'll be fine. She may be the makings of him.'

Once everyone was seated and the food served, Martha sat down herself, clasped her hands, bowed her head and thanked the Lord for the meal in a strong voice, while the children fidgeted. Isa herself never had much time for religion.

'The house you're to have, it's not much.' Martha sounded apologetic as she shared out the food.

'Ah, it's fine enough.' Sandy cleared his throat. 'My good wife here made a grand little home from it. We were happy there, weren't we love?'

Martha cast her eyes downward and gave a slight smile. 'We did our best. I was happier in Kirkwall. Do you ever go back, Isa? Have you been to Annie's grave?'

'Aye,' said Isa. 'There's a man that tends the graveyard.' It was partly true. She hadn't the heart to tell her mother that on her one visit back, she had found her sister's grave sadly overgrown.

'Go fill the glasses.' Sandy prodded Martha's arm.

'Sandy shouldn't. He gets tired.' Martha looked around the assembled company. 'And all the excitement...'

'Oh, woman, will you stop talking about me as if I'm not here. If the boy wants a drink I'm about to have one with him. It's a rare thing for a man to see his family after so long.' Sandy coughed several times.

Davie accepted the drink and sipped slowly as Sandy regaled him with further questions about home and, in turn, told stories about life in Canada.

After the women had washed the plates and re-joined the men, Martha grew quiet, her chin resting on her hand, her eyelids drooping, her face, pale. The clock on the mantelpiece seemed to tick more loudly as the night went on, its steady rhythm lulling the bairns to sleep and causing Isa's own eyes to tire.

She turned to Davie. His face was too flushed to be natural. 'It's been a long journey. We'll need to get to bed,' she said.

Martha blinked, started and sat upright. 'You'll have a coffee first. Tea is no good with Canadian water.'

'No thanks. It's late.' Isa had tasted coffee once and hadn't liked the bitter-tasting liquid.

Now that they were leaving, Martha became animated, the words rushing from her as if she wanted to delay their parting.

'Thank-ye for the dinner, Mam. It was a real treat. Come on bairns, say goodbye to your granny and granddad.'

'It was fine to see them.' Martha picked up the baby and kissed her cheek, pressing her to her chest for a long moment as if reluctant to let her go, before passing her to Isa.

'Are ye all right, Da?' Isa asked.

'I'm fine lassie… but you're right…it's been a long day.'

Outside, Pierre was chopping logs by the light of the lantern. When he saw them, he set the axe down and walked towards the cart.

Isa heard her name and turned to see Martha coming down the steps.

The two women faced each other in the light spilling from the window.

'It's been so long…' said Martha.

'I know.' Impulsively Isa opened her arms and for the first time since she had been a small child, the two women hugged each other, briefly and awkwardly.

'I am glad to have you here.' Martha pulled away, her voice broken. 'But your dad. I worry so and he doesn't sleep well.'

They studied each other's faces for a moment.

'I'm just so tired…' Martha's eyes filled and she turned away to shuffle up the steps. Isa watched her go and tried to understand. Her mother had been almost distant…and yet…she always had trouble showing her feelings. Had Isa really thought she would have changed?

The wheels of the trap crunched on the still-frozen ground. The sky above was a dark canopy with pinpricks of light. The moon lit the path before them. Suddenly an unearthly sound filled the air. A strange lament that rose and echoed and merged. Not even the hounds of Hell would make such a sound.

'Ghosties.' Wee Dan buried his head in his arms.

'No, no. It's the coyotes,' said Pierre.

'Will they come near the cabin?' Isa leaned forward, a cold finger tracing her spine.

'Ain't no one been killed by a coyote. Wolves…'

'Wolves?'

'A pack isn't bad. A lone wolf, he brings danger. Without his pack, he loses himself. And bears, they get hungry before their big sleep, come way down from the hills. You need a rifle.'

Isa shuddered, silently vowing to learn to shoot in spite of her fear of guns. She had not considered bears and wolves.

Pierre turned and glanced at Davie. 'The farm is sad. Land dying. Maybe you will make it better.'

'I'm sure we can.' Isa's natural optimism had been depleted. 'There's not a better worker than Davie when he's well. And till his arm heals, I can work.' She shifted on the hard seat. 'I grew all my own vegetables back home. Made butter and cheese and salted many a piece of meat. And I've taken a plough to the land.'

Pierre said nothing.

'Do my parents really have no money? How do they survive?' It had been obvious that her father was unfit to work, and her mother, too, seemed worn out. No wonder the farm was dying. What had she come to?

'They sell cattle, but now all gone,' said Pierre.

'There are no animals?' Isa felt her stomach tighten. 'But tonight we had roast beef.' On Raumsey beef had been a rarity, the diet being mostly fish and birds.

'Before winter we killed the last steer. We can the meat or store it outside where it freezes and lasts till spring. Now it is finished. They have three cows for milk, and chickens. They will share this with you.'

'Are there animals to trap?' She thought of the ready supply of rabbits and birds back home.

'Yes. Deer, moose, buffalo. And small animals. Rabbits, squirrels, beavers. Eat the meat, cure the pelts, sell them. And grow your own vegetables. There's a patch of land behind your shack.'

'What about fish?' asked Davie.

'The rivers have many fish.'

At least in this land it seemed they would never go hungry, thought Isa.

'What about the lake we passed on the way – with sand round the shores?' Isa had imagined taking the children for a picnic there.

'It's not sand. That's sulphur, no good for nothing.' Pierre fell into silence.

Isa had never heard of sulphur. The cart trundled on for what seemed like forever; the distance from the main house was almost the breadth of Raumsey. Finally they drew close to a small homestead, little more than a hut built of turf, the roof growing with grass.

'My hut,' said Pierre. 'Other times I stay in the Indian village.'

As they laboured on, Isa looked back once. While on the train, she had heard talk of the sod huts. When the settlers first came west, it was often the only shelter they had.

At last they pulled to a stop outside a shack smaller in size than her cottage back home. Around it towered the black shapes of trees threatening to hide all manner of unknown creatures of the night.

Constructed of logs, the cabin was pretty enough. Pierre lifted their luggage from the wagon and carried it indoors. For a minute they stood, listening to the sounds of a Canadian evening. Howling wolves, and nearer, melodious coyotes, croaking frogs, the soft swish of wind through the grass. To the north a pale curtain of light shimmered, a soft voile, pulsating into the night like a cold heartbeat. The smell of strong-scented pines filled the air. A fat, white moon watched it all.

Inside the shack, a wide bench, covered by animal skins, sat in one corner. A table, two hard-backed chairs and a settle made the room appear overcrowded. The fireplace, much wider than the ones on Raumsey, with a long iron stand full of logs in the base, dominated one wall. From a hook in the chimney-space hung a cast-iron container with a pot-belly and beside it, a kettle.

Martha, true to her character, had made this place into a home.

Floral curtains hung on the window with matching cushions on the settle, deer skins decorated the walls and covered the floor.

The other room was even smaller, barely space for the iron double bed and the dresser which held a jug and basin.

'It's a fine home,' she said to Davie. 'We'll be comfortable here, will we not?'

In spite of her words, she shivered and thought of her old house, of a blazing driftwood fire, of the sea washing over the stones outside, the cosy bed tucked in a recess in the wall, with a curtain across the front, Lottie's shop just along the road and the folks on the croft of Scartongarth no more than a step away, and she already missed them.

Pierre followed them in and handed her a basket. 'Food in here. And coffee.' He crossed to the fireplace, bent to his knees and applied a light.

'Thank ye,' whispered Isa. 'I'm … I'm pleased to have met ye.'

He looked at her with shrewd, beady eyes that missed nothing. 'You are a good woman. I will watch over you.' He turned and left.

Isa lifted the lid of her kist and took out an object folded in newspaper, unwrapped it and held up the picture of a dove. Her old friend Jessie's words came back to her, *'Follow the dove and ye'll never go wrong.'* It had been her symbol of hope ever since; the one thing, apart from clothes, she had brought with her from home, and she knew exactly where she was going to hang it. In pride of place on the fireside wall.

Chapter Four

Isa

Isa took Annie from Davie's arm. The baby-cheek pressed against her own, damp and cold. 'Come on, peedie wifie. Let's get you ready for bed.'

Davie drew in a sharp breath and winced.

'Your arm?' Isa asked, ashamed that she'd paid so little thought to his injuries this night.

'I've suffered worse.' He smiled but his hesitant voice told her he was in more pain than he was admitting.

Isa took the children into the small room and wrapped them in the woollen blanket. They fell asleep almost immediately.

Back in the living quarters, she lowered herself onto the settle beside Davie in the glow of the open fire. The flames flickered up around the logs and filled the room with their warmth. From outside, the dirge of the coyotes grew louder as if they were crying for some long-lost love, their hearts breaking. 'They're coming closer,' she whispered. She had never seen a coyote before she came to Canada, never seen a wolf, and only knew of them from the descriptions in her father's letters and the pictures in a book she'd once read. She thought of them as creatures with sharp fangs and death in their eyes.

'Come here, lass.' Davie held out his good arm and she sought comfort in the warmth of him.

'They won't come up to the cabin, will they?' She glanced at the door, checking the wooden bolt was firmly in place.

'If they do, they won't get in.' His breath was fast and his face against hers burned like a too-warm stone.

'You should lie down,' she said. 'Sleep some.'

'And leave you to the wolves?'

'Are you glad we came?' She already knew the answer, for

Davie had never wanted to leave the sea and yet she prayed she was wrong, that Davie would embrace this adventure.

'Early days, lass, early days. At least you got to see your folks again.' He kissed her head, her face, her hands, and struggled to his feet. 'Come and lie beside me.'

Too tired to undress, they lay on the bench and covered themselves with the skins, and Davie fell asleep like that.

Isa, however, could not settle. The hard wood of the bench below them was unforgiving and she stared into the darkness as the fire matured and dimmed in turn. The clock on the mantel struck midnight. From the other room, Annie cried in her sleep then fell silent again.

Staring at the dying embers, the concerns Isa had tried to extinguish rose to confront her. With her decision to come here, she had walked away from her past forever. She had no regrets, but only for her parents' sake. She had not expected them to be so impoverished, so spent. It had made her face their mortality, and in doing so, face her own.

How they were all going to survive was another matter. As sleep evaded her, she twisted to find a more comfortable position. Tomorrow, she thought with determination, she would find a means to fashion a mattress, something to make her sleep easier.

A few hours after finally drifting into deep oblivion, she was pulled awake by Davie's restless moans, his sweat soaking them both. The heat rose from him in waves, his teeth chattered. He muttered and struck out at the air as if he were being attacked by invisible demons. She had seen it before, the hot body, the shivering, the chattering teeth, the hallucinations. On rising from the bed, the chill in the room hit her, drying the sweat on her body to an icy sheen.

She lit the lamp and pulled Davie's arm away from where he clutched it to his chest. Carefully, she unwound the bandage.

'Davie, ye have to lie still,' she shouted. As if her voice penetrated whatever nightmare he inhabited, he settled, closed his eyes and clenched his jaw.

The scar ran from his shoulder to his elbow. The skin was

puckered, the arm red and swollen. Isa laid her hand against it and felt the heat. 'It needs a poultice,' she said. If only they were back in Raumsey she would go for Chrissie, her sister-in-law, who had a knowledge of herbs. Here she felt useless, adrift in a sea of snow-covered grassland and inhabited by strange howling creatures, with two children, a man in the grip of fever and her nearest neighbour a strange dark man who lived more than a mile away. She had never felt so alone in her life.

All she could do was to make a bread poultice. She boiled water and bathed the area, then prepared the compress hoping it would draw out the poison.

Back in Kirkwall, she had helped her mother to bathe her sister when the bronchitis had her bad. Martha had tried in vain to keep the shivering girl warm to the horror of the doctor when he called. 'You have to cool her down,' he had said. 'Otherwise she'll take convulsions and die.'

The fire was barely alight. Isa heaped on more logs and swung the kettle over the flames. As soon as the water began to make a rushing noise, she filled a basin, wrung out a cloth and bathed Davie, leaving him wet and chattering. All her instincts told her to wrap him up, yet her common sense told her to keep him cool. She opened the door, peered out into the darkness and, seeing no movement, let the cold wind fill the room.

Where could she get a doctor? Stony Plains? It was many miles away. Pierre Whitewater was her only hope, but with images of strange wild animals prowling around, she couldn't go out in the darkness of this strange land, she just couldn't. She continued to bathe Davie until the plains were lit by the first amber streaks of morning. Only then did she look in on the sleeping children, wrap her shawl over her jacket and walk outside into the early morning, inhaling air so cold it hurt the insides of her nostrils.

Where were the wolves and the bears and the coyotes, she wondered. Did they sleep when the sun rose, or did they still lurk around? Closing the door behind her, she squinted at the Whitewaters' sod hut, no more than a dark shape in the flat distance, and set out, gripping the shawl tightly around her. The trees looked less menacing in the cold light, their shadows less dense, and above her, the welcome music of early birds greeted the day. With her heart pounding, she hurried up the road, small and alone in the enormous landscape.

Pierre answered the door, dressed as he had been the night before and holding a candle, his face an eerie mask of light and shade in the flickering light.

'My man is ill. We need a doctor.'

'I come. What is wrong?'

'Fever.' Isa touched her arm. 'A wound – gone bad.'

Inside the sod hut was a bed, a chair, a stove and a wooden cupboard leaning against the wall. Pierre opened this cupboard and brought out a few small sacks. From the contents of each, he chose some leaves and twigs and filled another bag. 'Now we will go.'

'Bring me the pot and the knife,' Pierre said, once they reached the shack. He brought out a piece of bark and began to scrape the inner surface into the pot. 'White pine.' He answered Isa's unspoken question. He added young shoots, twigs and leaves, then water from the kettle. Stirring the mixture, he brought it back to the boil, muttering a strange tuneless dirge as he did so. Once he had made a tea, he strained it through a piece of cloth into a cup and handed the steaming liquid to Isa. 'Make him drink.' Then he emptied the mixture onto the table, pulled out the twigs and pounded the mush and leaves with a stone until it was a paste. He pulled the poultice from Davie's arm and applied his own concoction. Davie winced as the hot resin met his skin. Pierre covered the lot with more leaves from his sack.

'I've got a bandage,' said Isa. 'To make sure it stays in place, like.'

Pierre nodded. 'Now he will sleep. When he wakes give him more tea. I must go.'

Isa sank to her knees beside the bench and clutched Davie's limp hand. His skin was grey and slack, his breathing shallow. 'Don't leave me now. We've come all this way. Please don't leave me now.'

24

When the children woke her, she was still on her knees beside the bed, her head against Davie's arm, her body stiff and cold. His colour had improved and his breathing was more regular.

She dressed the children and fed them on slabs of buttered bread and milk.

'Finished, Mam,' cried Wee Dan, banging his tin plate on the table.

'Hush. Don't wake yer dad.' Isa turned and smiled. 'Come away,' she said. 'Let's go outside to explore yer new home.'

Crisp, silent air met them, welcome after the confines of the sick room. Although early, the sky was milky blue with not a stir of wind. From her house, the rough track stretched in a straight line as far as her eyes carried, snow still clinging in swathes over the sea of flat land before her. Forests spread like a dark scar to the west. The piece of ground Pierre had referred to, where she could grow vegetables, was the size of a small field and would need a fair amount of digging. Apart from the sod hut of Pierre Whitewater and the barely discernible collection of buildings where her parents lived, there were no other habitations in sight.

She needed to go to the store, yet she did not want to leave Davie for too long.

Torn, she lifted her face to the useless sun and closed her eyes.

Chapter Five

Sarah

Sarah woke to the sound of the stove being stoked up. At first she thought she was still in Liverpool and her father was showing her some uncharacteristic kindness, that he had forgiven her. Too suddenly memories rushed at her and she knew there was no forgiveness. Her heart contracted as the hopelessness of her situation rushed at her. She eased herself from her cramped position, her limbs stiff and sore. A chair had been placed under her feet, her boots removed and the deerskin wrapped around her.

'Ah, ye're awake, queen.' Paddy was crouching before the range, coaxing the fire to life. 'Get yerself up now and I'll show ye the work that's to be done around here.'

Sarah rose with a desperate need to relieve herself and a strong desire to wash. 'Is… is there an outhouse?' She was cold and she clutched the deerskin to her chest.

Paddy straightened up, wiped his hands on his dungarees and jerked his thumb in the direction of the door. 'Just outside, by the end of the cabin. And if ye need a wash, there's a pump in the yard.'

The water from the pump hit her with an icy splash causing her breath to contract. With chattering teeth, she rubbed it on her face and hands and, with no towel, she used the end of her skirt then dashed inside to where the kettle had already started to sing.

Paddy straightened up. 'There's eggs needing gathering and a cow soon to calf. I'll away and check the traps. Ye can cook a rabbit stew I'm sure?'

Although not sure at all, Sarah nodded. The only stew she'd ever cooked was from a piece of scrag end when she was lucky enough to be able to afford one from the market. She had been brought up in the streets of Liverpool, being a farmer's wife was as foreign to her as if she had landed on the moon.

'Good. After, we'll go to the store and get whatever supplies ye need. Go once a month – don't look so scared, girl, sure, ye'll soon get the hang of it.'

Sarah nodded again and rubbed one hand against the other. 'Where am I to sleep?' she ventured.

Paddy stared at her for a long minute. 'Ye were sent out here to be my wife and wife ye shall be. But ye seem the kind of wee girl who wants things proper, although I can't see why, the way ye are. We'll go and see the priest today after the store and set it up. Until then ye can have the bench yonder and I'll make myself up a hammock in the other room.'

Sarah nodded, relieved yet scared. She did not want to get married, but it appeared she had no choice. Wondering how her sisters and brothers were faring without her, wondering what they were doing this morning, knowing her dad would rip a letter up the minute it came through the door, she decided to write to them anyway.

After Paddy had gone, she explored the cabin. There was a wad of bread wrapped in a dishcloth in the cupboard and, in the box on which the water pail sat, she found a chunk of lard, surprisingly enough, in a dish with a lid. She made herself coffee, ate the bread and lard, then set about tidying the room. Unable to find a mop, soap or spare bucket, she gave up and wandered outside. The cow in the paddock gazed at her with eyes so sad that it tore her heart. She approached the animal carefully, reaching out her hand to touch the head.

'Are you hungry?' asked Sarah, noticing the prominent bones. The cow watched her, then lifted her tail, squatted slightly and released a steaming jet of liquid into the ground.

Sarah looked around but could find nothing with which to feed her. 'Maybe some water then.' She leaned over to pick up the bucket, horrified to find it almost empty, the small amount of water remaining frozen into a block of brown ice.

When she returned the full bucket, the cow drank, almost

emptying it in one go. She lifted her head, droplets falling from her mouth, and once more caught Sarah's gaze with her big, sad eyes.

'Don't worry. I'll get food for you as soon as he comes back, see if I don't.' No longer nervous, Sarah pressed her face against the gentle head and finally gave vent to tears.

Chapter Six

Donald

Back in Scotland, on the island of Raumsey, the Reverend Donald Charleston stepped out of his manse into a chill spring morning. Daffodils danced along the walls of the church, a dash of colour against the grey stonework. He turned up the collar of his greatcoat and rubbed his hands together. Strangely enough the churchyard was empty of graves, the dead being buried around a seventeenth century mausoleum on the south side of the island.

Today he did not want to meet with parishioners. Today he wanted to be alone to contemplate his future. Isa would be in Alberta by now. Although he wished them well, her departure had left a void in his life and a desire to move away from this island where he saw her everywhere. He hadn't meant to fall in love with a married woman, had known there could be no future, yet, just to be in her presence had been enough.

He walked a short distance along the metal road, past long, low cottages with small windows, thatched roofs and clucking chickens round the doors; past vegetable gardens, sad and still trapped in the sleep of winter; past swollen-bellied sheep who would soon have lambs running at their heels. Islanders waved at him from doorways, from gardens, from fields.

He veered off across the heather-covered moorland towards the coast. This part of the island to the south-west was largely uncultivated, the ground being boggy and peaty and, in other parts, pure clay on which nothing grew, so there would be less chance of meeting anyone. Here and there were stone-built circles erected to pen sheep, the walls coloured by moss and lichen and the excrement of birds. Suddenly his feet sank in soft ground and he realised he had strayed too far from the path. Brown water seeped up around his rough, country brogues. With a 'pah', he jumped from hummock to hummock until he reached a more solid footing.

There were shells scattered here, dropped by birds which had scooped out the soft innards. Across the sound lay mainland Scotland and the high towering cliffs of Dunnet Head. The sun flashed from the white surface of the lighthouse, stark and solid among the muted browns, pale ochres and faded greens of an earth waiting to be reborn. Clouds scudded across a wide blue sky causing shadows to race across the earth. Above him, those birds that had not left for warmer climes or had already returned, wheeled and yelped. The sea thundered dully against the rocks at the bottom of a sharp drop leading to a cove where once the fishermen landed their catch before the days of havens and piers. On an outcrop, he could see two boys fishing with hand lines. One turned, saw him and lifted a hand in recognition. Donald Charleston waved back, tightened the coat around him, breathed in the salt air and realised in his time here, Raumsey had seeped into his bones. He loved this island.

'Be happy, Isa,' he said into the wind. He had promised to write, to reply to the letters she had sworn to send, but he knew he never would. That particular dream was over. Time to move on.

***

At the same time as Donald Charleston stared at the waters of the Pentland Firth, Isa tied Annie on her back with her shawl in the way she had done back on Raumsey. With her booted feet striking the frost-covered ground and Wee Dan running beside her, she set out to trek to her parents' cabin. She had left Davie reluctantly, but he had slept for fourteen hours straight and when he awoke, the fever had gone.

In the daytime the clutch of buildings rose from the flat landscape, the towering red barn, the long, low outhouses and the cabin itself rising from its raised foundations, its walls weather-beaten in the pure light. Wooden-fenced paddocks, one holding a grey pony and another, two goats that ran towards her bleating and shoving their noses through the bars, had been erected to one side.

Martha was in the yard, a bucket in her hand. From the distance she made a stooped figure, her thinness hidden by a buckskin jacket several sizes too large, a far cry from the immaculately dressed woman who held her head high in the streets of Kirkwall and supplemented the family income with her skill as a seamstress. She straightened and raised a hand to shield her eyes.

'How's dad?' asked Isa as she drew nearer.

For a moment Martha stared at her as if she were a stranger. 'He sleeps late.' Then her eyes, filled with distance, turned away. 'We were fine back in Kirkwall. There was Annie and you.' She gave a little laugh. 'And your dad was the handsomest man in the town. The herring fishing served us well. He was never a farmer. We shouldn't have left.' She turned to stare at Isa. 'I imagined us here, you know. Annie growing strong in the dry air and you...' Her voice broke and she stopped for a minute. 'I was going to feed the hens. We have to keep them in the barn. Too many predators in this country. Even with them shut inside, weasels and skunks still get them sometimes. Some varmint broke open the pig box last year and it high up and all.' Martha indicated a wooden box slung half way up the side of the house. 'We kill a pig at the year end, it stays frozen outside until the thaw. By then we've eaten most of it anyway. Was Davie everything you wanted?'

Isa hesitated. The suddenness of the question had thrown her. Davie, everything she wanted? No he was never that, yet she loved him in spite of his faults.

'I wouldn't have changed it. Don't you salt your ham or smoke the pork?'

'Sometimes, but just for the taste of it. Gets so cold here food doesn't go off as long as we keep it outside.'

Isa thought about that. Pierre had said as much.

'Tell me what's expected of us.'

'Questions, questions.' She shook her head. 'You've come just in time for the sowing. The thaw has set in and the frost could vanish overnight. All the ground will have to be used since we grew little last year. The cattle can graze on the prairies, but there's dangers; a pack of coyotes can bring down a cow. For now they're in the byre ready to calve. I've only the three left, and one is for you. We bring them fresh water and clean out the stalls every day.' She held out her blistered hands, 'And this is my pay.'

'Do you have seed?'

'We've saved enough from last year's vegetables, but we've nothing for wheat or corn. You'll need to buy some fresh.'

Isa thought of her dwindling cash reserves. 'Don't ye have any money, Ma?'

Martha lowered her head. 'Barely enough.'

A sudden distant crack followed by a boom filled the air. 'Oh my.' Isa clutched her chest. 'What was that?'

'It's the ice thawing in the rivers. It's more than a mile away but the noise carries. Great lumps of it break away from the tributaries. It's frightening at first, even more so to see, the water rushes so fast. You'll get used to it.'

'There's a lot to get used to. Ma, I need to go to the store. Could ye lend me the trap?'

'We use the oxen and the cart and buy a month's supplies at a time. The pony can't pull the cart. He's too fine boned. Not like those great beasts we had in Orkney.' For the first time she lowered her eyes to Wee Dan, who stared at her and chewed on his finger.

'I don't need much. I can't leave Davie too long.'

'I guess then the trap will be fine.' Martha's voice trailed off. Then she added more forcefully, 'The farm will be yours one day. Make it work.'

'I intend to,' said Isa, with enough energy to make her mother believe her.

'Good. Selling up would break your father's heart.' Martha patted Wee Dan's head. 'How is Davie?' she asked, as if she'd just remembered him.

'He's still asleep. Can I have the trap, then?'

'The tack's in the byre beside the horse stall. The store is that way.' Martha pointed up the empty road.

Isa yoked up the horse, trying to forget the thoughts which plagued her. Her money would not last long, cultivating the neglected acres in time for the sowing seemed an insurmountable task and she needed Davie to be fit and working.

She drove up the track for what seemed like miles. From time to time she saw animals; buffalo, deer, antelope, always far away, the vastness of the landscape filling her with awe. Finally, in the distance, she saw a gathering of wooden buildings. The church was easily spotted because of the steeple. Next to it was the school, a long low structure with a bell outside and small windows. From inside, came the voices of children chanting something indecipherable.

Several shacks and cabins were strung out along a wide earthen street with frozen ruts. She carried on until she came to a hotel and then the store with the name 'McArthy's' printed on a board above the door. She hitched the pony to the rail outside, next to where a heavier horse was yoked to a long cart, and lifted the children from the trap.

The remembered smell of earthy potatoes, oatmeal and paraffin met her as soon as she opened the door and for a moment she was transported back to the wee shop on Raumsey. But there were other smells here, smells of coffee, pine, of cut wood and of something she could not identify. It was easily four times the size of Lottie's wee shop and sold pelts and blankets as well as many products available back home. Several open sacks of a grain which Isa did not recognise sat along one wall. On the counter was the familiar scales and cash register and on the shelves above were various goods and lengths of material. At one end of the counter was a glass partition with the words 'Post Office' printed above it. Against the far wall stood a few tables. A couple of old men sat there drinking coffee and playing cards. Neither looked up as Isa passed.

The shopkeeper, a young lad with a pale face and hair the colour of dead hay, glanced at her and nodded, then turned his attention to the couple in front of her. The man spread a collection of pelts across the counter. 'How much?' he asked.

The assistant sorted through the skins. 'Not enough. Pelts aren't worth a lot any more. Now if you could get me mink…' He shrugged his shoulders. 'You still owe me.'

The man lifted a basket from his feet. 'Enough in here?' he asked.

The assistant counted out a dozen eggs and several large jars of what looked like jams. 'That should about cover it,' he said.

'For the love o' God, it's a crook ye are.' The man slapped the palm of his big hand against the counter.

'Aye, Paddy, there's not a bigger crook than yourself.' They both laughed.

'You folks got everything you need now?' the shopkeeper asked, grinning as he moved the pelts and jars to somewhere beneath the counter.

'Sure, this should see us out the month,' said the man.

The woman turned slightly and Isa recognised her.

'Sarah!'

The girl twisted all the way round. A smile lit up her face and it was as if the sun had risen behind her eyes. It was only then Isa noticed how desperately young the lass was, even younger than she had initially thought, perhaps fifteen or sixteen at most. The man with her was squat and beefy. His broad, rounded shoulders and short neck reminded Isa of a bull.

'How're you settling in?' Isa asked.

'Sure, she's settling in grand.' The man threw a sidelong glance over his shoulder. 'Is that not so, queen?'

Sarah's coat hung open and she smoothed her hands over her apron, her cheeks reddened and the hands sprung away, but not before Isa realised with a rush of heat that the girl was going to have a bairn.

'Ye…ah,' Isa caught herself. 'We're neighbours – well near enough. Come over, visit sometimes.'

Paddy looked at Sarah and a softness filled his eyes. 'D'y hear that, Sarah? This fine girl wants me to take you visit and drink coffee. What d'y think?'

A smile lengthened and quivered on Sarah's lips. 'I thank ye.' Her eyes turned to Paddy. 'Maybe…maybe I could go soon.'

'The Muirison place. Do ye know it?' asked Isa.

Paddy grinned. 'Ye're kin o' Sandy Muirison?'

'He's my dad.'

'Then we'll be over real soon. Grand man, Sandy, grand man.' Paddy seized Sarah's arm. 'Come, lass, help me get the supplies to the cart.'

She threw Isa a look which was both hopeful and dismayed, reminding Isa of a forsaken child.

So he was the man this girl was going to marry, thought Isa, and in spite of Paddy O'Brien's gruff but kindly manner, her heart went out to Sarah. He must be more than treble her age.

When it was her turn to be served, the assistant smiled at her, showing nicotine-stained teeth. 'You new round here?'

'Just arrived yesterday,' replied Isa.

'Irish?'

'I'm from Scotland.'

He held out his hand. 'Hector MacLeod. You'll fit in pretty good round here, then. Most folks are from Scotland. There's Duncan MacKinnon two doors down. Speaks the Gaelic and plays the bagpipes.' He gave a hoarse laugh. 'He even wears the kilt on Sundays! My own folks came from Skye way back in 1870.'

'That sounds grand, but I'm from the north.' Isa didn't want to admit she did not speak Gaelic, nor had she ever heard the bagpipes being played and had never seen an island man in a kilt. The young lad wanted to chat, but she was keen to get her goods and return to Davie.

'It was a man MacDonald who founded Stony Plains, you know. Called it after the stone people, some say.' Hector seemed determined to regale her with information.

For once she was glad the children were growing fractious giving her an excuse not to dally. Nevertheless she was curious. 'Stone people?' she asked.

'Sure, the stone people. The Indians built them long before the settlers came, stones piled in the shape of a man, arms pointing the way to go, like markers.'

'Markers for what?' asked Isa.

Hector shrugged. 'Maybe to places where the bison roamed. Maybe to find their way back to their hunting grounds. No one knows really.' He leaned forward as if to impart something confidential. 'You know, they're moving the town. Moved most of it already. Up to where the railway ends.'

Isa remembered the houses being rolled along on logs. 'The store too?' she asked, horrified at the thought of having to drive for so many more hours just for supplies.

'The store's busy with homesteaders round here. I reckon as long as it stays that way, we'll not move.'

Another couple of men in Stetsons and heavy jackets came in and drew Hector's attention.

Isa thanked him and made her escape. Stone people, she thought. Interesting. She had wondered why the area had been called Stony Plains when the ground was reputed to be green and fertile.

Back home she found Davie sitting on the settle drinking coffee, his shoulders hunched, the marks of the pillow still on his cheek.

'Pierre left a milk cow with a calf at heel and he put a few chickens in the barn. Said they were all laying.'

'That's good. Where did they come from?' Happy to see him up, she put her hand on his forehead. He was cool. 'They belonged to yer folks. Yer ma told him that it would be too much bother for you to trek over there every time ye want an egg or a drip of milk.'

With her optimism returning, she gave the children bread and milk as she chatted, telling Davie about the store, the stone people and the man Sarah had come to marry. 'We mightn't need much money after all,' she said. 'Paddy O'Brien paid his bill with skins and other stuff.'

'We might need to do that and all, the way things are going,' replied Davie.

After putting Annie down for her nap and leaving Wee Dan playing in the yard, she returned the trap to her mother.

With the horse in the paddock, Isa went indoors.

The aromas of baking bread and stewing meat met her. Sandy sat in his chair, puffing his pipe.

'You're back.' Martha busied herself making the coffee. When she next spoke her voice sounded hollow. 'It's a hard life out here. The summers are hotter than you've ever known. You almost kill yourself tilling the land and planting the crops, only to have them die in the drought and if they do survive, the plagues of grasshoppers and dragonflies come down from the north. It's not like home.'

'Don't heed her, lassie. You'll do well here.' Sandy removed his pipe and leaned back, blowing smoke rings in the air. 'Where's the bairns? I mightn't be good for much, but I could watch the bairns for you, aye, I could do that.'

'Thank you, Dad.'

Isa knelt beside him and clasped the arms of his chair. 'I met Paddy O'Brien and Sarah at the store. He said he'd come for a visit.'

Martha opened a drawer in the dresser, pulled out a cloth and began polishing the dishes from the shelf.

'Mam, please sit down.' Isa remembered Martha had always cleaned rigorously when she was under stress.

'Oh, Isa, I should have wired you. I should have never let you come. But I said nothing. My own selfishness. I wanted to see you again, and the bairns. It's lonely here, being the only woman for miles around, and your dad, he missed you sorely.'

Isa felt a small frisson of warmth at her mother's words. 'Why shouldn't I have come? Seems like it's no harder than the life we left behind.'

'But out here, sucks the life from a body.' Martha came towards her, the cloth still in her hands. 'Everything's gone. With your uncle dead and your dad laid up, the land has fallen away. You'll have to start again.'

'Hush, girl,' Sandy's voice cut through the air, sharp and stronger than it had been. He cupped Isa's face in both his hands. 'The ranch needs more folks like you. Pierre's growing old, like us all. But young blood, it can bring the ranch back to life.' His eyes scanned her face.

'Davie's a fisherman, he never really took to farming; if things are so hard maybe we could sell up, move to town,' Isa said. 'I heard on the journey here that there are plenty of other jobs.'

'Aye. Logging, paddle boats, it's a land of opportunity for the young.' Sandy patted her hand and as if reading her doubts, continued, 'Give the ranch a try first, eh? The price of wheat is soaring. Ye didn't make a mistake by coming here.'

'Listen to him.' Martha pursed her mouth. 'We've no money for seed. The cattle are so thin we'd get not a penny for them. It was the cattle that made your uncle his money. But it's the wheat where the money is now, and that needs hands to work the land.'

'We've got a bit of money left.' Isa's eyes fell on her father's downcast face. 'I guess we've got enough for seed. Don't worry about us, we're going to make it work, see if we don't.' Please God make it work, she added in her head.

Chapter Seven

Sarah

That night Paddy brought a rabbit home and slapped it on the table. 'Damn varmints got to the traps before me, but I reckon ye can rustle up a stew from this.'

Sarah stared at the rigid body. One leg kicked out, the nostrils quivered with quick terrified breaths. The bloodied leg which had been caught in the trap hung limp.

'Ye do know how to cook a rabbit?'

Unable to speak, she nodded. She had cooked a rabbit on the odd occasion, but it had been skinned and readied and bought from a butcher's stall.

'Good, then.' Paddy nodded, and went out the door, leaving her staring at the petrified body on the table.

Realising she was expected to kill it, Sarah pressed her knuckle to her mouth. She had never had to clean and skin anything before. Laying her hand against the chest, she felt the racing heartbeat. 'No, no,' she said, and, grabbing a towel from where it hung over the range, she wrapped it round the rabbit, picked it up and laid it before the fire. Then she lifted her skirt, tore a strip from the bottom of her petticoat and bandaged the leg as best she could. She trembled at the thought of Paddy's wrath, but she could not kill this animal. 'Better?' she asked, stroking the ears. 'Are ye hungry?' As she spoke, the eyes glazed over, the nose stopped twitching and with a final kick of its leg, the rabbit lay still. Horrified, Sarah rubbed its chest, tears leaking from her eyes.

At that moment the door swung open and Paddy's voice thundered into the room. 'What are ye doing?'

'It's not dead,' Sarah leaned back, her mind desperately scrabbling for some way to fend off the expected rage.

To her surprise, Paddy let out a loud guffaw. He bent down

and inspected the corpse. 'Sure it's dead. It's a soft heart ye have, but we've got to eat. Come on, I'll show ye.' He picked the corpse up and laid it on the table, laughing again when he saw the bandage.

A rush of blood reddened Sarah's face. How stupid could she be?

'For the love of God, girl.' Amusement crinkled in Paddy's eyes, 'Have ye never cooked a rabbit afore? Ah no, ye're from the streets.' He took the knife in his hand and demonstrated, deftly slitting the animal's belly open and with one hand, he scooped out the steaming entrails. 'Get the bucket, lass.'

Glad to escape, Sarah ran outside and grabbed the wall, her stomach heaving. When she returned with the new bucket, just bought that day, Paddy was parting the animal from its skin.

Trying hard not to associate this piece of meat with the dead rabbit, Sarah put it in a pot with water and vegetables. But the image stayed with her and, although she was hungry and the stew smelt good, she couldn't bring herself to eat a bit of the flesh. Instead she filled her stomach with gravy and bread.

Paddy smacked his lips and wiped his mouth on the back of his hand. 'That was a grand meal lass,' he grabbed her hand. 'It's a fine cook ye are.'

The warmth from his praise lifted her slightly. The corners of her mouth twitched.

'Ah, that was nearly a smile,' he said.

She rose and began to clear away the dishes.

'No, no. Leave the plates for now. Come sit with me a while.' He took her hand and pulled her onto his knee.

She went without resistance, but could not stop her body from stiffening.

'Speak to me, me fine girl. A man needs a bit of conversation once in a while.'

Her face grew pink. 'I don't know what to say.'

'Now don't you be feart. I'm not a man to be forcing my attentions on a woman. Like I said, it'll be wedding bells for us first.' Running his fingers up her back, he felt her draw from him.

He lifted his hands in the air. When he'd received the letter from his old pal about the lass being in trouble, it seemed his prayers had been answered. Sarah was a loose woman, her father had written, and had got herself in the family way.

She's a disgrace to me were his very words *and you'd be doing me a kindness by taking her off my hands.*

Paddy had always longed for a family and he had loved his native wife. Since she died, he missed a woman around the house. Missed her for everything; cooking, cleaning, rubbing his aching limbs after a hard day in the fields. And she had been a woman who never said no to his manly needs in bed.

Now here was a sixteen-year-old girl with loose morals and already carrying a babby. It didn't matter that it was not his, if she could carry one live child, she could carry many more. Out here in the wilds she wouldn't have much time to pass her favours around, oh no, he would make sure of it.

Young or not, her father had painted her as a woman of the world. Paddy had expected someone brazen, a sixteen-year-old who would gladly open her legs to him. Instead he got a shy girl who shrank away from his touch and had hardly spoken two words since she arrived. Oh, she could cook alright and she had made a good start to tidying up the house, but how long he could allow her to sleep on the makeshift bed in the kitchen, he was not too sure.

The priest would fit them in in a week's time, but the girl sneaked around as if he were a wolf or a coyote. Maybe he'd hold off till after the child was born. Maybe that's why all his other babbies died. Nakota liked the pleasures of the flesh, yes, right up until the day she went into labour. But ah, it was hard lying in bed at night knowing a woman with all her softness was only a wall's breadth away. After all, if it hadn't been for his kindness, Sarah would be out on the street back in Liverpool, plying her trade for a crust. By Jaysus, she was one ungrateful hussy!

He regretted that he'd drunk so much the day she arrived that he'd fallen into a stupor and failed to collect her. If only she knew how nervous he'd been. Cleaned the house, had had a wash, then just one for the Dutch courage. That was another thing he had hoped she would help curb in him – his love of liquor. To be sure, it was the loneliness that drove him to it.

As Sarah busied herself washing the pans, he turned his eyes to the whiskey jug on the sideboard. What point was there in trying to abstain? Imagining his drunkenness had repelled her, he had remained sober since her arrival. But it appeared it was he himself that repelled her, the ungrateful hussy. If he could not have the love of a woman, if she would not even give him the pleasure of conversation, then he might as well get good and drunk.

'Get me a wee dram, will ye?' His voice was harsh but what did she expect, for the love of God?

Sarah jumped, wiped her hands on her apron and took a tin mug from the shelf. She filled it almost to the brim with whiskey from the jar and silently handed it to him.

'The cow,' she said.

'What about the cow?'

'She needs more food.'

'By Jaysus, woman, is it telling me how to run a farm now is it? Sure I feed that cow every night on what little grain I have left, give her hay too, in the byre. Ye'd do well to keep yer opinions to yerself.'

Sarah's face reddened. 'I…I didn't know you put her inside,' she mumbled.

'Is it leaving her for the wolves ye believe I do? D'ye think I'm an eejit? Get me another whiskey.' He drained the mug and thrust it at her.

She scuttled away, her face aflame.

He instantly regretted his harsh words and softened his voice. 'Since ye're so interested in the animal, maybe ye'll keep an eye on her. When ye see her arch her back and lift her tail, come and find me. I'll not be far away. Means she's going to have her calf, see? And just before she does, there'll be a bag of water sticking from her rear end. She's never had a problem in the past, but I like to be here in case. Will ye do that for me?'

'Yes, yes I will.' Her hand trembled and she didn't look sure at all.

'God help us, what have I let myself in for,' muttered Paddy and held out the mug for more, silently vowing to make sure the trapped animals were dead before he brought them home. Although her softness had irritated him, it was also endearing, child-like, so different from the strong women of the prairies.

Sarah filled the mug, hoping Paddy wouldn't pass out. Although ashamed to admit it, she was afraid to be left alone with the night noises. The coyotes' eerie serenade, the hoot of an owl, the scuffle of tiny feet on the roof which sent the dog into a frenzied barking. Once she heard something snorting and snuffling just outside the cabin, and she had pressed her back against the wall, frozen with fear. She was glad the cow was safely inside.

From then on, the big, gentle animal became her confidante. She brought her water each day and spoke to her, pouring out her sorrows, telling her things she wouldn't dare mention to another human being. And the sad eyes watched her, non-judgemental and kind.

Chapter Eight

Isa stared at the hard ground still covered with a layer of frost. Almost as wide as a field back in Raumsey, the area allocated to her to grow vegetables appeared barren and sad. The land beyond also needed cultivating and only she and the aging Pierre were able-bodied. Compared to the soft, yielding earth of her homeland, these wastes were unknown and unforgiving. She thought of Davie with his damaged arm, her father with his bad heart, her mother, worked to a shadow of the woman she once was, and she looked at her own hands, softened by weeks of travel.

She returned to the barn and searched through the array of tools there. A hoe, a rusty scythe, a spade, a rake and a pitchfork. She took the spade outside and tried to force it into the earth but it barely broke the surface. An hour later, she had managed to turn over the top soil of around two yards in each direction. She straightened her back and flexed her muscles. Her hands were already raw, one beginning to bleed; she would have blisters by this evening. Eventually her skin would harden, calluses would form and the rents would pain her no more.

Behind her she could hear the steady drumming of a woodpecker somewhere within the cottonwoods growing to the side of the homestead. A strange animal, larger than a squirrel, with round black eyes appeared at the edge of the shack roof and peered down at her.

At first she started, thinking it was a rat, but then she remembered someone telling her there were no rats in Alberta. This animal had a whitish face and a dark brown body and the hair was fairly long. Its appealing looks and shy curiosity made her smile. She held up her hand and the creature didn't move, as if knowing it was in no danger.

Behind her she heard the thud of hooves and the animal disappeared in a flash. She turned around to see a rider galloping towards her. Pierre reined in his mount and the horse pranced where it stood, its breath smoking before it.

He dismounted, walked towards her and took her hand in his, turning it palm upwards. 'You must rub with the sap of the white pine.' His gaze fell on the earth she had disturbed. Something lightened his eyes, surprise, admiration? Isa was not sure.

'It is foolish to dig. Rake the topsoil. Crops grow just as well.'

'That's about as much as I can do,' said Isa, relieved. She laid the spade on the ground and spat on her burning hands. 'It's still so cold. Are ye sure the vegetables will grow?'

'It will get hot quickly.'

She gazed around her and felt her throat thicken. 'Everything's so different from my country.'

'The seeding has to start soon,' he said, after a few moments. 'Your uncle had many cattle once. Grew enough grain to feed them over the winter. And then he got ill. He sold the cattle, all but what's left now, and he forgot the land. Your father, too, is a sick man. Now the wild animals are claiming back what was once theirs, a place to roam free.

'We will make it work,' said Isa. 'See if we don't.'

'I will come with you to buy the best seed when you are ready.' With a nod, he swung onto his mount and galloped away.

Davie came out of the house, looked at the departing Pierre then at Isa and said, 'I've been thinking, we don't have to stay here. I was talking to a man on the ship who was going further west, to the coast. Prince Rupert. I could build a boat, fish there.'

'I can't leave my parents like this. I owe it to them to give it a try.'

'I don't like the land, Isa. Ye know that. There are other jobs I could do. We could take your parents with us.'

'Let's give it a year. One year, and if things don't improve, I promise I'll think about it. Uncle Jim was prosperous once. We can make the farm that way again.' I'll have to, she thought, I will. She looked up at the clear blue sky now filling with birds returning from wherever they had wintered, and knew she did not regret coming. But she had to find a way to carve out a better life for the family. They still had cows and in a few weeks, they all would have a calf at heel. They could build the herd up again. Her dad loved this farm. 'We can make it work,' she said, but with more confidence than she felt.

'One year then.' Davie held her gaze.

'Maybe two.'

Davie nodded. 'I'll go round the ranch with Pierre tomorrow.'

Isa shook her head. 'Yer arm, you can't risk re-infecting the wound.'

'It's just to see what's what, lass.'

Above their heads an arrowhead of geese winged their way southwards, their yapping reminiscent of the same flights they had witnessed back in the islands of Scotland.

In the distance Isa saw a horse and cart travelling towards her parents' ranch house. 'Davie, look,' she shouted. She had already gathered it was a rare thing to get visitors. 'Let's go over there.' The thought of seeing other faces, hearing other voices stirred her blood.

Isa was delighted to find Paddy and Sarah sitting with her parents before the large range. Martha was making coffee and on the table sat a tray of home-baked scones.

Paddy and Sandy both relaxed in the fireside chairs, sipping moonshine.

Paddy lifted his mug. 'So this is yer lass? Nice to see her again. A fine looking coleen, near as pretty a picture as yourself, Martha.' He turned to Isa. 'Jaysus, your mother fair pulled the eyes outa my head, so she did, when first I saw her. Damn good job auld Sandy here is such a fine fella.'

A blush crept up Martha's cheeks.

Isa laughed. 'It's good to see ye again, too,' she said, loving his cheerful banter.

'It's an invitation to my wedding I'm bringing ye. Ye and this strapping young man here.' He nodded at Davie who looked anything but strapping.

Sarah's hands twined together. She shrank back into the chair, reminding Isa of a small animal, hounded into a corner and too scared to move.

'Me and Davie'll be right glad to come,' Isa said.

'I'm fair sorry I'll not be there.' Sandy set his hand on his chest. 'But ye see how it is.' He sucked in some air, looked Paddy in the eye and jerked his head towards Sarah. 'Bye, but she's a young lassie, man. Are ye sure ye want to marry her?' He had dropped his voice as though by doing so the others in the room could not hear him.

Paddy made no such concession. 'For the love of the almighty, she'll be the talk of the district soon if she's not got a man.'

Sarah reddened and hung her head.

'I'm about to put a wedding ring on her finger, make her decent, like.' Paddy leaned forward and dropped his voice. 'But not a word outside this four walls. The priest'll not be happy about marrying us if he knows the truth.'

Martha sniffed and set the coffee down on the table in front of Sarah. Her eyes showed her disapproval. 'I'll not be coming, either.'

'Ye go, love,' said Sandy. 'Just because I'm an invalid there's no need for ye to stay at home. Ye see little enough of the outside world as it is.'

'I'll not leave you,' she replied.

Isa said nothing. She understood her mother well enough to know the real reason lay in what she saw as the girl's wantonness. That and the fact Paddy's crassness had offended her.

Without asking, Paddy lifted the keg at his side and refilled his mug. 'Here's to a good harvest this year.' He held up the drink, wiped his lips on his other hand, then swallowed the liquid in one gulp.

'It's good to see ye.' Isa leaned towards Sarah. 'Maybe ye'll come to my wee cabin over yonder a ways, some day.' She waved her hand in the direction.

Sarah turned nervous eyes towards Paddy who had begun an earnest debate with Davie on what was the best method to distil whisky. 'I'd like that,' she said.

47

'Ah, but there's nothing like the poteen.' Paddy settled back. 'Made it out of praties, me old fayther did. Fair warmed the cockles.'

He swallowed the drink and poured himself another.

Davie gave a laugh. 'Liquor made from tatties?'

'Aye, they needed it on the cold nights back in Ireland. But I have to say, the rye is a fair bit tastier!'

Sandy leaned over to the drawer and took out a pack of cards. 'Have you time for a game? I may get the better of you this time.'

'There'll be no gambling in this house,' said Martha. 'The devil's pictures, that's what cards are.'

'A game of gin rummy, how about it Isa? Davie, do you want a hand?'

They gathered round the table. In spite of her earlier words, Martha took a seat as well. 'As long as there's no money involved,' she said.

'I don't know how.' Sarah looked perplexed.

'Ye'll soon get the hang of it, queen,' said Paddy, as Sandy shuffled the deck. 'I come over to beat this fine man once a month or so, aye, Sandy?'

Isa picked up her cards. 'I hope we get an invite to your games. We played many a hand of cards on a winter's night back home.' Warmed by the easy banter as much as the coffee, Isa relaxed. Maybe Canada wasn't going to be so bad after all.

Chapter Nine

The Wedding

For the next two weeks Isa and Davie drove the oxen and harrows over the fields, breaking up the topsoil, while Pierre followed with his pony pulling a seeding machine which spilled the seeds they had bought with the last of their money, in straight rows. The land had not seen a plough, but both her father and Pierre assured her it made little difference. Davie tired easily and, although he never complained, she could see by the greyness of his skin that his arm still caused him pain. The ground had been badly neglected and there was neither the time nor the money to plant more than just enough to feed animals come the following winter. But spring came quickly and the seeds seemed to germinate overnight.

***

On the day of his wedding, Paddy rose and washed, wetting his hair and plastering it down, yet still the determined curls sprung up. With no suit, he dressed in a clean pair of dungarees and shirt. His jacket, well-worn, had holes in the elbows, but it would do.

'Get yerself ready, girl,' he said gruffly. 'We need to be at the chapel in an hour.'

'I am ready.' Sarah spoke to the floor.

Paddy couldn't say whether or not she was wearing anything other than she had worn every day since she came here. What he did notice was how desperately young she looked. Standing there with her scrubbed, freckled face and her hair hanging loose round her shoulders she could pass for a twelve-year-old. He suddenly saw himself as others would see him, a middle aged man with a child bride and the realisation did not sit easy with him. He grunted and went outside. From the edges of the house he gathered a few bluebells, then wandered further into the forest to where he knew the blue columbine flourished. He brought the bouquet inside and thrust them at her. She stood where she had been, smiling that irritating little half smile of hers that never reached the eyes.

Taking the flowers from his hand, she nodded. 'Thank you.' Her voice was no louder than a whisper.

'Come on, then.' Grabbing her arm, and realising she was shaking, he led her outside. Mother o' God, he thought, the girl looks like a frightened rabbit. Her very timidness annoyed him, almost drove him to lifting his hand to her at times.

He winked at the buxom women who flitted in and out of the barn. Aye, he might not be the most popular man in the district, but the immigrants would not pass up a good ceilidh; there was little enough entertainment in these parts. Most around here were Protestant and would not go to what they saw as a papist house of worship, but the celebrations now, that was a whole different matter. Furthermore they were filled with curiosity about Paddy's young bride.

A few of the temperance ladies with sober clothes, stern faces and hard eyes, stood whispering outside the small wooden building, surrounded by graves marked with white wooden crosses. The priest, Father Flannigan, an elderly man, with a pronounced wheeze and a florid face, didn't get around very much, unlike in the streets of Liverpool, where the priest was active within the community. Sarah had not met the Father before.

With her chin pressed to her chest and the flowers clutched in a trembling hand, she climbed from the trap. Paddy offered her his arm and prayed she wouldn't stumble as they walked past the onlookers. 'Straighten yer shoulders, girl,' he ordered, 'and for God's sake lift your head.'

She didn't answer, but her face grew red and her lip quivered.

The priest had brought in a couple of field hands to act as witnesses and they too stared at her with curious eyes.

After the service, the field workers shook Paddy's hand and

gladly accepted his invitation to the dancing later. Not so the priest who wished them both every happiness with disapproval in every line on his face.

Outside, the small knot of onlookers had grown and Sarah scanned the gathering briefly, hoping to see Isa's smile, but, only meeting what she saw as judgemental stares, she lowered her head again and clambered into the cart, wishing herself anywhere but here.

'Well that's that.' Paddy climbed in beside her. 'Pay no mind to them – I never have before.'

Sarah said nothing, but clutched the now-limp flowers more tightly, wondering whether to throw them away. If only her mam had lived, she would have stuck up for her. True she would have been right angry, but she wouldn't have let her father send her away. The tears leaked from her eyes, ran freely down her face and quivered on the end of her chin.

Back at the homestead, the barn had been cleared. Storm lanterns hung from the rafters and chickens roosted on the beams. A group of settlers from Ireland and Scotland arrived with musical instruments; bagpipes, an accordion, a violin, a piano which someone brought on the back of a trailer; a skinny, acned youth who played the spoons came from the village and Davie, who had been roped in with his mouth-organ. The sounds of music mingled with voices and laughter. Couples birled arm in arm with their partners up and down the rows of men and women standing facing each other, waiting for their turn to dance down the aisle in the conventional fashion. Smoke and music rose to drift along the roof space and disturb the chickens, some of which flew down in a panic to land among the dancers causing much screaming and hilarity.

There was food, too. Traditional Scottish stovies – mostly gravy and potatoes but some beef as well – and a wild boar turning on a spit outside and, of course, a ready supply of Paddy's moonshine.

Memories of island get-togethers brought a flood of nostalgia to Isa, who loved to dance. 'Come on, lazybones.' She grabbed

Davie's hand and dragged him onto the floor. 'Ye mind how we danced on Raumsey?'

'Aye, ye could dance a spring lamb off its feet.' Davie twirled her round the floor until his face was red and damp. 'Mercy, lass, don't ye ever tire?' He said at last.

Isa laughed, she had not felt so gay since leaving home. She continued to drag him up every reel until, declaring exhaustion, he refused to put another foot on the floor.

'We dinna do this often enough,' said Maggie, a buxom red-haired woman from Glasgow, who had come with her family to manage the hotel. She set one chubby hand on Isa's shoulder. 'That's ma lassie,' she pointed to a slim girl who had joined the band and was now singing in a beautiful lilting voice.

Oh! Rowan Tree, Oh! Rowan Tree!
Thou'lt aye be dear to me,
Entwined thou art wi mony ties,
O' hame and infancy.

'Wid that no bring a tear to a glass eye?' Maggie wiped her cheek.

Isa had to admit that it brought a lump to her own throat. The mood shifted, the tempo slowed and heavy-eyed immigrants sobbed about their homelands so far away.

It was then Isa realised Sarah had not been seen for some time. The sad melody finished, the band struck up a faster tempo. Isa looked around the barn and saw Paddy, his face ruddy and sweating, flinging his legs about in his own version of an Irish reel.

She slipped outside. A dim light glowed from the cabin window. Inside she found Sarah, crouched in a corner, her eyes red, her cheeks wet.

'Sarah, lass, what is it?' Isa hunkered down beside her.

'I don't want to be his wife.' Sarah wiped her nose on the back of her hand.

'It's maybe not so bad. Paddy seems a fine enough man in spite of his rough ways.'

Sarah shook her head and stared at the fingers twisting together in her lap.

'What's it like?' she whispered. 'What will he want?'

'Ye're having a bairn. Ye know what it's like.'

'It hurt.'

'It won't hurt this time. Did ye love him a lot, the father of yer baby?' This was a question she had not felt able to ask before. It still felt as if she was treading on a territory where she had no right. 'I'm sorry, ye don't need to answer that.'

Sarah covered her face with her hands. 'No, no. I didn't know them.'

Isa's breath stopped. 'Them?'

'Three. I think it was only three. I barely saw their faces. I was walking home and it was dark. They came up behind me. And they laughed. I still hear them laugh when I close my eyes.' She had stopped crying and now stared stricken-faced at the far wall, as if she could see her degradation being re-enacted there. Her voice was trapped behind her teeth and barely escaped her parting lips. 'I passed out after three, there might have been more. I woke up lying in the street. It was raining and I was wet through. And I was bleeding.'

'Oh, Sarah.' Isa placed her arm around the other girl's shoulders, felt how cold she was, felt the tremble. 'What did your parents do?'

'My mam died four years ago. My da would have blamed me. He was right mad that I was late home. He used his belt.'

'Maybe if I talk to Paddy, explain...'

'No, no, please. I'm so ashamed! I'll do what I have to do.' Suddenly agitated, she stood up and began to tidy away the skins from the top of the bench in the main room with quick, nervous movements. 'You can go home. I'll be fine.'

Isa hesitated. 'I don't want to leave ye like this.'

At that moment an almost unconscious Paddy, supported between two others, was carried into the shack and deposited roughly on the floor where he rolled onto his back and began to snore loud enough to make the rafters quiver.

Sarah collected the skins and re-made her bed on the bench.

Davie shoved his head round the door. 'I was looking for you, Isa. Everyone's leaving and the bairns are tired.'

'You go, Isa, I'm fine.' Two red dots had appeared on Sarah's cheeks and her eyes held a faraway look as if her mind was detached from her body.

'It was a grand night, was it not?' said Davie as he made a bed in the back of the cart for the children.

'Aye, it was.' Isa was still abuzz after the dancing, but her mind was in the shack with Sarah. She thought of her own first sexual encounter, of the love and tenderness shared with the lad she loved, and she thought of Sarah and her eyes burned.

'Let's just curl down in the back,' said Davie, 'The bairns have dropped off, and the horse'll find his own way home, so yer da said.' He winked at her and trailed a suggestive finger down her arm.

Isa didn't doubt it, and another night she might have tested the truth of his words, but now the pleasure of the evening had been tarnished, and her heart bled for the new bride.

Once they had carried the children indoors and laid them, fully dressed, on the bed, Davie took her hand. 'Don't be too down about Sarah,' he said. 'Paddy's not a bad sort. I'm sure she'll be fine. Let's go outside. Look at the moon.' He wore a sly grin.

Isa was tired, but knowing she would get little sleep this night, she followed him willingly. It was one o'clock in the morning, and a full moon sailed high above them. The dry heat of summer had baked the ground beneath their feet.

'Remember the night I taught you to dance?' He gazed down at her. 'A fine summer night outside Jessie's wee but and ben to the music from the Mains loft.' His voice was little above a whisper now. He slipped an arm around her waist. 'I couldn't exist without ye.' He led her across the yard. And then, while the call of the coyotes filled the night, Isa and Davie danced under a prairie moon, to music only they could hear.

***

Sarah did not sleep that night. She lay staring into the dark-shadowed corners as the moon cast its light through curtainless windows. This was not the wedding night of her imaginings when she had been foolish enough to dream. She had seen herself walking down the aisle and her Jamie waiting for her at the altar, his black curls flopping over one eye, his mouth curving at the corners, his blue eyes full of love for her. She turned her face into the pillow and wept, wishing she was dead and praying the man on the floor would not wake up. However, with Paddy not opening his eyes till well into the next day, Sarah spent her wedding night blissfully alone.

'Grand night last night.' He wiped his mouth on his sleeve after eating a breakfast of eggs, bread and dripping washed down with several mugs of strong black coffee. 'Ah well, this'll not do.' He rose, belched and without another word, left the house.

Sarah set about doing her chores with heavy heart. All day, she dreaded the coming night until she felt physically sick. She stared over the flat prairie land and wondered where she would end up if she started to run and kept on running. Then she turned and contemplated the darkness of the forests behind the shack thinking that maybe, in there, she would be killed by a wolf or a bear. Death might be preferable to what lay ahead. She shuddered, horrified by the thought. Having been brought up a Catholic, the very notion of causing her own death was a mortal sin. She crossed herself hurriedly.

Suddenly a great moose moved from the shadow of the trees. It turned its head, the large antlers catching the light. The nostrils flared and contracted, its eyes fixed on hers. Seemingly unafraid, it turned slowly, chewed some grass and ambled across her path onto the rich grasslands of the prairie. A little way behind him came his mate, heavily pregnant. The sight of them awed her and somehow calmed her. She returned to the house, resolving to bear whatever the coming night would bring. What did it matter? When had she ever mattered? Even her siblings, by now, would have turned to her sister, Eileen, for the nurture she once gave them.

Beyond the confines of the yard lay a wasteland where nothing grew but weeds. If she cleared it she could sow vegetables; eating the small animals she had watched running around on the forest floor was still abhorrent to her. Forcing her mind on this task, she searched the outhouses until she found a spade. Here in the shadow of the trees, the frost remained reluctant to surrender to the warmer weather and the earth was loath to submit to her blade. By the time Paddy returned, she had barely managed to clear a very small area.

'Ah, I've been meaning to clean that myself,' said Paddy when he saw what she had done.

'I'll get seed from the store tomorrow. What would ye like to grow? I've never had much of an inkling for vegetables, except for the praties, and they need dampness to make them sweet, aye that they do.' He handed her his sack of small, dead animals and took the spade from her.

'I don't mind.' Sarah flinched as she took the bag, her insides already churning.

An hour later, Paddy had turned over half the patch.

Sarah cleaned and skinned the animals and began to cure the pelts by laying them flat on a board and rubbing them with salt as Paddy had instructed her, bearing the stinging pain as the salt found small rents in her fingers and hands. She no longer cried over the fate of these creatures, but had developed a way of detaching herself from the reality. Soon the aroma of stewing rabbit filled the kitchen.

She was tired. Her hands were blistered and sore. Hopefully she would be so tired she would be able to sleep after the ordeal awaiting her this night. She began to gather the deerskins from her bench again.

Paddy watched her. Since he had come home she scuttled around him like a panicky mouse, never meeting his eye. God, the girl drove him to distraction. At that moment it hit him, the foolishness of marrying her. He had never forced a woman in his life and if he took Sarah to his bed it would amount to no less. He now saw her as a frightened child, because that was what she was.

A child. At least by making her his wife, he had given her respectability. When the babby came early, tongues would wag, but let them. Let them wag until they fell out.

'What are you doing, me girl?' Paddy grasped her wrist and turned her to face him. 'You'll sleep here until the babby is born. Yes, ye do that.'

Relief was like a wave washing across her face. She lifted her head and he gazed into the grey-green, solemn eyes, at the small, slightly upturned nose and the pale, wide lips beneath. Someday, with a bit of flesh on those bones, she'd be a lovely woman.

A sudden anger filled him at the man who had impregnated her. It rose in him like a tide which had to be squashed lest it erupted. Last time he'd felt like this was when his wife had died; then he'd smashed up the house. Now he turned and headed for the door. He would take his adrenaline-fuelled energy out on the land; he would dig until he was weary and only fit for sleep.

'I'll finish turning over the garden,' he muttered.

'Thank you.'

With a sigh, he batted the air, turned away and lumbered outside, slamming the door.

***

Paddy was not there the day the cow went into labour. The animal stood with her back arched and bellowed into the early air. When Sarah went to check on her, a bag of some sort was protruding from the cow's hind end, a sign the birth was imminent, Paddy had said. *Look out for that. If you see it, come and get me,* were his very words. But he had left early in the morning with his rifle and his sack, without telling her where he was going.

She grasped the wood of the paddock fence, her head turning desperately as she scanned the unbroken road to either side. 'Don't worry, girl, don't you worry.' She stroked the cow's head. Where could she hope to get help? She couldn't go to the village; she didn't know any of the people who had danced at her wedding. The only other person she could go to for help in this

57

limitless country was Isa. She looked down the track in the direction the trap had taken the day Isa and her family had brought her here. Pushing her hair back from her hot face, she set off.

***

It was the end of May. Isa filled her bucket with water from the pump to top up the tin bath she kept at the side of the fireplace. That way she had a continuous source of warm water for washing. It seemed these days, she was constantly carrying water. The weather had grown hotter, the sun a ball of fire in a white heaven, and they'd had no rain for a week or more. The ground was hard and cracked, young shoots in danger of withering before they had a chance to flourish. Now the earth sucked up moisture as soon as the dew of the night formed or Isa emptied her bucket over the plants. With sore arms and an aching back she wondered how the other farmers coped, some poorer than they were. She had met them in the store, clothes so old they barely stayed together, faces drawn with sad, hungry eyes, as they desperately bartered a few pelts for food or seed.

Wood splintered beneath Davie's axe as he hewed logs into kindling. A solitary figure stumbled towards the homestead. Isa squinted into the fierce light and, recognising Sarah, she ran forward to meet her.

'The cow, the cow.' She could hardly get the words out before slipping to her knees and taking great gulps of air. 'I don't know what to do.'

'What's wrong with the cow?' Davie, dropped his axe, hoisted Annie, who had toddled towards him, onto one hip and offered Sarah his free hand to help her up.

'I think she's going to have the calf. Paddy's away. I don't know what to do.' Her eyes were fixed on Davie as if he could be her saviour. Tears left trails down her flushed cheeks.

'I'll come.' Davie passed the child to Isa.

'I'll take the bairns to my parents, for what use would you be, a man of the sea? That poor cow was a huddle of skin and bone. She looks a might old to be having a calf. I think maybe you, Davie, had better find Paddy or Pierre,' said Isa.

'Will I not do?'

'I mind many a difficult calving back home and as many times as not, more than one man's strength was needed.'

Davie was still fragile and she often saw him rubbing his arm when he thought no one was looking. No, she feared he would not do. 'Come with me, Sarah. I'll no leave ye alone. It would be a sad day if ye went into labour on me too.'

Sarah's face reddened and she looked down at her stomach, covering it with both hands as if the child might at any moment decide to make an entrance.

'Come away,' said Isa, 'I wasn't serious.'

Sarah looked blankly at her, as if confused, before falling in step beside her.

'Ye're no to worry,' said Isa. 'When's the bairn due?'

'I … guess…' Sarah lowered her head. 'I don't know.'

Isa stopped and looked at her. Her stomach wasn't very big, so it would be a while yet. How innocent Sarah was compared to herself at the same age, Isa thought and hoped Paddy had been gentle.

For the rest of the journey Isa tried to engage Sarah in small talk, but getting a conversation was like training a snail to run. In the end she decided it was best just to leave her be.

'Have ye no idea where Paddy might be?' asked Isa when they got to the O'Brien's place. One glance told her what she had feared, the beast was far from the best of health. She did not want this responsibility on her shoulders alone.

Sarah shook her head. 'I don't know where to look.'

'Go and make a pot of coffee, then.' Isa guessed the girl would be of little or no use anyway.

Isa pushed her sleeves up. Her hand and arm disappeared inside the great body of the cow. She found the head of the calf and gave a cry. 'It's an awful big calf.' But at least it was the right way round. A breach would have been a disaster. Gently she manoeuvred the front legs into the right position and withdrew her arm, washed it in the water-barrel and dried it with bundles of straw.

About an hour later, when the men rode in, the cow still arched her back in long slow spasms, but despite Isa's efforts, the calf was no nearer being born.

Without a word, Pierre completed his inspection, then turned to Sarah. 'This animal is too sick to have a calf. Probably been bitten by black-fly.'

'Is that bad?' asked Isa.

'They destroyed half the cattle in Alberta last year.'

'We have to do our best.' Now even more anxious, Isa ran her hand down the flank.

Pierre grabbed the rope which Isa had already tied around the calf's front legs and slowly pulled. Nothing happened. Pierre indicated for Davie to join him. Together he and Pierre strained until the sweat ran down their faces and the veins stood out on their necks. Then all at once, with the squelch of blood and fluid, the head was free and the upper torso followed.

'Some size of calf,' said Davie. 'They should get a good price for this one.'

Isa marvelled at his optimism. The cow had been in labour too long. The men continued to pull, but the hind end of the calf did not budge. It had stuck at the hips.

Isa joined the men on the ropes. 'Alright,' she said. 'Let's try again.' All three gave one almighty wrench until their muscles burned and their bones ached and the cow let out a long, low bellow. Finally, in a rush of blood and water, the slippery young bull landed on the straw. Pierre and Davie fell backwards as Isa fought to retain her balance, gave up and tumbled on top of the men. With the instinct born from years of farming, one look told Isa that the calf would survive.

Pierre struggled to extricate himself from the other bodies.

Isa rolled over into the straw and, fuelled at relief that the tense moments were over, the ridiculousness of the situation struck her as immensely amusing. Her hand landed in something unpleasant. A giggle started in her throat and burst from her mouth. That ripple of laughter infected Davie and he too began to laugh.

'So you think that's a laughing matter, eh?' Feigning anger, Isa rubbed her dirty hand across Davie's face.

He yelled. 'Hey! That's not funny.'

Pierre, on his feet now, glared at them.

Davie paused. 'Pierre almost smiled then.' He looked at Isa. Laughter rocked them in its grip once more.

Sarah stared at the couple on the ground as if they were crazy.

Isa laughed some more, then sobered and struggled to her feet, helped by the still-smiling Davie. 'Is the calf alright?' she asked, although she could see he was a fine sturdy animal already fighting to stand up on shaky legs as the cow extended her great tongue to lick him clean. Isa crossed to the water barrel and began to wash the muck from her hands and clothes.

Suddenly, the cow's hind legs folded beneath her and she crumpled onto the ground. At once she raised herself onto her forelegs, but her struggles to stand upright were in vain. Any remaining laughter plunged into an abyss. Isa had seen this before, back home where the death of an animal was a disaster. If the cow's hips had been damaged she might not survive and the bulk of the livelihood of the O'Brien family depended on this one creature.

'What can I do? I don't know what to do.' Sarah reached forward and pulled nervously at the halter.

'Lift the calf to her head, let her clean him. We'll milk her and feed the young one.' Davie joined Isa at the water barrel. 'Pray to God that she'll rise afore two days are gone.'

Pierre turned to walk from the byre.

'Shouldn't you look for Paddy?' asked Isa.

Pierre did not turn around. 'This is not our business. I must find your own cows.'

Her eyes met Davie's. His face knotted in pain as he rubbed his arm, but as soon as he realised he had been seen, he caught himself and straightened up.

Isa's joints ached and she felt a might too warm. 'Is your arm still paining you, Davie?'

'Tis nothing,' he made light of it. 'Just a twinge. All that pulling.'

Sarah knelt in the straw, stroking the animal's head, murmuring softly. 'Don't worry, girl, ' she said. 'You'll be fine.'

'Paddy should be home soon.' Isa was torn between wanting to stay and help this inept girl, but needed to change her clothes, collect her children from her parents and start the evening meal while the men brought the Muirison cattle home for milking and into the safety of the paddock. She hesitated a moment longer before climbing into the trap beside her man. 'I'll come round tomorrow.' She waved to Sarah, but the lass did not see her. She was staring at the calf.

***

When Paddy returned he found Sarah sitting on the hay stroking the cow's head, the young calf beside her.

'What the…? Get that cow to her feet.' His voice was slurred and the smell of whisky hung around him.

'She won't rise.' Sarah lifted worried eyes.

'What have you done, girl?' Paddy grabbed her by the arm and dragged her roughly upright.

'Nothing, I got help.'

'Help? Who from?'

'The Muirisons. I went to them for help.'

'God Almighty! Why didn't you come for me?'

'I didn't know where ye were.'

Paddy raised his hand and brought it down sharply across Sarah's face. She screamed and staggered back. The ridge of the stall struck her across the spine.

He was immediately on his knees beside her. 'Oh God, I'm sorry. I shouldn't have done that. But if this cow dies, there'll be no milk, none for any of us.' He tried to put an arm around her, but she drew away, holding her face.

It was three days later before Isa found the time to return to the O'Brien's. She took the bairns to her parents where she borrowed the trap and drove towards the yellow distance, down the narrow track between young grass blown sideways by gritty spring winds. A herd of antelope, partly concealed by their colouring in the long grass, raised their heads and sprung away in a graceful fluid motion. Isa watched them until once again they became one with their surroundings.

She walked into the byre to find the cow dead and hanging from the beams by her hind legs, her throat gaping open. Buckets of blood mixed with oatmeal sat to one side. Crouching beside the calf, Sarah was tempting him to drink from a pail of milk.

Dry-eyed and puffy-faced, she glanced up as Isa entered. 'It was her time.' She looked through the door at the sky. 'Do ye think cows go to heaven?'

'I'm sure they do. Here, let me.' Isa knelt beside the calf and allowed him to suck her fingers. Then she slowly lowered her hand into the milk pail. The calf, still sucking, now drew in on the milk. Once she was convinced he'd got the hang of drinking, Isa removed her hand. 'You'll need to get more milk from somewhere soon.'

'She was our only cow. Paddy says we might have to kill the calf and salt the meat.' Sarah continued stroking the calf's head. 'I've called him Bobby.'

'Are you alright?' Isa watched the wan, slight girl tickle the calf's ears.

'I'll be fine.' Sarah didn't raise her eyes.

***

That same night, Paddy sold the calf. Sarah accepted it as she accepted everything in her life, with outward calm and inward frustration. As she watched him lead the young animal away, she wished she could slit the throat of her husband as easily as he had slit the throat of the cow. She suffered the pain of parting as if she had been torn from a dear, much loved friend. That night, while she prepared a meal of black pudding made from the blood of the cow mixed with oatmeal as Isa had instructed, she kept her eyes averted from Paddy. She could not bear to look at the man who had so callously drawn a knife across her cow's throat. In her head she knew there had been no other option, that Paddy had done his best to get the cow back on her feet, but her heart was torn and angry.

Paddy ate without comment. He had accepted the silent disapproval of his wife although it agitated him greatly. He shouldn't have hit her, had never raised a hand to his native partner, but the lass, with her silent ways, coupled with the desperation of losing his last cow, brought out the worst of his nature that night. He seriously regretted he had ever brought her over from Britain and even more so that he had actually made her his wife. His normally optimistic temperament sank as low as his boots.

Under Paddy's direction, Sarah had reluctantly learned how to skin an animal and cure a pelt. Since she had come here and been faced with the raw reality of slaughtering living, breathing creatures to fill a man's belly, she found it hard to eat meat, and only did so as an alternative to starving. Subsequently her face grew gaunt and her arms and legs, stick-like. She missed the busy streets of Liverpool, the neighbours and their gossip, the little shop along the road, the comfort of her bed and horsehair mattress, and most of all, her brothers and sisters. Thankfully, Paddy, although a rough man, was kind enough, kinder than her father, even when he had a drink or two in him. At least he'd only raised a hand to her once.

She knew, as a married woman, certain things would eventually be expected of her and she constantly lived in fear of that moment. As long as the bairn grew inside her, she would be safe from Paddy's advances. If only she could hold it within her for ever.

Paddy had said he would teach her to ride once the child was born and she had smiled, but quaked inside. Truth was, she was afraid of horses, afraid of their size and strength. There were many things in this land she was afraid of; wolves and bears and creatures that snuffled round the cabin at night; the swarming insects the heat brought and the mosquitoes that loved her flesh.

Isa was her only friend and Sarah missed her if weeks passed without a visit. Yet the visits were becoming shorter and further apart.

Paddy seldom took her to the store now and no one else called by. The priest had come once to berate them for not attending mass, but he was an old man with large brown spots on the backs of his hands and silver hairs protruding from his nostrils and the journey had tired him. She would have loved to go to mass, she missed the Sunday mornings and the closeness of the congregation, but Paddy was not a man for religion and she had never picked up the nerve to ask him if he would take her anyway.

In her loneliest moments she sat outside on a thick length of tree trunk, delighting in birds as bright as jewels. Cedar waxwings flitted among the sunlit leaves and shier, smaller birds, as yellow as buttercups, crept among the twigs. But her favourites were the bluebirds; a flash of vivid sky fallen to earth to sweep among the branches.

Chipmunks ran in and out of fallen trunks, gophers sat up and stared at her, different kinds of squirrels scuffled about in the trees. Emptying the traps of dead animals was the one thing she refused to do, despite Paddy's urging.

Chapter Ten

Davie

'Ye're not eating,' Davie searched his wife's face for signs of illness as she scuttled around the room.

'I'm not hungry,' she pushed her fingers through her hair. 'I've not been sleeping well since the O'Brien's cow died. I keep thinking how much more we have than them and we have little enough. This new land will take a fair bit of getting used to.'

This was not like his Isa. He rose from the table and crossed to where she stood. 'You're not keeping a secret from me?' he asked as he nuzzled her hair.

She pushed him away, impatient. 'There's no secret. There's no another bairn on the way if that's what you're thinking.'

He dropped his hands with a slight twinge of disappointment. 'It would be nice though, a new bairn born in Canada. 'My arm's better now, I guess I can match Pierre for work.' He looked into her face and gave a cheeky grin. 'What d'y think? With Annie sleeping and Wee Dan away with Pierre we could make a start now.' He wrapped his arms around her, his lips tracing the outline of her jaw and settling on her neck.

'Will you stop that.' She jerked away and to his horror, burst into tears.

'Och, lass, lass, what is it?' He pulled her to him and this time she allowed the embrace.

'I'm so tired. I've never felt so tired. And I miss home. I miss the sea and the mist and the folks and the cool evenings. It's so sticky and hot and at times I can't breathe. And ye, ye should be away with Pierre learning what ye can, no still here playing the invalid. I'm sick of trading skins and eggs for whatever I need.'

In spite of being stung by her words, he held her for a long time as she sobbed into his shoulder, then led her to the bench. 'Ye lie down. Take yer rest while the bairns are sleeping and I'll see to fire and the traps. It'll be fine, ye'll see.' He kissed her cheek, her eyes, her neck, helped her down on the settle and pulled the skins over her.

It wasn't true he was playing the invalid. He chopped wood, mended fences and did what he could to fix up the cabin. He had helped break the earth with the horse and harrows and planted seed for next season's harvest. Plans were already in his head for adding another room to the cabin once his arm was strong enough to fell a tree.

At that moment, Annie woke up, crying out for attention.

'Stay where you are,' whispered Davie. 'I'll take her to yer Mam's, and I'll find Pierre. I'll learn how to be a farmer, ye'll see.' He had never seen Isa like this. Usually she kept his spirits up.

In truth his arm still pained him and the strength he had once possessed had all but deserted him. He too missed the taste of salt on his lips, the cry of the gulls and the exhilaration as his boat plunged and heaved at the mercy of a swelling ocean. Before another year was out, he had promised himself he would build a yawl in the style of the Islands. *The rivers are full of fish and there are lakes not too far from here,* Sandy had said. *'You'll feel at home here.'* Yes, lakes without the tempestuous waters, swirling whirlpools and unpredictable tides of the Pentland Firth. But it was the best Alberta had to offer. Davie winced as he picked up the child, cursing the weakness in his left arm. The weakness he would never talk about, never admit to. 'Hush wee wifie,' he said into the softness of the dark curls. 'We'll leave yer mammy in peace for a peedie while.'

He walked outside and stared over the flat landscape, miles and miles of nothingness. All the farmers in the area grazed their cattle on the prairie but from where he stood, Davie couldn't see one beast.

After delivering Annie to Martha and Sandy, he returned to find Isa with her arm plunged in a basin of water.

She looked up quickly as he entered, extracted her arm and pulled her sleeve down, but not before he had seen the red swelling on her forearm.

'What's that?' He reached forward and grabbed her hand.

'T'is nothing.' She tried to snatch her hand away. 'Just a midgie bite.'

He pushed her sleeve up. 'Some midgie bite.'

'I've been scratching it.' She yanked her sleeve down.

'How long've you had it?'

'Only since yesterday.'

'There's strange beasties in this country. Maybe we should see the doctor.'

'No, no doctor. We don't have the money. Pierre'll have something.'

He felt uneasy. Isa did not normally react badly to insect bites.

The door opened behind him and Martha entered. 'Davie said you weren't feeling well. What's wrong with you?'

'I'm fine.' But Isa did not feel fine.

'Have ye seen the like of this before?' Davie grabbed her arm and pushed up the sleeve.

Martha gasped. 'Black-fly. You've got to keep your arms and legs covered. Did no one tell you?'

A cold dart hit Isa's heart. Black-fly. Was that not what had weakened the cow and killed half of the cattle in Alberta the year before? Was she going to die too?

''What'll happen?' She looked at her mother's worried face, suddenly thankful for the woman's presence. The woman who nursed her as a little girl, who surely would know what to do now.

'You'll be fine. Davie, boil some water, go and ask Sandy for witch-hazel.' Gone was the indifferent Martha and in her place was the mother Isa had known in her early years. The mother who watched two of her children die and her one remaining child become rebellious and ungrateful causing a separation which had lasted for years. Wrapped in her weakness and vulnerability, with aching head and limbs, Isa gave herself up to her mother's welcome ministrations.

During the course of that night, Isa's temperature peaked and waned, but by morning she was able to sit up and eat porridge.

'You must keep the arms and the legs covered,' instructed Pierre when she told him about it later. 'And eat well.' He handed Isa a mug of his home-brewed tea. 'Drink,' he ordered.

Isa shivered. She clasped her hands around the mug and forced the foul tasting liquid down her throat.

'Ye take it slow,' said a worried Davie. 'I'll away with Pierre and learn what I can about this country.'

Remembering how Davie often winced and rubbed his own arm, Isa gave a weak laugh. 'Aren't we a pair, only two decent arms between us.'

***

That first summer was the hottest Isa had ever known. Annie often slept in the shade of the cottonwood trees, while Isa washed in the tub in the yard with the chickens round her feet, birds and graceful butterflies above her head, squirrels watching her from the roof of the house and skunks and possums sometimes venturing into the grounds to steal chicken feed or examine the contents of her midden. She learned to cope, too, with the unwelcome visitors, the mosquitoes, the flies, the wasps. Wee Dan's arms and face grew brown in the sun and he seldom spoke of home. Afraid lest he might forget completely, her bedtime stories were of Raumsey and how it had been there.

Canada wasn't just hot, it was dry. In the fields, the crops struggled and the cattle grew thin. Work was different but no easier than it had been on Raumsey, although there was no shortage of food here for those who hunted. There were deer, rabbit and squirrel to shoot or trap.

In spite of the hours she spent nurturing them, the vegetables in her garden fought to survive and Isa and her family, for the first time in their lives, lived mainly on meat. Pierre taught her how and when to extract syrup from the maple tree, how to cure a pelt, how to set a trap, how to shoot a gun and ride a horse. But the battle against the lack of water and the plagues of insects raged on. In spite of all that, they salvaged enough crops to get a good return and, since the government actively encouraged wheat growing on the prairies, seed was cheap.

However, it was the sense of desolation that got to Isa. The sweeping miles of land with hardly any human habitation. The Canadians she met in the store were different than the folks she knew back home. They were friendly enough, but none seemed interested in her life before she came here and, afraid of being thought nosy, she avoided asking them about theirs. The talk was superficial, about crops, about drought, about where they would relocate to if there was another failed harvest. They were a nation on the move, still without lasting roots in this country.

She tried to help Sarah, frustrated when she could not convince her to snare a small animal for the pot herself or get over her horror of killing it by her own hand. 'I hate it as much as ye,' said Isa. 'But we must eat.'

Sarah shook her head defiantly. For hours she carried water to her vegetable patch to supplement the diet, yet never managed to sway Paddy from his love of meat. She unnerved Isa by following her with eyes not unlike a trusting hound and hanging on her every word without offering much conversation in return.

Wee Dan had taken to Pierre and, when he could, trotted at his heels. The nearest thing to a smile Pierre could manage was when he played with the child. He brought Wee Dan a pony and taught him to ride round the yard. One day when Isa opened the door to call Dan in for some bread and syrup, she stopped and instead watched the picture they made. Pierre led the pony with one hand, the other gripped Wee Dan's thigh. 'No, hold the reins, like I showed you.'

Wee Dan lifted his hands. 'Like this, Pierre? Mam thinks yer strange cos ye don't talk much.'

Isa shrank inside. She should have known to watch her tongue around the children.

Pierre didn't react. 'Some men speak too much.' He spoke slowly. 'The beasts don't have words, but I reckon they know a lot more because of it. See a wolf – he knows his place in the pack – knows what the leader wants, and do they have words?'

Wee Dan looked confused. He shook his head.

'This is something you must learn,' said Pierre.

Isa stifled a laugh. Surely Pierre didn't expect a five-year-old boy to understand the logic of what he just said.

Pierre noticed her and stopped.

'I made coffee,' she shouted, then turned and went indoors. It should have been Davie teaching his son to ride, but instead he had gone to the store with a long list of supplies and a bag full of eggs, pelts and wild honey to trade. She poured the coffee and as the aroma permeated the air, she longed for a fine cup of tea.

Pierre never seemed to be far away except for the times when he took himself back to the Indian encampment for days at a time, days when either Davie or Isa had to do his chores as well as their own work.

Isa soon got into the habit of stocking up on supplies once a month with the oxen and wagon. She enjoyed the visits to the store as it was the only time she had to mix with the other homesteaders. Occasionally she met women who, like herself, had left close-knit communities to be forced to come to terms with the vastness and loneliness of this land, women whom she had met at Paddy's wedding, and they would promise to visit or organise get-togethers which never happened given the distances and the amount of work it took just to hold body and soul together. Sometimes they would talk of their homelands with such fondness that Isa returned to the shack wondering why they had ever left in the first place. And once in a while, late at night when silence fell over the land, Isa fancied she caught the shadow of something or someone skulking in the cottonwoods and her skin crawled with the strong sensation of being watched.

Chapter Eleven

Sarah

Summer matured and by August the heat was oppressive. Sarah sat in the shade of the doorway trying to get her calloused fingers round the needle as she sewed a garment for a child with whom she felt no connection. Isa had given her some clothes which Annie had outgrown, but which would be too big for an infant. 'Who are you, what are you?' she whispered touching her stomach, talking to this unwanted burden that had ruined her life. Not that she had had much life back in Liverpool. But there had been Jamie, the lad she hoped would marry her one day. Their friendship had been no more than fleeting glances and a once-only touching of lips, both innocent and unsure.

Then, after the bad thing happened, she couldn't face him, couldn't face anyone. She had felt so dirty. Now she wondered whether, if she had told him, would he have married her anyway? Neither of them had any money, but his family had been nice. Maybe they would have taken her in if he lied, pretended the baby was his. But what would the baby look like, be like?'

Suddenly she was back in the horror of the day her father had found out.

'Are you in there, our Sarah?' Her sister, Eileen, tapped on the outhouse door. 'Da wants you. He's real mad.' Her voice was low, a whispered warning.

Sarah's stomach rose as she retched again. Strings of bright yellow liquid hung from her lips. She wiped her mouth on the back of her hand.' Just coming.'

Eileen stared at her when she came out. 'Ye look a right sight. Da knows you were sick again. Are you going to die like Mam?' Eileen's eyes watered, her lip trembled. Less than a year younger than Sarah and as thin as a reed, with the same red-gold hair and freckled skin, the terror of losing yet another member of her family shivered in her eyes.

Sarah's throat burned. Desperate for a drink of water, she ran past her sister and into the house, to be met with her father's fist. 'Whore!' he yelled as she fell to the ground. 'Who was it? Who did ye open yer legs to? For the love o' Jesus, is it not enough mouths I've got to feed?'

'Please, Da.' Clutching her throbbing cheek, she struggled to rise. 'I've got to catch the market.'

'Market! Ye'll not leave till I say so. Ye'll not find shelter in this house and bring shame on me. I'll be writing to my old pal in Canada. He's in need of a wife.'

Terror squeezed her heart. One thing about her da, he did not make idle threats.

'Please, Da, no!'

One hand grabbed the front of her blouse and he yanked her towards him so that his face was inches from hers, his other hand bunched into a fist which he brought up between them. 'Is it more of this ye're wanting, ye slut?' Drops of spittle flew from his lips. She could smell him, the oil on his clothes, his nicotine breath, his heavy sweat, all combined to make her heave again.

Her younger siblings, skinny, snotty-nosed and dirty-faced crowded in the doorway behind him, looking terrified.

A few strands of what was left of Da's red hair had fallen forward across wild eyes that bulged.

'Is it that Jamie? I'll whip the little bastard for laying a hand on my daughter.'

'No, Da, no. I promise, it wasn't Jamie.' Now her fear was for the boy she loved.

'Then who?'

'I don't know. I don't know,' she cried as her knees grew soft and she sank to the ground in a faint. When she came to herself, she was in the scullery. She tried the door but it was locked.

It was dark and she was cold, sore and hungry. 'Da,' she sobbed, pressing her face against the wood, 'Please let me out. I'm sorry.'

When she heard the key in the lock, she scuttled backwards, pressing her body tightly against the wall furthest from the door. If it was her father, she could expect more of his temper. Eileen, carrying a candle and a blanket, edged her way in. 'Da's gone down the pub. I've been warned not to let ye out. He's written a letter to someone in Canada.' Her eyes filled. 'Oh, our Sarah, he's going to send ye away. He is.' With their hearts breaking, the two girls hugged each other as they had done often since their mam died.

'Don't worry.' Sarah stroked Eileen's hair back from her brow. 'It might be nice there and I'll write, and one day I'll come back for ye.' The words were said to comfort her sister while her own heart fluttered and terror held her in its grip. She could escape now, run away, for surely life in the poor house would be better than being cast into the unknown. Even as the thought raised itself, her courage failed her. Furthermore, the punishment on Eileen would be severe.

She had been in her fourth month when the letter from Canada came, the letter which was going to shape her life.

The voyage had been bad. She travelled steerage and the quarters had been cramped and overcrowded. When the weather was fair, people went up to the deck to exercise and clean themselves, but otherwise they were forced to remain below in their own stench. A woman who had befriended her died of the cough and her body was thrown overboard sewn in a canvas bag. Sarah, sore with her own sickness and terrified of the future, had coiled herself into the foetal position and prayed to die also.

A sharp pain brought her into the present, causing her to throw her sewing aside and crouch on the floor. Inhaling quickly, she struggled to her feet and crossed to the window, petrified of all the empty miles between herself and any assistance. Then a new contraction gripped her, clutching with steely fingers, forcing the breath from her. Fear of what was happening filled her up. She knew about childbirth. Had seen her mother produce baby after baby in grunting agony. But there had always been a midwife. Then there was the last baby, the baby who died and took her mother with it.

She stumbled to the forest where Paddy was clearing trees. The air was dank here, the trees closing like a hot canopy over her head.

Passing into the shadowy darkness, she followed the sound of chopping wood. After the episode of the calf, Paddy had always told her where to find him should she need to. Today he was clearing the land to give him more agricultural space. 'The early settlers had to clear all this to grow any crops at all,' he explained. 'I'll build us a better house, with room enough for the bairn and all the rest to follow.' He had winked at her and she had silently panicked, seeing her future as a bleak unending nothingness in which she was little more than a brood mare with no choices of her own.

'Sarah, what is it?' He set down his axe and wiped the sweat from his brow.

'Please, I want Isa. It's the bairn.' This time the contraction brought her to her knees.

'For the love of the almighty, girl, is it having the child here in the woods yer after?' He gathered up his tools. 'Get yerself back home, I'll fetch you a woman from the native village.'

'No, no. Please get Isa.' Sarah had no knowledge of the Indians, only those she had seen hanging around the store with their skin jackets and long braids. Their dark eyes on her had made her feel uncomfortable and she still thought of them as savages.

'The wee woman from the settlement is as good as any ye'll find. It'll take too long to ride to the Muirison place.' Paddy grabbed his gun and straightened his back.

Sarah slunk home, tears blurring her vision. The pain was now almost constant, bringing her to her knees with every onslaught, but somehow she managed to drag herself through the front door. She wanted her mam, she wanted Isa, she wanted Eileen. When she felt the urge to push she grabbed the leg of the chair and her scream rent through the house. She was aware of her body ripping in two, then there was only blackness.

By the time Paddy returned the still body of a baby lay on the floor, cold and uncovered.

With her knees under her chin, Sarah stared blankly at the far wall, dimly aware it had been a boy. The native woman said nothing, but pulled off her own jacket and wrapped it around the child. She rubbed his chest and blew in his mouth but he remained unresponsive. She offered him to Sarah, who closed her eyes and turned away.

Paddy walked outside and put his hands to his head. What curse was on him a live child could not be born in this house? In this case, however, it was as well the child did not survive. In spite of his previous beliefs, Paddy knew he could never have accepted him, never been able to treat him as his own, for what he had just seen had shattered his dreams.

The Indian woman brought the tiny body to the door.

'Take it with you.' Paddy averted his eyes. 'Do what you want with it.'

Without a word, the woman walked away towards the village.

That night, Paddy brought in another keg of whiskey and without looking at Sarah, he downed jar after jar until he swayed in his chair as if he were on a boat in the ocean. For once he did not talk, but lifted his hand towards her in such a gesture of helplessness that she began to cry. And then Paddy did too, covering his face and filling the room with great shuddering sobs. As soon as he caught himself, he poured another drink, splashing the moonshine over the can rim and raising it to lips he could barely aim.

The dog lay beside Sarah, his head on her knee, his eyes turned up to fasten on her face. It was the warmth of his tongue against her hand which brought her out of her stupor. She became aware of Paddy, head hanging forward, a ribbon of saliva dangling from his open mouth. As she watched he fell forward, caught himself, pulled himself upright, slumped and fell forward again. After repeating this action a few times, he tumbled onto the floor and began to snore.

Sarah waited a few minutes, stood up and limped outside into the night. Ben followed her, whimpering.

Chapter Twelve

Isa put the last of her supplies into the cart and returned to barter with skins, eggs and milk as part payment.

'It's wheat you should be growing,' said the young assistant when she made her plea. 'The price is rising. The big companies in Stony Plains can't get enough to fill their towers and are paying top dollar.'

'Towers?' asked Isa, interested.

Grain towers. Several of them next to the railway station.'

'I remember seeing the towers. I asked what they were at the time. Ye think wheat pays better than dairy farming?'

'I sure hear a lot of talk standing here all day. You need a hell of a lot of cattle to make a profit on milk. A lot of folks round here are taking up more land so that they can grow a new strain of wheat.'

'But the droughts.' Isa mentally shuddered at the thought of carrying water to the large expanses of land. For now they only grew enough to feed the animals.

'Marquis Wheat, they call it. Farmers are trying out a new method. Leave a field fallow for one year – get two crops from it the next. Winter grown wheat is more successful, they say. No drought or flies in winter.'

Isa thought of the freezing conditions of winter. 'How can wheat grow in snow?'

'You sow it into the stubble of the spring wheat after the harvest, so I've heard tell. The idea is, the stubble protects the young shoots from the snow, keeps them warm. See, it's like this,' he puffed out his chest as if happy to have an audience for his new-found knowledge. 'The shoots germinate before the big freeze, then as soon as the weather warms up in the spring, it grows like billy-ho. It's ready for harvesting by April. Some of these old guys think it's a new-fangled idea that'll not work, but the government's sure having a push on.' He leaned forward and glanced both ways as if he was about to impart a mighty secret. 'I ain't going to serve here all my days. No siree. I plan to have my own farm one day. By then I'll know everything there is to know.' He nodded and stood upright.

'And this growing of grain in the winter, does it work?' Isa was more than interested now. She was familiar with the practice of leaving one field fallow every year back on the island, but it hardly seemed possible here with such dry summers and the need for every morsel of crops they could produce, but two crops a year from other fields would more than compensate. It was true spring was a wet, warm time and crops grew quickly. If a second growing was possible...ideas rushed round her head. She would not stop her efforts to build up the herd, but they could graze on the prairies. There was little to fear from the coyotes in summer when there was plenty easier prey for them to eat.

If a double crop of wheat could be grown and sold, they might yet make a profit from the farm. She decided to put it to her father this night, though she suspected he would be too set in his ways to agree right away. He only knew about the traditional methods of farming, like they did back on the islands of Scotland. The other problem would be raising the necessary cash for the initial sowing.

***

Sandy shook his head. 'I have heard more grain is needed, but the risk's too great. If we sink everything we have into wheat and the crop fails, we're doomed.'

'But there'll be two crops,' Isa insisted. 'We can't go on like this. We're living hand to mouth and nothing will ever change. We took a chance coming here, you've got to let us make the most of it.' She grasped his hand and looked into his eyes. 'I've got a good feeling about this. If we've nothing better to look forward to, I don't think I can stand it.'

Sandy shook his head. 'We'll not rush into this, lass. You're too impulsive by far. But I'll make enquiries, aye that I will.'

Later, after she had put the bairns to bed, she settled down with a ball of wool she had bought from the store earlier. It would soon be winter again and the bairns were growing out of all their clothes. Davie was still working. She lifted her eyes and looked at a darkening window.

There was a timid knocking at the door.

Isa set her knitting to one side. Davie didn't knock, so it had to be Pierre. She opened the door a fraction and peered round the jamb, instantly aware of a white face and dark-shadowed eyes and Sarah tumbled towards her.

Isa grabbed her arms, half carried her into the house and laid her on the bench. She noticed the blood seeping through her clothes.

'The baby…'

'Gone.' Sarah's eyes stared blankly ahead.

'What happened?' Isa covered Sarah with the skins and went to stoke the fire. 'Let's get you cleaned up, lass.'

'There is no bairn. Not any more.'

Later, after having gleaned the facts, Isa sat holding Sarah's hand. 'I'm so sorry.' She stroked the damp brow. 'But there'll be other bairns.' A young lassie left to give birth alone was unimaginable. Isa had been scared enough with a strange midwife and Davie's mother in attendance. She remembered how she'd cried for her own mam. But in O'Brien's shack with not even a decent bed…and the baby dead…her heart ached for the girl before her.

'It's my fault.' Sarah lay on her back staring at the ceiling. 'My fault for not wanting him in the beginning.'

'I know it was bad, the way it happened. But it's not your fault.'

'It is. That's why the baby had to die, see?'

'Oh Sarah, what do you mean?'

'It was as well. The bairn was black.' Tears rolled across her face and pooled in her ear. 'He was as black as the black-hearted man who fathered him.' Only her lips moved. 'It was as well,' she repeated.

'Ye're not to worry. I'll look after ye.' Dismayed, Isa went to collect a woollen blanket and tucked it around Sarah. 'Sleep now.' As Sarah's eyes closed, Isa tiptoed away and tried to pick up her knitting, but her heart was aching, her mind too full of shocked sorrow to knit a stitch.

When Davie came home, tired and dirty, the last thing he expected was Sarah asleep on his bed. Isa led him outside to where the air was still and mild and they were out of earshot. There she told him the story in brief. 'We can't send her back.'

'I'm right sorry for the lass and all, but we can't keep her here,' said Davie. 'Where's she going to sleep?'

'I'll make a bed for her on the floor tonight.' Isa paced the ground for a moment. 'Tomorrow we have to speak to Paddy. Once he knows the whole story, I'm sure he'll look more kindly on her. He doesn't seem like a bad man.'

'Aye, it's still a shame. The poor lass, she's but a bairn herself. I wish there was more we could do, but ye see the impossibility of it?'

'I do.' She twiddled with the material of her skirt. 'But Paddy's old enough to be her dad. I can't imagine him touching her…like that.' She shuddered. Their eyes met in the fading light.

Davie shook his head. 'She agreed to marry him. No one forced her.'

'Mayhaps she'd little choice.' Isa inhaled. 'There's something else I want to talk to you about.' She glanced to where the clouds had begun to pile on top of each other over the horizon and stopped, mid-sentence. A slash of crimson divided the sky from the land and turned the distant grasslands into a sea of orange and gold.

Before her eyes, the clouds moved and became a rolling blackness which gathered strength and density. They began to move in circles as if chasing each other around the heavens, before merging and turning into a cone shape. From the centre of the forest rose a black, pointed column which joined the downward funnel. Suddenly the roar of thunder filled the air around them. Lightning flashed from the frenzied mass. Distant trees fell like stacks of dominoes; branches, dust, leaves and timber swirled through the air. Wind rose and rain drummed into their faces and soaked her clothes within seconds.

She grabbed Davie's arm in terror. 'What is it, what's happening?'

'Indoors, quickly now,' said Davie. 'It's a tornado, Pierre told me about them.'

Unable to move Isa stared in horrified fascination as the inky column headed their way at a terrific speed.

The door swung open and Sarah rushed out, crying, straight into Davie's arms and clung to him like a limpet. 'It's the damnation of hell. It's come to get me. Come to get me for my sinful ways,' she cried, as Davie dragged her towards the house, the wind strong enough to knock them off their feet. 'Get the bairns, we'll need to lie under the bed, it's the safest place,' he shouted to Isa above the roar.

Jolted out of her nightmare, Isa struggled with them into the house, where she leaned against the door to shut it against the determined gale.

'Mammy, what's happening?' cried Wee Dan, from where he crouched in the corner in terror.

Isa picked up Annie from the floor, and, grabbing Wee Dan's arm, pulled them into the back room.

By now Davie had pushed Sarah before him and all three adults and two children crawled under the iron bedstead just as the tornado struck the end of the cabin. The roar filled their minds and heads and drowned the screams of the children. The ground beneath them shook. There was crashing and splintering, something fell, hurtling onto the top of the bed. The room trembled, there was a great ripping sound and then, just as abruptly, the roaring died away. After a few seconds, Isa lifted her head and dared to open her eyes. Miraculously, the room was still intact, but filled with dust. 'Is everyone alright?' she asked.

Davie was already crawling from their refuge. He sat up and

pulled a screaming Annie from her mother's arms. 'The roof's gone,' he said.

'It's over now.' Isa hugged Wee Dan, who still clung to her, whimpering, and passed him into his father's waiting arms before clambering out herself.

'Sarah,' shouted Isa.

Sarah lay still, with her arms over her head.

'Sarah, it's over.' Isa shook her arm. She didn't move.

'Let me.' Davie reached in, and, grabbing Sarah by the arms, pulled her out. She lifted her head, eyes round and filled with naked terror, she pushed Davie away and struggled to her feet. She ran from them and threw open the door, where she stopped and covered her mouth with her hands.

Isa and Davie came up behind her. Isa gasped. One end of the cabin had been completely destroyed, the wall where the chimney had been was now an open space, littered with timber, her pots and pans scattered, the table lying on its back, remarkably unbroken.

'It's all my fault.' Sarah's fists grabbed handfuls of her hair which she pulled and twisted. She started to scream.

Isa tore Sarah's hands away from her head, slapped her, then, grabbing her by the shoulders shook her several times. 'Stop this,' she shrieked. 'The bairns are scared enough.' She turned to Davie who was standing by the gaping void that was once a wall. 'What's happening out there?'

'Everything's gone,' he said, 'All the outhouses.'

'The animals...'

Davie went outside and looked around. Everything had gone eerily quiet. No birds sung, no dogs barked, no chickens cackled round his feet. 'They're not here. They must have escaped. They'll be terrified, probably miles away.'

Isa left the shivering, sobbing Sarah and joined her man. Nothing remained of the tornado except a fading funnel in the distance. 'It could...could have...' Her voice wavered and failed.

'They don't happen often, they say, thank God.' Davie's face was white, his voice uncertain. He swallowed. His eyes slid past

Isa to Sarah. 'Come on, lass.' He crossed to where she stood, eyes and mouth clamped shut, her body jerking as she fought to keep panic at bay. He hugged her. 'It's over now.'

She flung her arms around him and buried her face in his chest. His eyes met Isa's over her head and he shrugged.

'Are we safe?' Wee Dan rubbed his eyes. Isa stroked his hair and kissed his cheek.

Davie took Sarah by the shoulders and set her gently aside. 'Ye're alright now, everything is alright now.'

Sarah hiccupped and wiped her eyes on the back of her hand. 'I'm sorry,' she said again. 'I've been a bad person. My baby died and I was glad. I thought…I thought…' she started to sob again, but quietly now. 'I brought this on us.'

'Don't be daft. Tornados happen in this country.' Davie turned to Isa, 'Come on, let's get ye all to your parents' place.'

As they approached the main building, Martha ran to meet them. 'You're alright?' she cried, 'Thank God. What happened? I was so worried.'

'We're fine,' said Isa, 'but the shack has gone. We'll have to move in here.'

'Yes, of course. Until it's rebuilt.' Her eyes fell on Sarah. 'Why's she here?'

'Oh, Mam,' Isa's legs suddenly began to shake. Now the danger was over, she had no power to argue. 'Can she stay here tonight? She can sleep on the floor. We'll talk tomorrow.' The full impact of what had happened struck her, her strength failed her and tears burned the insides of her eyelids. Davie put an arm around her and she leaned against him, realising that he too was trembling.

'Yes, tomorrow. Come in. Your Dad's worried.' Martha took Annie in her arms and led the little party indoors.

After her parents were in bed and the children settled, Isa returned to the main room. Davie and Sarah were sitting one at either side of the table. Sarah still shook, her small white hands clasping and unclasping. Isa heard her teeth chatter, saw the pallor in her face and the tangles in her hair. 'Come away. The danger's over. Let's try and get some sleep.'

'Do … do ye think Paddy'll be alright?' asked Sarah.

'I'm sure he'll be fine. He's seen more tornados than we have. We'll check on him tomorrow.'

'I hope he's fine, but I can't go back.' Sarah slowly lowered herself onto the rug which Isa had placed on the floor for her and curled herself into a ball under the red wool blanket.

Outside, the wind had died leaving an utter silence. Isa sat on the bench that would serve as their bed and buried her head in her hands. She couldn't start crying now, she couldn't.

'Come on, lass, tomorrow's another day.' Davie pulled back the blankets and helped her into bed. She lay down, but stared at the ceiling. Sometimes it seemed to her that the problems in this land were insurmountable. One more fright like that, and she'd pack up her family and find a way to take them back home where the sturdy wee houses clinging to the shoreline stood fast against the strongest gales. How she wished she had the security of quarried stone and broad walls around her now. Even Sarah was snoring gently by the time she closed her eyes.

Isa woke in the early morning to the sound of the fire being stoked up and the smell of coffee.

'Ah ye're awake.' Sarah immediately poured a cup of the steaming liquid and placed it in Isa's hands. She peered at Davie who opened one eye, uttered a curse under his breath and turned away.

Isa pulled herself upright. 'Thank-ye, Sarah.' The coffee was welcome, the presence of the girl less so. She was used to having the house to herself in the time it took for her family to wake up.

'I've brought a bucket of water in, too. It's easy having a pump so close to the house.'

Isa looked at the clock on the mantel. Five-thirty. It was barely light. The girl must have been up for at least an hour.

'I could be a real help.' Sarah lowered her eyes. 'I would milk the cows, but I don't know how. They're making a fair bit of noise out there.'

Isa swung her feet out of bed. 'Aye, ye would be a help, but ye can't stay.'

Sarah's face fell. Her fingers raked her hair. 'I could sleep in the barn. I'm sorry about last night – I was scared.'

'We all were. But it's not up to me. This isn't my house and ye've got a man. He'll be looking for ye.'

From behind the wall came a child's cry. Sarah immediately jumped up. 'I'll get her.' She rushed from the room.

By now Davie was fully awake. 'She can't stay here another night, ye know she can't.' He struggled out of bed and began to pull his trousers on and was hopping about on one leg when Sarah returned, Annie in her arms. Her eyes widened, her face reddened and she turned away. 'I'm sus… sorry,' she stammered.

'Good God,' muttered Davie. Struggling to make himself decent, he fell over and landed sideways on the bed, one leg of his trousers still round his knee.

Isa laughed.

'No laughing matter.' Davie's own face grew more scarlet than Isa had ever seen it.

Sarah stood with her head hanging. 'I'm sorry. It'll not happen again.'

'Ye're right, it'll not. Isa's parents can't give shelter to another man's wife.' Davie's voice was strained.

Isa turned from Sarah's stricken face, crossed to the range to find a pan with porridge already there.

Davie swallowed his coffee. 'I won't wait for anything more, I have to go, check the damage.' He kissed Annie's cheek and swung out the door.

'But you always eat your porri… 'Isa's voice faded as the door slammed.

Seconds later he returned. 'Look at this.' He held the door open. There, tied to the paddock fence was their cow, calf and pony.

'Who…?' Words failed her.

'Pierre?' Davie shrugged. 'We'll find out later. But I'm right glad the pony's here.' He walked over and grabbed the halter.

By the time Isa came back indoors, Martha was also out of bed, and accepting a cup of coffee from Sarah.

'Davie doesn't want me here,' said Sarah.

'Aw, lass, ye can't stay. But ye can come over as often as ye like.' Isa looked at Martha, who, for once, remained silent.

Sarah stared at the ground for a second, then rushed to the cupboard, bringing out the milk pitcher and filling a mug for Annie. 'Can ye show me how to milk the cows? I can do that for ye.'

'She's right. She could be a help,' said Martha. 'Things are hard round here, and my back's paining me badly. I don't know how much longer I can go on. If she doesn't want pay…'

'She's Paddy's wife.' Isa sighed, surprised at her mother's words. She had not stopped to think of how Martha was coping with her father's bad health and all the extra work expected of her. Now she took a long look at the woman before her. Her skin was grey, her eyes heavy, weary and downcast.

'I'm a hard worker.' Sarah looked up with pleading eyes.

'I'm sorry. Ye can't stay unless Paddy allows it.' Persuading Sarah to return to her husband was not going to be easy especially since Martha had warmed to the idea of having unpaid help around the house.

She tried to imagine how it would feel to be raped by three men, to have a father who sent you to the other side of the world to marry a middle-aged man you didn't know, to have no one to turn to but strangers. Her heart went out to the girl, but she didn't want to fall out with Paddy. She could see no way to help her other than by being her friend.

***

As it was, Paddy came looking for her. He rode up to the homestead about an hour later. 'What a twister last night. Rattled right by the house and woke me up. I didn't know where Sarah was, sent me clean out of my mind with worry, so it did.'

'She came to us,' said Isa.

Paddy slid from his horse, removed his hat and ran his hand over his head. 'Aye, I thought as much. I went by yer place first. What a mess. I spoke to Davie. Where is she?'

'She doesn't want to come back to ye.' Isa looked up at his bloodshot eyes and grizzled hair, saw the worry pucker his forehead.

'She should be thankful to have a roof over her head, being as she is.'

'She's not a bad lassie. She was raped back in Liverpool, did ye know that?'

Paddy stopped for a beat, his eyes opening wide. 'Forced ye say?' His fingers tightened round the brim of his hat. 'She's no more than a bairn hersel.'

'Aye,' said Isa. 'She needs caring for.'

Paddy shook his head. 'She's not what I expected, no she is not. That wee girl'll never make a wife. I could no more touch her now than gouge me own eyes out.' He put a hand to his chin. 'God help me, I want no more of her. She scuttles round me like a mouse, won't even speak and I'm afeart I'll lift me hand to her when I'm in my cups.'

'You've already done that,' said Isa, her voice cold.

'To my great regret,' Paddy lifted his eyes to hers and she saw the pain in them. 'Sure it was a mistake, taking this girl for my old pal.'

'But take her ye did.' Isa thought about offering to let her stay where she was, but saw the sense in Davie's objections. However, if Paddy was going to abandon her there would be no other option.

'How do you know she was raped? Eh? She slept with a black man. Could be it's just an excuse. But I'm not a man to shirk my responsibility. Every time I look at her I'll see that babby with his hair like wool. And how did he die? A fine healthy-looking lad.'

'What do you mean?'

'There was not another soul with her when the babby came into the world. She shoulda cared for him. She can come back with me to live if she keeps my house clean, but apart from that...' He shook his head. 'There's houses in Stony Plains which cater to the needs of a man like me.'

'She told me the bairn was stillborn.'

'Could be she's telling the truth.' He looked doubtful. 'But she didn't want the child and that's a fact. I aye wanted a bairn of my own, but I can't take the risk of her harming another.'

Isa's blood ran cold. She couldn't believe what she was hearing. A child in danger from his own mother. But she had to admit, there was a strangeness about the lass. And Paddy's suspicions planted a seed in her mind. Would Sarah really have hurt her own baby? She had admitted she was glad the child had died. If there was the slightest chance that was true, how could Isa leave her around Annie and Wee Dan?

'Where is she?' Paddy asked.

'She took Annie to feed the hens.' Isa turned into the yard. 'Sarah,' she shouted, but there was no answer. She ran round the cabin. The hens pecked in the yard, scattering when they saw her. There was no sign of Sarah or the baby.

'She's gone. She's taken Annie.' Isa grabbed Paddy's arm and shook it. 'Do something.' She ran across the yard and spun around. Wee Dan played in the dusty earth with a wooden horse and cart Pierre had carved for him. 'Did you see where Sarah went? She asked. He shook his head and returned to his play. Except for the distant forests, everywhere was flat land without anyone moving across it. Sarah and Annie hadn't been gone more than ten minutes, they couldn't have disappeared. She ran indoors. Martha sat in her chair rubbing her hands with oil.

'Did Sarah come in here?'

'No, she took the bairns out. She's not come back since.'

When Isa went outside again, Paddy was coming out of the barn, shaking his head. 'No sign of them in the outbuildings.'

They couldn't just have disappeared into thin air. 'Sarah,' Isa screamed. 'Annie!'

'Are there any wells or ponds near here?' asked Paddy, furthering her panic.

'No, I don't know.' For the first time Isa realised she had not investigated what lay around the homestead, other than the track to the village or the one to her own shack.

She raised her hand to her head not knowing which direction to take. 'I'll go back to the shack, maybe she's gone there.'

But she was not there and Davie had not seen her. He immediately dropped the length of timber he had been holding and joined Isa. 'What are ye saying? She couldn't have just vanished.'

'The Whitewater's hut,' Isa exclaimed. It was the nearest place. Together they ran all the way there, until Isa's breath was laboured and her lungs were sore. The hut stood empty as she knew it would.

'I can arrange a search party, but I'll have to go to the village. It'll take a while,' said Paddy.

A new thought struck Isa. 'Would a wolf have taken them, a mountain lion?'

'Not very likely.' Paddy shook his head. 'There's plenty food in the forests this time of year, they wouldn't come near the homesteads.'

'But possible?' Isa scanned the vast prairie. The knee length grass waved and undulated in an unseen breeze. Cupping her hands to her lips, she called again. 'Sarah, where are you?'

She looked helplessly at Paddy. 'Go get the search party, it's all we can do.'

'I'll come with ye,' said Davie.

Returning to the ranch, her eyes swept over the land once more. Suddenly she saw a movement in the distance. Like a wraith, a figure rose from the wheat, the heat shimmering around her. Then Sarah, carrying a tearful Annie in her arms moved towards her.

'Where were you?' Isa ran towards them tripping on the hem of her skirt, fearful lest this was an illusion conjured up out of her own desperation. She tore Annie from Sarah's arms and pressed her to her breast.

'We were playing. Hide and seek. I was peeking at her through the long grass.'

'Didn't you hear me shout?' Isa was so angry the words shrieked from her. She wanted to slap the girl before her.

Sarah shook her head.

'I don't believe you. Paddy was here.'

Sarah lowered her eyes. 'I know.'

'Is that why you hid?'

Sarah nodded.

'We were frantic!'

'I'm sorry, but I'm not going back to him.'

'Well, ye're not staying here. Paddy's yer man and it's there ye belong. If we hurry we might catch him before he gets a search party together. Do ye know the trouble ye've caused?'

Sarah covered her face and started to sob. 'I'm sorry. I didn't think...'

'Let's get the trap. I'm taking ye home.' She pushed the girl before her all the way to the main house.

Still shaking with rage, Isa drove to Paddy's shack. The last sight she had of Sarah was of the dejected figure standing in the yard, head hanging, shoulders hunched. Then she headed towards the clutch of buildings in the distance to divert the search party.

Chapter Thirteen

Donald

While Isa and Davie settled into their new life in Canada, black clouds were gathering in the skies above Europe.

In Raumsey, Reverend Donald Charleston sat across the kitchen table from his friend and fellow debater, schoolteacher William Smith.

'There will be war.' Donald sipped at a raw whisky. 'Mark my words. Germany's been made a new state and the Kaiser won't stop there.'

'Let's hope it stays well away from our door.' William tossed his whisky back and reached for the keg to pour himself another.

'If there's trouble in Europe it will affect the world. America's banking system is already in panic.'

'Maybe be better, all those wee states under one ruler.'

Donald shook his head. 'The Prussian emperor rules by a divine right, or so he believes. And his policies, well, no one knows what he's going to come up with next. The attempt to gain land in Africa insulted Britain.'

'Aye, there's too much distrust now,' said William.

'He's a dangerous man right enough. All that trouble with France a couple of years ago, now they say he's looking at Russia. He's delusional, I tell you. Another whisky, minister?' Andra, an old fisherman and the third member of the debate team held out the keg.

Donald covered his glass with his hand and shook his head. 'Can't have a minister drunk,' he said with a smile.

Andra took out a pouch and stuffed tobacco into the bowl of his pipe with a nicotine-stained thumb. Although he had little book learning, he was astute and sharp as broken glass.

'He's trying to get a better navy than us,' continued William. 'Britain won't stand for that.'

'There'll be a fair few fine young men lost,' said Andra. 'I was in the Crimea myself and hoped never to see anything like it again.' He leaned back and puffed at his pipe. 'And he'll turn his eyes to Britain, as sure as eggs is eggs.'

Donald swilled what was left of his whisky round his glass and stared into the amber liquid. 'If there is war, I'll volunteer to be an army chaplain.' He rose and walked to the window. 'There's a big world out there, maybe one which needs me more than the folk on this island.'

'Ye don't know what it's like,' said Andra.

'But I do. My father fought in Crimea. The stories were terrible. These poor men will need spiritual guidance more than ever.'

Through the window he watched the black ribbon of riptide divide the firth, the clouds thicken and pile on top of each other, sun rays escaping from beneath and hitting the ground in long shafts, highlighting the coats of sheep grazing contentedly beyond the kirk-yard wall. His father had made his money as a merchant banker and had expected his three sons to follow in his footsteps. Donald had neither the stomach nor the cut-throat instincts for a life in high commerce. What he had was a strong belief in the equality of man and an inherited good speaking voice. The church had given him the means to escape from his father's domination and, as a young man with high ideals, to work among people of lowly birth, to somehow enrich their lives. In truth, he now believed that it had been the people of Raumsey who had helped him understand the true resilience of the human spirit.

'It'll only take a wee spark now to light the fuse.' Andra studied his glass. 'Life's hard enough for us common folks as it is.' He removed the pipe from his mouth and pointed the stem at William. 'If I was to meet the Kaiser face to face, I'd put a bullet right between his eyes. Murder it might be, but it would be for a greater good.' He replaced the pipe and drew deeply. Clouds of smoke rose above his head. 'Would God condemn me for that?' he asked after a short silence.

Donald said nothing and continued to stare through the glass. The grassy tops of hummocks waved in a wind which never seemed to cease and the first large drop of rain of the day smacked against the pane.

Chapter Fourteen

Isa

Hector MacLeod, the young assistant in the store, was glad to see Isa, loved the sound of his own voice and always had a wealth of information to impart. 'How're you getting on with rebuilding your shack?' he asked on the first day of August, his face lighting up to see her.

'We're not.' Isa handed him a written list of supplies. 'There's no time. We've few hands. Pierre and Davie are making a start on the harvest today. Takes a time with only one scythe.'

'What you need is one of those harvester machines.' He weighed out some flour, dumping it onto the scales. A small cloud puffed upwards.

'Aye, I've seen them. I suppose they cost more than we can afford,' said Isa.

'Have you given thought to the winter wheat?'

'I have that. But we need money for the seed.' Then a sudden idea struck her. 'If I could have it on credit, we could pay it back once the harvest comes in.'

'I would sure love to help you, lady. But McArthy now, he's a mean old guy. Wouldn't trust a coyote to eat a rabbit. He leaned forward, his elbows on the counter. His pale eyes, slightly prominent, bore into hers. His breath smelt of peppermint. 'Go speak to McArthy. The Department of Trade and Commerce are keen to develop what they're calling the wheat basket of Canada. That's right here.' He tossed back his reed-straight hair. 'Help's easy to get and McArthy knows how to do it. Best send your man though. Some folks ain't too keen on dealing with a woman.' He straightened up and poured the flour into a brown paper bag.

As he collected the supplies on her list, her mind was already racing ahead. Since she had been staying with her parents, she had realised just how hard her mother found the daily grind. She tended to her husband religiously, but often fell asleep sitting upright in a wooden chair. Once Isa had caught her crying and clutching her back.

With so much work to do on the farm, and her parents' declining health, staying where she was seemed the wisest option despite the cramped conditions. Davie and Pierre had moved the brass bedstead from the ruined shack. It now stood in the corner of the main room of the big cabin.

***

'Are ye sure?' said Davie when she told him about the winter wheat. They were standing at the edge of the cornfield, looking over the golden acres.

'A double crop would never work on Raumsey, but seems things are different here.' Isa looked at him hopefully. She needed him to agree, to do business with the men who ran the county. It was true what Hector had said; they would never take a woman seriously.

He set his hands on her shoulders. 'Ye've a wise head on that neck of yours, Isa, and never a day passes that I don't give thanks I found ye. But sometimes ye can be a bit rash.' Their eyes met and held. The vivid blue that had once entrapped her appeared to have faded and lost its lustre. He slipped his hand to her cheek. Those eyes grew smoky with desire. 'We've not got the privacy in your parents' home, but here...' He lifted his hand and indicated the miles of emptiness.

As he bent towards her, she set her palms flat against his chest and pressed him away. 'There's little time for this, Davie. We've to speak to my dad, convince him this is the thing to do.'

He jerked back. 'It's not a good idea, Isa. I'll not settle here. I've been thinking about joining a paddle steamer or going to the logging.' He dropped his hand and straightened up. 'I don't like farming and well ye know it. We could make a good living if we moved further north.'

She gritted her teeth, swallowing her despair. Davie had always been the same. Always looking over the horizon, his dreams chasing something he would never catch.

'Ye promised me ye'd give it a try.'

'Give it a try, yes. But ye're talking about tying us to a loan that may take years to pay back. Sounds to me like ye're planning to stay. It's a big country and I'm not sorry I came, but this place is not where I want to put down roots.'

'A couple of years, Davie. We owe my folks as much. And in the meantime we've got to do the best we can.'

'Ah, Isa, forget about that for now.' His eyes flicked over her face and down her body. 'You look real bonny with the sunlight on yer hair.' Once more he made to pull her towards him, but she stepped back.

With a snort, Davie turned away. 'Ye've no time for me anymore. Ye're always too tired or too busy. I might as well go north on my own.'

'It's not that I don't want ye, I don't want another bairn. I was so ill last time.' She reached out, grabbed his hand. 'There's a good life for us here, but it takes money to start off. We've both got to work. We can move later, once we know the country better. And my folks…we'd have to take them with us. But I promise I'll think on it.'

He shook his head, 'I don't know…'

'Believe me, this is what's best for us.' She watched the indecision race across his face and grabbed the advantage.

'Come away. We have to speak to my da.' She turned towards the cabin, pulling him after her, ignoring the slump of his shoulders, the shadow of defiance in his eyes.

***

'No, no.' Sandy rose from his seat. He combed his fingers through what was left of his hair. 'The bank would want the farm as collateral. I can't risk being thrown out with my bad heart and all. I doubt if I'd survive it.' He walked slowly to join his daughter by the window. Martha was washing in the tub in the yard, bent at the waist, her arms submerged in a tired lather, her skirts hanging loose over thin hips. She stopped, straightened up and rubbed her back, her face twisting as if she were in pain.

'And I doubt if your mam could take much more.' Sandy's voice barely rose above a whisper. 'It's little enough I've given her.'

His words only filled Isa with renewed determination. 'We've got to do something, make life better for us all. Hector says the government is helping farms to expand.' She had had a vision of acres of waving wheat and Davie driving two heavy horses yoked to one of the latest harvesters. Since the dream had taken hold, it had grown and sunk roots deep into her consciousness. Furthermore, if they were to do it, it had to be soon.

'Only when the men are fit to guarantee them a good return.' He lifted his hands. 'I doubt they'd take a chance on me, and Davie doesn't want to tie himself to the land.'

'Yer Da's right,' said Davie. 'The risk's too great. If I go north and ye and yer folks run the farm as it is, we'll get by.'

'Is that the best we can hope for – getting by?' Isa pulled her shoulders back as tears of frustration pricked her eyes. She'd had had a glimpse of what could be achieved and felt it within her grasp. She couldn't let it slip away now. She just couldn't.

'Ah, lass, don't be like that.' Sandy turned to face her.

'Ye said there was opportunity here. Ye said me and Davie could do well. But now ye won't help us.' Isa dropped her head, vexation shortening her breath, her fingers curling into fists.

'Och, lass.' Sandy reached out and squeezed her arm. 'We're in a country with no kin to give us shelter if things go wrong. I've seen droughts and insects that eat the crops, the like you've never known. Give yourselves a few years to learn what's what. We've got three fine calves and next year we'll have more. It won't take long to build the herd up again.'

'Listen to yer da, he's been here a lot longer than us. And who's going to do all the work? There's not enough hours in the day as it is,' said Davie.

Determination closed Isa's ears and drove her forward so much so that she ignored him and dropped to her knees before her father. 'At least let me find out what this Trade of Commerce is offering. If I can get the seed will ye agree then?'

'Aye,' Sandy said with a sigh. 'I reckon I will, if it means so much.'

The smile lightened her heart as she hugged him. She did not see Davie's face tighten, did not see him shake his head in resignation or the flush creeping up his cheeks. But she did hear the slam of the door as he left.

For a moment she thought of going after him, then changed her mind. Davie's concerns were not a problem. His choices in the past had been poor, he had often admitted as much. She was sure she could win him round in the end. If she spoke to McArthy, maybe she could somehow persuade Sandy this was the way forward.

***

'I need to see McArthy.' She pressed her hands against the store counter.

Hector grinned. 'You really think you can do it, huh?'

'Ye said yerself it is a good idea. Just let me try.' A pulse beat in her ears. She didn't expect it to be easy, but she was willing to give it her best efforts.

Hector shrugged and raised his eyes to the clock on the wall. 'McArthy part-owns the hotel too. I reckon he'll be taking his morning tipple in the saloon about now. But hey, don't say I sent you.'

All eyes turned to Isa when she walked into the bar-room. The smell of beer and wood and dust filled her nostrils. She stopped and swallowed, realising she was the only woman there. 'I'm... I'm looking for Mr McArthy.'

'That would be me,' came a voice from her right.

She turned to see a big man with scant hair, hard, sharp eyes and a square jaw. He was dressed in the manner of most of the men around here, buckskin jacket, kerchief and a Stetson lying on the table before him.

She bit her lip, with no knowledge what to do in these situations, she wondered whether or not she should sit beside him.

Finally he drained his glass, stood up, grabbed her arm and led her outside. 'A bar-room is no place for a lady. Now, what do you want with me?'

She cleared her throat and glanced up and down the wide street, thinking this was no place to do business. 'I need seed. I want to grow winter wheat.' She said the words through a dry throat, her voice less than confident.

'Sure, talk to young Hector in the store. He'll see you all right.' He turned as if to go back into the hotel.

She spoke hurriedly. 'Thing is, we've little money. I believe there's loans to help farmers expand. I don't know how to go about it.'

McArthy's eyes rounded, his mouth opened slightly as he stared at her for a moment. Then he heaved back his head and guffawed. 'What would a slip of a girl know about farming?' he asked, once he caught himself.

Indignant blood heated her face. The tremble that had started in her legs now ran the length of her body. 'I ran a farm by myself back in Scotland. I can gather a harvest and plough a field if need be.' She held out her hands, callused palms upward. 'I didn't get these knitting socks.'

McArthy studied her, no longer laughing. 'I sure admire your audacity. Where is your farm?'

'The Muirison place.'

'Sandy and Jim Muirison? Good farmers, solid workers. But didn't Jim die a while back?'

'I'm Sandy's daughter. My man and me, we're here to help.'

He rubbed his chin. His hands were thick, his fingers short and blunt. 'Winter wheat, eh? The spread's big enough. Why is your man not doing the asking?'

Isa took a deep breath and lied. 'He didn't want to take time from the harvest to come all this way. He trusts me to talk on his behalf.'

He looked thoughtful. 'Maybe I'll take a ride out and see Sandy myself.'

'Then…then you're interested?'

'I admit the winter wheat is a great idea. Would do it myself if I was a full-time farmer.' He tilted his head to one side. 'Tell you what, I'll think on giving you the seed, but I get sixty per cent of the takings.'

'I don't know.' Isa was taken aback. She wanted a loan, but with no knowledge of percentages or business, she had not expected this. 'I'll have to speak to my father.'

'Of course you will.' He tipped his hat at her and turned away laughing. At that moment she realised he had not taken her seriously. A wind had sprung up and stirred the dust round her feet. A few horses with carts made their way along the road. She didn't want to walk back to where her own mount was tethered; with her blood racing, she wanted to run, leap on his back and gallop back to the farm, the heat of her anger spurring her on.

***

As she rode into the yard, Davie, his hair hanging in his eyes, a sheen of sweat covering his skin, came towards her from the field. 'Where have you been?' He grabbed the horse's rein. 'We need someone to gather the hay. We can't do it all ourselves.'

'I went to speak to McArthy.'

Davie stared at her. 'What? Do my feelings count for nothing now?'

'Trust me, Davie. This is for our future.' She slid from the saddle. 'It'll be fine, you'll see.' With McArthy's derisive laughter still ringing in her ears she reached for him, wanting him to hold her, forgive her, but there was to be no such comfort.

He grabbed her hands and pushed her from him. 'No, it's not fine. I'm not settled here, not by a long way and you know that.'

He turned and marched towards the house, leaving her staring after him.

She stood still in the soft air where the bluebirds sang and the horse snorted and swished his tail at the gathering clouds of flies. Something was dying between herself and Davie and she felt unable to stop it. Why was he so resistant to a plan that promised them a better future? She couldn't give in and risk starving just to pander to his masculine pride.

She would get the seed, the rains would come and the harvest would be a success. McArthy would be paid off and subsequent profits would be theirs and theirs alone. Then Davy would come round and see that she had been right all along. And he would forgive her. All these things would happen for no other reason than she had willed them. She could not contemplate anything less.

She found him in the cabin, slicing a wedge of bread from a day-old loaf. 'What is the matter? Even McArthy thinks winter wheat is a good idea.' It wasn't a lie, not exactly.

Davy lifted his head and glared at her, his eyes glinting with an edge of steel. 'It's a man's place to make decisions, Isa. Ye'd do well to remember that.' Pushing the bread into his mouth he strode towards the door.

'Davie, wait.' She put her hand on his arm. 'Please, ye have to deal with McArthy. We can do this, we really can.'

His muscles tensed beneath her grip.

'We've come through so much before,' she whispered, her eyes searching his face until his expression softened.

'Can ye do it alone, Isa?' he asked.

A cold finger touched her heart. 'I won't be alone, will I?' She flung her arms around him, pressing her breast against his chest, hoping to get a positive reaction, but he remained cold and indifferent. Tonight, she thought, tonight I'll make it up to him. She would risk having another child if it meant making things right between them.

At the end of the day, when she returned from the fields, she found McArthy sitting before the fire nursing a mug of whisky.

'This fine gentleman, here, has talked me into agreeing with you,' said Sandy. 'And he's a man with a good business head on his shoulders.' His fingers were steepled together, veins standing out like blue worms on his white hands.

'Ye mean you'll advance us the seed?' She sat on the arm of her father's chair, looped one arm around his shoulders and felt the fragility of the bones. It seemed he had lost more weight since she had arrived in Canada.

'You didn't tell me your paw was ailing,' said McArthy. 'But nevertheless I'm willing to take a chance. There's money available, but you need a sound business plan. You'll not be able to do it yourselves. I want a percentage, and I'll make sure we all do well.'

Isa swallowed, looked at her father then back at McArthy. She breathed slowly to hide her nervousness, knowing the man's small, sharp eyes missed nothing.

'I rode round the farm. You've sure got a good acreage going to waste.' He leaned forward and stared at Sandy. 'Here's the deal. I get you the seed, sign fifty per cent of the crop to me and I'll pay the wage of a couple of seasonal workers to help with the harvest. I'll oversee the work myself.' He slapped his knee and sat back.

'Ten percent.' Isa knew nothing about business, but it seemed to her the man was asking too much. If it was true that the government would advance the seed, all they were paying McArthy for was his expertise.

McArthy's smile faded. He looked at Sandy.

Sandy reached up and took Isa's hand. 'The lass here knows what she's about. If she thinks ten per cent is a good deal, it's fine by me.'

McArthy licked his lips. 'I'm taking a chance here.'

'We all are.' Isa clutched her father's shoulder to stop her hand from trembling. She had a strong feeling that McArthy saw a sick old man and a young naive girl as easily taken advantage of. At the same time she knew nothing of the way things worked and this might be the only chance she had.

'Then there's no deal.' McArthy's eyes hardened. He set his hands on the chair arms and made to push himself up.

Isa held his gaze. 'Ye might as well go. I can find out how to get the seed myself.' She squeezed her father's hand, willing him to keep quiet. Undoubtedly she could do that, but McArthy was right, she knew very little about farming on this scale, and with Davie's lack of interest, her hands were tied.

McArthy's face turned red. 'Hold on there.' He held up his hand. 'You don't have the time. The seed has to be sown as soon as this harvest is over. You'd have to go to Edmonton, see the right people. Hire men. *You* can do that?'

Isa stood up. 'I'll bid you good day, Mr McArthy.'

'Damn it all girl, land is cheap right now. I could get acres up north for very little.'

'Aye,' Sandy sat upright. 'Acres you'd have to clear of trees before you could grow a blade of grass. Fifteen percent and we've got a deal.'

McArthy drew in some air through his nose. 'Thirty-five and that's my final offer.'

'Twenty,' said Isa before she could stop herself.

McArthy shook his head. 'Twenty-five or I walk through that door.'

'Dad.' Isa looked at Sandy, willing him to agree.

He caught her eye and sighed. 'Guess I won't be around much longer, so it's your gamble, Isa.' She hesitated. It was either this or give up the whole idea, and that she could not do. After years of poverty, she was finally being given the chance to make money, if not for herself, then for her children.

'Then I accept,' she said, before he could change his mind.

McArthy held out his hand to Sandy.

'I'll have to read the paperwork when you've got it drawn up.' Isa held out her hand, too.

McCarthy shook with her on the deal, gave a deep, rumbling laugh. 'What a minx. I can see why your menfolk let you do the talking.' His eyes flicked over her as if he'd really seen her for the first time. Was that a look of respect or something quite different? She felt a moment of unease.

Flushed with success, she rode back to the homestead,

surprised to find only Pierre gathering the grain. 'Where's Davie?' she asked.

'He says to tell you he has gone north to get a job on a paddle steamer.'

The breath stopped in her throat. 'But he can't go. I've got the seed.'

Pierre said nothing, but continued raking.

'What am I going to do now?' she cried.

Pierre stopped and rested against the handle of his rake. 'We can manage to finish the harvest and plant the seed.'

Davie had asked her whether she could do it alone. Had he already been planning to leave then? She needed him. McArthy had promised to pay men to help with the harvest, she'd be damned if she'd go begging for help with the planting too.

That night, long after the others were asleep, she sat alone, listening to the call of the coyotes. Closing her eyes, she pulled the curtains against whatever might be out there. With only herself, the children and ailing parents in a cabin miles from anywhere, her nervousness heightened. It was as if a great burden had been placed on her shoulders. The responsibility for the survival of them all was now hers and hers alone.

For the first time she doubted the wisdom of her actions. Had she pushed Davie too far? So carried away had she been by her own optimism, that she failed to consider just how deeply this would wound his pride. He would come back, once he's cooled off, she thought, aye that he would.

Because of her, a man she barely knew now owned twenty-five percent of their profit, and yet the remaining wheat would be more than enough to keep them in comfort if things went well. As the night wore on, her mood swayed from fear of the future to anger at Davie's thoughtlessness. Eventually she grew weary of her own anguish and brought her fist down on the table. 'Damn you, Davie Reid,' she said. 'I survived without ye before and I can again.'

The following morning she rose before dawn. When the clock struck six, the cows had been watered and milked, the eggs gathered and the hens fed. By the time she had done all that, Pierre was already in the fields, raking up the last of the barley. By the end of the week, the new seed had been planted in the stubble, every bone in her body ached and she was so tired she feared she would fall asleep standing up, but it was done.

Isa looked up at the hard blue sky. If they were to have a successful crop, they needed rain. Once more she felt self-doubt. If the rain did not come, all would be lost and she could not contemplate the thought. That night she was too tired to even eat and too tired to curse Davie. As she watched her mother feed the bairns, her heart hardened against him. How could he do this to her? She wanted to scream, to thump her fists against something solid until they bled, but her outward appearance had to be calm, in control, strong.

***

By the end of October, the winter feed had been stowed in the barn, and wild honey and maple syrup stored in jars. Pierre had killed a young steer and shown her how to can the meat. The winter would be long and hard and extensive preparations had to be made.

Thankfully the rain did come and the young seeds began to germinate.

Within weeks the temperatures plummeted bringing an icy sharpness on the wind, and still there was no word from Davie. By now her anger had been replaced by fear. What if he had met with some kind of accident? What if he was dead? It was because of her actions that he had gone, and whatever happened was her fault.

The nights grew colder still and her longing to hear from him replaced every other emotion. She stood on the decking and watched the nightly display to the north, of red, mauve and turquoise, like fine gauze blowing in the breeze, wafting to and fro across the vault of night and reflecting on the distant, snow-covered ground, turning it into a field of colour.

One morning she woke up to a strange stillness in the air. The fire was low and her breath smoked before her. She rose, pulled her shawl around her shoulders and padded to the window where lacy patterns decorated the panes. Touching her fingers to the glass, she felt the roughness of ice which had formed inside as well as out. One hand clutching the shawl at her throat, she opened the cabin door to be hit by a wall of cold that stopped the breath in a way she'd never experienced before.

A blanket of white covered the ground. Colours of gold and copper merged to shroud the wide prairie sky and reflected on the virgin ground. The world was filled with a bright pure cleanness in which there was no sound and nothing moved. Standing in the splendour of an Alberta winter sunrise, Isa realise for the first time that Canada was seeping into her bones. She was beginning to love this land.

From the shadows of the cottonwoods, she saw a movement, and a black shape emerged. For a second, she flinched. A caribou, his antlers catching the early light lifted his head. Isa watched, enthralled. Then suddenly, as if sensing her presence, he stopped and with one wild bound, disappeared back into the darkness of the trees.

The snow melted with the morning's sun, leaving a scattering in hollows and alongside the road. Isa was carrying water to the byre when she saw a figure she could not fail to recognise in the distance, trudging towards the homestead. Around him the prairie spread into nothingness on every horizon, making him appear small and insignificant. He was hatless, his familiar lean features beneath the thick tumble of blond hair. She saw the fatigue in his eyes. His jacket flapped open, his trousers clung wetly around the bottom of his legs. Slung over his shoulder was a haversack. He stopped. They faced each other. He had put on some weight and looked good enough to make the breath catch in her throat.

'Davie,' she said.

He lifted the corner of his lip in an anxious smile.

She tried to stop the flutter in her heart, the flutter that still gave him a power over her.

He dropped his haversack.

She waited.

'Did you do it, plant the seed?'

'Aye.'

'I'm sorry I went like that.' He took a step towards her. 'I've got a job. On a paddle steamer, *The Bonnington*. Sailing from Arrowhead to Robson West. Oh Isa, it's grand to be back on water.' He searched in his pocket and drew out some bills which he thrust towards her. 'Wages. Here, take it.'

Isa looked at the notes. There were so many things needed for winter, the money was a godsend. It was enough to make her almost forgive him.

'I'm sorry too, Davie. I should have paid more mind to what ye wanted.' But her body remained tense. 'At least yer back. We'll have a good harvest come spring.'

He cleared his throat. 'I'm only back for a few months. The boats stop sailing for the winter. The lakes freeze, ye see.'

She stared at him. 'Ye're not home for good?'

'I'm going back in spring. When there's enough money, I've got a mind to move us up to Prince Rupert on the west coast and get myself a fishing boat.'

The word, no, sprung to Isa's lips but she trapped it behind her teeth. By her efforts they were going to be better off, perhaps even well-off, and he wanted to move them to a strange, wild place where the railroad did not reach. She would not tell him about McArthy's cut. She doubted he would care. Tonight was not the time for conflict, but his words had dampened the pleasure she felt at his homecoming.

Chapter Fifteen

Isa

'What are ye doing, lass? Come in and shut the door,' shouted Davie. From behind her, she heard the sound of logs being piled on the fire. She returned indoors as a red morning light began to fill the room.

His hands closed over hers. 'Ye're frozen. We'll need to buy warmer coats.'

The thaw did not last long. The following day a wind rose and heavy, black clouds formed in the sky. By night the wind fell silent, and large snowflakes, soft as moths, began to fall. Next day the ground was covered by a hard, shiny white.

Davie set a match to the fire and she huddled before young flames struggling for existence. 'I'll go water the beasts.' Each word was accompanied by a cloudy breath. 'You sit here and keep warm.' Since he'd returned, he'd been overly attentive, as if he needed to somehow make up for the fact that he could never be what she wanted.

Once he left to begin the tasks of the day, Isa poured herself another coffee. Since she had moved in with her parents, they lay longer in the mornings and she relished this time to herself, before even the children were awake.

An hour later, she went to the byre to check on the animals, horrified to find the water Davie had given them already frozen over. Seemed they would need a fresh change several times a day and, as well as that, the icy bedding beneath them would have to be swapped for fresh straw.

Another hour had gone before she fed the children then fetched the galvanised tub. She needed to do the washing before the sun lost its heat.

'I want to play in the snow.' Wee Dan was desperate to get

outside. Isa wrapped her son in every stitch of clothes he possessed. He ran through the door, kicking up the snow. The sun was high and warm and had softened the frozen ground. 'Mam, come play with me,' he shouted.

Pulling on her gloves, Isa followed him and scooped a handful of snow, packed it into a ball and threw it at the lad. Giggling, Wee Dan retaliated.

The snowball fight ceased. Let's build a snowman,' she said. 'I did this with my own sister, back in Orkney.'

When she first came here, she'd been surprised to learn dinner was at ten o'clock in the morning, lunch at three in the afternoon, and supper at seven. It seemed to be the way it was for everyone and Isa soon adopted the regime.

When Davie came down the track, beating his hands together, Isa rolled a snowball and hit him in the shoulder. He yelled and laughed. Grabbing a handful of snow, he chased her and rubbed it on her face and together they fell, laughing onto the ground. A giggling Wee Dan joined them.

They were still laughing when they returned to the house.

'Have ye made the sandwiches? I'll be home late.' Davie pulled off his gloves and stamped his feet.

'I've made them, and scones,' said Martha from where she bent over the stove.

Wee Dan followed them in, trailing snowy footsteps in his wake, his face red, his nose running. 'I'm frozen,' he exclaimed.

Scooping him up, Isa kissed his cold cheeks. It had been good to laugh again.

Chapter Sixteen

Isa

The day her father died, Isa was canning berries in the barn. He lived for a year and five days from the date when Isa set foot on Canadian soil. The death wasn't unexpected. Sandy's strength failed daily of late, his life trickling away, water over stone.

She felt it, like a shadow on the air, like a cold breath, a mist that hovered above and left so quickly she fancied she'd imagined it.

She hadn't disturbed her parents that morning. Sandy had had a restless night, and Isa had expected them to sleep late.

Carrying baby Annie, she ran from the barn to the cabin. Wee Dan spent his days out on the range with Pierre, who had taken a strong interest in the boy. She found her mother sitting in the main room staring at the stove, rocking slowly, her fingers clawed around the arms of the chair as if the woman and the seat were one, as if she had grown like a plant whose roots were of wood and anchored to the ground. Her face in its deathly whiteness did not move, her eyes did not acknowledge Isa.

Isa set the baby on the floor and knelt by her mother's side.

'He's gone,' said Martha.

'I know.' The ticking of the clock, the crackle of burning logs and the whispering of a warming kettle became loud in the stillness of the room. 'There are things to be done.' Isa took Martha by the hand. 'Come on.' She raised her up.

Her mother moved slowly, rising from her sanctuary reluctantly. Talon-like fingers clutched at Isa's. The lips drew back, the head tilted, the mouth widened and a low cry, not unlike that of a wounded animal, began in her throat, rising in volume until it found release; then became a loud keening, terrifying the child on the floor, causing her to scream in unison.

Isa could only clutch her mother to her chest in a desperate effort to quieten her. Once Martha gained control of herself and the howls subsided into hiccupping, gulping sobs, Isa released her and picked Annie up. 'Hush ye now. It's all fine.' She looked around the room, as if help would materialise from the blank walls. On a ranch this size there was no knowing where the men were, or when they would return.

At that moment her heart called out to Chrissie back on Raumsey. She saw her in her mind's eye, practical, sympathetic, taking charge and dressing the body with care. Here there was no Chrissie. Isa had only herself, a crying child and a woman who appeared to have lost half her mind.

'I'll attend to Da,' said Isa, once Annie ceased her wailing, the wolf-skin rug having drawn her attention. Isa rose and walked slowly to the door behind which her father lay, finally at peace. 'Da,' she said, before drawing the blanket over his face, 'Sleep well. I'll take care of Mam.'

It occurred to her that, without her man, Martha would be lost. Sandy'd always been a dreamer, always talked about what he was going to do. He was the perfect antidote for her mother's sharp edges, her over-practical nature. They had done well from the herring back home, yet he had to drag them over here, chasing an elusive future, which, it seemed, had not materialised.

Isa imagined the relief that Martha must feel to have her family here, relief to have the support as Sandy slipped away, like the slow sinking of the sun.

For that reason, if for none else, she was very glad she had come.

***

On the day of the funeral, the stove had gone out and Isa's breath feathered in the air, her numbness insulating her from the cold. She hadn't shed a single tear. She wasn't ready for that. Standing at the window, she watched as the neighbours departed.

For the first time since she'd left her standing in front of

Paddy's shack, she saw Sarah. She had put on weight, but her eyes were filled with pain. 'I'm so sorry.' She reached for Isa's hand but changed her mind. 'It's a sad thing to lose someone you love.' She lowered herself to the floor beside Annie and cupped the small face in her hands. 'But ye're so lucky to have bairns.'

Isa felt that perhaps Paddy was wrong and Sarah could have loved her child. 'You'll have more babies,' she whispered. She became aware of the broken nails, the calluses and rents and the painful redness of the small hands.

'Naw, for Paddy won't come near me.' She stood up and turned away, her shoulders stooping, her step slow. Isa had the feeling that this child had turned into an old woman without any years between.

'Goodbye, Sarah,' she said, but the lass did not turn.

Isa remained at the door as the mourners left. Some drove motor cars, but most came in a horse and trap. Some still had oxen. She hardly knew any of them, having only seen them in church; although never a churchgoer, Isa sometimes attended out of a desperate need to interact with other human beings. She watched them until they disappeared into the far distance. The distance which had so awed her and Davie when they had first arrived. Images drifted like smoke across her consciousness as she fought to put the pain of this day to the back of her mind.

She returned indoors and Davie tried to wrap his arms around her, but she batted him away. 'Stay with my mam,' she told him. She wanted to be alone, to have time to think, free from Davie's well-meaning platitudes, free from her mother's misery and Pierre's indifference. Time to grieve in her own way.

***

The following day Davie rose and dressed slowly. He knew it was a bad time to leave, but the hiring of the crew for the paddle steamers would be starting and he had to go north. He had delayed it long enough already. For a time he watched Isa, still asleep, her hair spread out on the pillow, one hand thrown out, fingers curled like a child. The winter wheat would soon be ready to harvest, but, as promised, McArthy had kept a steady eye on production and he had no concerns about Isa's ability to cope. Isa had been right. This was a grand crop, and with a market screaming for more, they would manage well, money-wise.

Davie experienced a stab of guilt. Had he stayed, been more of a farmer himself, they would have never needed McArthy's help. All he could do now was put his wages by until he had enough to realise his dream and go west to Prince Rupert. For a moment he considered just leaving, forego the pain of parting. He sat on the side of the bed causing it to dip and creak and stroked a strand of hair from her face.

Her eyes flickered and opened. 'Davie?' she said, the question in her voice.

'I have to go,' he whispered.

She sat up with a start. 'Go?' Her hair tumbled down her back, she smelt soft and warm.

'North.'

Her shoulders slumped. 'I hoped....'

'Will ye be alright?' He knew the question was pointless, for what would he do if she said no?

'I've always been before.' Her eyes trapped his and he bent forward to kiss her forehead, but she lowered her head, moving away from him. For a second he was tempted to crawl back in beside her, to stay and harvest the wheat, but the pull of adventure was strong.

He stood up and adjusted his clothing. 'I'll be back when I can.' Again his eyes lingered. 'Someday soon, we'll be together always.'

'In Prince Rupert?'

'Aye, in Prince Rupert.' He turned and left without looking back lest she saw the tears in his eyes, lest he gave in to the pull of her, lest he lost his dream for her sake and grew to blame her for it.

Part Two

1914

Chapter Seventeen

Donald

On the 4th of August 1914, Reverend Donald Charleston knocked on Raumsey's schoolhouse door. William Smith opened it and stood back to allow Donald to enter. 'I assume by the look on your face that the news is not good,' he said.

'The Germans have invaded Belgium. We are now officially at war with Germany.' Donald removed his hat and entered the kitchen. He was the only person on the island to own a radio.

'But Belgium's neutral,' said William.

Donald took a seat at the white-wood table. 'The young men of the island are all set to go, undoubtedly like young men all over the empire. I was talking with Charlie and Angus. They see it as an adventure, think they'll be home by Christmas.'

'Ah, the optimism of youth.' William poured hot water into the teapot, then went to the cupboard to collect cups and saucers.

Donald rubbed his hands together and studied his fingernails. 'I've applied to the Caithness and Sutherland Division of the Seaforth Highlanders in Golspie to serve as an army chaplain.'

He hadn't needed to think about it. From the first hint of trouble in Europe, he had known this was what he had to do. 'I'm young and fit, and the brave soldiers are going to need spiritual support more than ever before in the coming fray,' he said. The truth was he had become restless those last few years. His younger and much-loved sister had given her life as a suffragette, starved herself in a prison cell for a cause in which she believed. Ever since, he had suffered for what he saw as his own cowardice, had questioned his reasons for joining the church. For Donald Charleston it had been less of a calling and more of a means of avoidance. Although he loved the island and its people, and this parish in such a remote place had sufficed for many years, he now felt he had to follow the dictates of his conscience. Since the first rumblings over Europe, Reverend Donald Charleston had been ready.

'It doesn't surprise me. I'll miss our chats.' William set the cups and teapot on the table. 'When do you leave?'

'First thing Monday morning. I want to give a final sermon.' He looked up at his friend. 'Maybe my last in this kirk, eh?'

William raised his eyebrows but said nothing.

'From Golspie we're being moved to Bedford. That's as much as I know. I'll write you once I get there.'

However, it was the following May before William received a letter stating that Donald was actually getting ready to cross the Channel into France and the regiment had been retitled the 152nd Brigade in 51st Highland Division. In the same regiment were two other Raumsey lads, Georgie Sinclair and Dondie Bain.

He finished the letter with a promise to write again when he could.

***

Packed like herrings in a firkin, Donald stood shoulder to shoulder with the soldiers in his regiment. He held onto the boat rail and looked over the black, angry waters of the English Channel. His cork life-jacket was too tight, causing the corks to dig into his back. Above his head, the moon peeped through shredded clouds. In spite of the air of excitement, the men were quiet, each lost in his own thoughts, each alive with anticipation of the turmoil to come, yet knowing they might never return. Once the outline of Southampton faded in the distance, the moon disappeared and they were plunged into a dark void of sea and sky, only the grey froth flying like smoke from the wave tops broke the blackness; only the splash of water against the sides of the boat, an occasional discreet cough, and the hoarse rumble of the engines broke the silence.

'Is that France?' someone asked after what seemed like forever, his voice hollow and low, his finger pointing towards a dark, solid outline, barely visible.

Donald strained his eyes, peering into the gloom. 'I believe it is,' he whispered.

By the first early light, they sailed into Le Havre harbour. The first thing Donald saw was a long queue of walking-wounded, men caked with mud, with white, drawn faces, their uniforms hanging loose on skeletal bodies, waiting to be ferried back home. Smiling in spite of bandages covering half-faces, waving in spite of arms in slings and leaning on crutches, they shouted the good news of the British advance. The men on the boat cheered. It seemed to Donald his regiment had just got in at the beginning of the end. Maybe the lads had been right. Maybe they would be home for Christmas after all.

They disembarked amid the rain and spent the night in tents in a muddy rest camp. In the morning, they boarded a train of cattle trucks, with only straw to lie on, arriving the following day at a small station. Although weary and hungry, Donald and his comrades, with backs breaking beneath the weight of their packs, marched until they came to a village. Donald and two other Highland lads were directed to a nearby farm beyond a long line of motor wagons resting by the side of the road, ready to deliver supplies to the troops under cover of darkness.

The farmer beckoned them inside and indicated that they should sit at a long, white-wood table. A woman Donald assumed to be the farmer's wife, served them bread and bowls of strong black coffee. For once, Donald was glad his father had insisted his sons had a good education, because his schoolboy French, although dormant for many years, meant he could communicate with the family, a Marcel and Marie Belisle, and their daughter, Odelle.

Next morning, the rain had stopped, but the sky above remained grey. Donald wandered into the yard where chickens clucked and stretched their necks as they strutted around him. Odelle was leaning over a fence, feeding a goat. She stood up as he approached and turned to face him.

'Good morning, Padre.' She smiled up at him. She had a pretty face, round with dimpled cheeks and a turned-up nose. Her eyes were blue and large.

'My name is Donald.' His attention was immediately drawn to the skies. Although several miles from the front lines, the constant dull thud of gunfire carried towards them from the trenches. To the east, shrapnel burst like little spots of black ink dropped on blotting paper, spreading and hanging suspended in air for several minutes before dispersing.

'You'll get used to it,' said Odelle, as the steady putt of guns and rat-a-tat of machine-gun fire continued mercilessly. 'Come, help me collect eggs, then you will have breakfast.' She tilted her head a little and her lips lifted in a seductive smile.

'We have to leave soon,' he said. As their eyes held, he realized with a start, that she was flirting with him and the thought that such a young girl found him attractive lifted his heart and made him smile.

'Stay safe,' she replied, and they stood like that for a long moment as the shells exploded in the east and the chickens gathered round their feet. She turned away, rubbing her hands down her skirt. 'Le petit déjeuner,' she shouted to Murray and Alexander, two men who had shared a shed with Donald the night before and now stood looking up at the sky watching the devilish display. Odelle skipped ahead of them and into the farmhouse.

'You will come back this evening?' She asked as they left to join their regiment in the village. She was looking at Donald.

Donald took her hand and just as quickly let it drop. 'I don't know. I believe the front stretches for many miles and orders can be changed at any time.'

'Ye made a hit there,' said Murray as they walked away. 'And ye a minister o' the kirk.'

'Aye, that he may be.' Alexander punched his arm playfully. 'But a man's a man for a' that and she's a bonnie looking lass.'

Donald smiled and said nothing. For the first time since Isa had left the island, he had felt a stirring of attraction for a woman. His heart had finally healed. He breathed in the damp air. There was no way of knowing what lay ahead, but he believed that God had brought him here and whether he lived or died, he would do the best he could.

Alexander lit a cigarette and, with a shaking hand, offered one to Donald, which he declined.

'Are ye scared?' asked Murray. His faced was white and thin. He looked very young. A bead of sweat lay on his top lip.

'We wouldn't be human if we weren't.' Donald changed his mind and accepted the cigarette, coughing after the first draw. He had not smoked since he was sixteen with his brothers behind the potting shed in the garden of the house in Bearsden, Glasgow, where he had grown up.

'Can you ride a horse?' the transport officer asked Donald when they joined the others. 'It would be better for you if you could. You may be asked to cover many miles in one day.'

'I haven't for many years, but I'm sure it's something you don't forget.' Riding made sense.

'Your job entails helping with the deliveries, burying the dead and providing spiritual comfort. But for now we'll travel along with the water wagons.' A slim man with a florid complexion and a large, reddish moustache, his words were sharp and clipped.

Luckily the horse was docile and plodded along behind the cart without any sudden movements. By the time they reached the trenches, Donald began to feel fairly secure on his mount in spite of the fact that he had discovered muscles which had not been used for many years.

At last they reached the dumping ground and were met by a meaningless confusion of men and stores. From here bullets whistled overhead and the roaring shriek of shells was much louder. Mud-engrained groups collecting rations for many different regiments gathered round the transport carts. Others with empty petrol cans waited by the water carrier. Once full, the cans would be transported to the firing line. Horses grazed, waiting for their wagons to be emptied. Other smaller carts were pulled by dogs, strong hounds that bent to their task enthusiastically.

Flares and lights of all description lit the scene of this muddle of waiting and working soldiers. To one side sat a heap of stores; separate piles of sandbags, ammunition and tins of bully beef; to another, a pile of barbed wire on drums. A group of mud-covered soldiers were crouched on the ground playing cards, grabbing what respite they could. Others slept where they lay. Behind the tents was a rectangular piece of land almost full of little wooden crosses.

A queue of wounded men waited for the trucks to take them to a place of safety. New regiments, burdened with their back-packs, waited to relieve those who had done their stint in the trenches, their cigarette ends glowing in the fading light.

'Soldiers fight for seven to ten days in the front line before falling back for a spell in the supporting trenches, then back to the front line again, after which they move here to the reserve areas for a spell, giving them time to build up their depleted energy,' said the sergeant, answering Donald's unspoken questions.

As these old regiments staggered away for that few days' rest, Donald scanned the sorry faces drained of hope and energy, and decided raising the spirits and morale of these souls was going to be no easy task. All around them was the tremendous, ceaseless roar of the guns, the hum of bullets, and the evil tapping of the machine guns as they played their part in Satan's concert.

'This is where you'll conduct your services.' The sergeant led Donald to one of the larger tents. 'You should find everything you need in there. Any problems, you'll find me around camp.' He pointed to another tent. 'Mess hall there. Food will be served in an hour.'

Inside his tent, Donald found some empty ammunition boxes, candles and jars, a hammer and nails. With the boxes he erected a pulpit, and used the wood from another to make a cross. By the time he had finished, he was ready to get something to eat.

Dinner that night was corned beef and weak tea that tasted faintly of tar. He met some of the men and was amazed by their high spirits. 'I'd like to conduct a service as soon as possible,' he said.

'That's good,' replied a squaddie. 'You'll find no atheists in a war zone.'

His first ceremony was for the officers and it seemed every available man of rank attended.

Given the exhausted state of some of the enlisted soldiers, he was surprised and pleased at how many turned up for his second service, and even more so at the queue who waited afterwards to be confirmed, every man turning to God when he faced death.

'Reverend?'

Donald turned to see a tired-faced fellow, hatless, his uniform open at the neck. He offered his hand. 'I'm Doctor Ferguson. I have three bodies waiting to be buried and a lad who won't make another hour. I would be obliged for any comfort you can offer him.'

In the misty cold of the evening, while the guns sounded the death knell, Donald buried four bodies.

That night he spent under canvas, surrounded on all sides by other tents, but he could not sleep. His mind was still full of the young man for whom he had written what was to be the lad's last words; a lad who looked no more than sixteen. George, his name had been, George. The note was still in Donald's pocket. He would enclose it with the letter of condolences he would write to the boy's mother. He ran his hand over his face in an effort to take away the tiredness and thought of the lads from the island who had left before him, so full of hope and optimism, waving a cheery goodbye as they passed the manse. He wondered where they were now and how many would return home.

'My God,' he whispered. 'Why do you allow such evil?' He went outside and lit a cigarette knowing that, in this place, more than ever before, his faith would be tested to its limits.

The sky had cleared and there was a full moon. Stars twinkled, little blobs of light peppering a navy sky. A heavy ground mist hung all around and, rising above the mist, the barely pencilled tops of fir trees. Every few minutes the sky was lit by the terrible beauty of bursting shells.

A light spilled from the open flap of the hospital tent. An anguished cry rent the night and then faded into silence.

Chapter Eighteen

Isa

Back in Canada, Isa and Davie sat at either side of the table.

'The other immigrants are going.' Davie twisted the coffee cup around in his hands.

Isa stared into the dark liquid in her own cup and said nothing. She had heard talk in the store and he was right; a lot of the young men, not just immigrants, were joining up to help fight the war in Europe. And she knew it wasn't just because of national pride or any lasting loyalty to Britain. Although he had enjoyed the paddle steamers, Davie always yearned for change. She knew that, had she followed him to Prince Rupert, it would not have been long before his wanderlust drew him somewhere else. On the few times he returned home during the summer months, she had the feeling of him slipping away from her; and a new fear, that if he returned to Europe she might never see him again, filled her with dread.

She rose, walked to the window and folded her arms across her chest. 'I know it's been hard here, but with the wheat doing well, you don't have to go, do you? I thought farmers didn't have to.'

'I will sooner or later. It's you and Pierre who run the farm, not me. There's talk of conscription starting soon. Better we all go now and stop the Boche before they go further. The folks back home are having a hard time. Sounds like most of the boys from the island have gone. Wonder how the women are coping?'

'Like the women in Canada will have to cope without the men. Like the women in Europe and everywhere else.' Her voice broke and she covered her face.

Davie was beside her in an instant. He put his arms around her and held her so that she felt the beat of his heart against her cheek, breathed in the scent that was his alone. 'Don't cry.' He nuzzled her hair. 'It'll be over before we know it. And you know, if you were to go back to Raumsey, you'd be closer, if I got leave and that. I believe it's ten days a year, not enough time to come to Canada.'

'I can't go back! Dan loves it here and there's no assisted passages the other way.'

Apart from anything else, survival would be so much harder. Alberta had done well from the wheat, prices were peaking to a dollar a bushel, and life had never been so good. Isa and Davie had used their extra income to extend the homestead, so it now boasted an extra two bedrooms and a pantry. They also had more secure outhouses and fences, and additional livestock. In a few years, Isa dreamed, perhaps they would even own a motor car.

Back in Raumsey, things were not going well. In Chrissie's last letter she had talked about food shortages.

They've built a naval base at Scapa Flow, she had written. *Now the floating shops don't come. The waters are too dangerous. Lottie's shop can't get supplies. All the young men have gone and the women are having to learn to fish lest we starve.*

'Sorry, I didn't think,' said Davie, breaking into her thoughts, his eyes riveted on her face. 'Please understand. It tears me in two every time I leave you, but this is something I've got to do.'

'You still miss Raumsey, don't you?'

'I always will.'

Outside, behind the barn, he had built a boat, a replica of the one he sailed on Raumsey. 'I'll need a boat when we go to Prince Rupert,' he had said. For now he used it on the lake several miles east, transporting it on a trailer he had made for that purpose. During his periods home, they ate many a good fry of fish.

The day he left, he kissed the children and hugged Isa, holding her as if he would never let her go. 'My Isa, my beautiful, strong Isa. Please be strong for me now.' There were tears in his eyes, yet there was also an excitement about him she hadn't seen for a long time and she believed he was looking forward to this as if it was going to be some great adventure. The way he clicked his heels and saluted her the first time he dressed in his uniform, the way his lop-sided smile lit his face, the way he didn't look back when he walked from the shack and joined Pierre on the trap that would take him to the station.

What she didn't know was that he was afraid to look back in case he would not have the strength to go.

She watched the trap until it was no more than a shimmer on the horizon. Turning away, she tried not to think of that other time, when she had stood on the step of her wee cottage in Raumsey and waved her man goodbye, expecting him to return before the sky darkened. Only he hadn't returned, not that night. He hadn't returned for a long, long time. But now, as then, her early years of hardship gave her strength. Keeping fear hidden inside her had been part and parcel of being a fisherman's wife, and it was still there, forever part of her core.

She thought of her children and considered their future. At fourteen Dan was a fine strong lad who loved the land and Canada. Isa studied his ruddy features and gave silent thanks that he was not old enough to fight a war.

Ten-year-old Annie was growing as wild as the terrain around her. She could ride as well as any boy and spent a lot of time with the native children, appearing to prefer them to her own race. She was beautiful with her raven hair and flashing eyes. She looked up from her coffee cup. 'Why did Dad have to go?' she asked, her mouth pulled down in a pout.

Isa had no words for her. She turned her head away to hide her own distress. Summer had not yet relinquished its heat to a cooler autumn, or the fall as she had learned to call this time of year, but another winter loomed before them, cold and lonely. And she grieved for the lover she had lost, as if he were already dead. Except that he wasn't and he had not been ripped away by conscription, it had been his choice to leave her – again.

***

The following spring came in a rush as it always did. The sheets of snow melted in the yards. In the lakes and creeks the thick ice began to break up with loud booming and cracking noises startling Isa and making the dogs bark, officially declaring the end of winter. In the forests, the golden oriols built their nests and the bluebirds filled the skies. The winter wheat had survived well and now grew rapidly. As predicted, the wheat had continued to rise in price, the market constantly growing. Dan, Pierre and two itinerant employees worked tirelessly from dawn to dusk, cutting and gathering the crop.

Letters from Davie came intermittently and she saved them all, wrapped in a ribbon in the drawer of her desk. She often stared over the waving ocean of grain, her heart empty. She knew he had to go, that he would always go, and some day, he would not come back.

Chapter Nineteen

Sarah

Sarah brought a bucket of water into the cabin where she stripped and washed with the blue-veined soap that never lathered. Paddy walked in as she was drying herself. She felt his eyes on her, but made no move to hide her nakedness and continued to towel her neck and arms.

'Cover yourself,' he growled, turning away to lift his rifle from where it hung on the wall, but not before she saw the sorrow in his eyes.

'Going hunting.' He held up the rifle. 'Maybe bag a deer. Venison for supper, eh?'

'Sure.' She dropped the towel and pulled on her drawers and vest, her loose shift and badly-knitted cardigan. 'Is that better?' she asked, but he did not look her way.

What was the point in her trying to entice him? He would not touch her, never had through all those years. At first she'd been grateful, still was, for she had no desire for the man, but she yearned for a child of her own, as if having someone to love would in some small way compensate for the waste of her life. As the years passed and her body grew and matured, the yearning had almost become an obsession. Even a letter from home would have gone some way to ease her loneliness, but in spite of the many she'd written, no one ever replied. Eventually she stopped writing, but never a day had gone by that she didn't wonder about Eileen, Bridie and the boys.

Sometimes Paddy left the house and returned with the smell of drink and other women on him. Sometimes he would stay at home and sink a few jars. She looked forward to those nights, because he would talk to her, tell her what was going on in the outside world. She had little of interest to tell him, but was a captive audience. From time to time, she thought that he was not aware of her presence and spoke only for the pleasure of hearing his own voice. At those times, he could be funny, making her laugh with tales of his boyhood, especially stories of the O'Flaugharteys who lodged next door to him in the streets of Liverpool after his family had moved from Ireland. 'Old Ma O'Flaughartey.' He shook his head, his face creased with laughter. 'As mad as the banshee. Once a month, come the full moon she'd go crazy. Twelve of a family, like steps on the stairs they were. And my, when the auld man went on the poteen, they would scatter like cockroaches in the light for fear of her temper. Aye, a fearsome devil that woman was. Sure, the streets of Liverpool often rang with her yelling.'

In a blink of an eye, his mood could change and his talk would turn to the war in Europe. Rumour was that all the young men were going to be conscripted, those who hadn't signed up already. 'Sure, I would never fight for the English.' The laughter slipped from his face. 'T'was a sad time for my family in the owld country, praties rotting in the fields, bairns dropping dead from the starvation. What did the English do? Carried on taxing folks that didn't have a crust to their name, and when they couldn't pay they threw them out, pulled the houses down around their ears. The work houses were full to overflowing. The Irish peasants died in ditches with not a rag to keep them warm. A quarter of the population of Ireland died that way, and many more left. It was before I was born, but I've heard many a tale. No, no, I'll take a knife to me own heart before I take up arms to help the English.' Then great tears would roll down his cheeks and he would begin to sing some desolate song that wrenched at the heart.

Sarah listened to the stories and the songs until she knew them, word for word. When she cried with him though, it wasn't for the plight of the Irish, it was because she had never forgotten the baby she had borne, the fear and horror when it forced itself from her, the pain and the distress: how she cried herself to sleep night after night, blaming herself for his death, and worse still, having Paddy blame her too. In her head she still heard the whimper, felt him move against her leg. Was it her memory or had she imagined that he had been born alive? The next thing she remembered was the Indian woman rubbing the child's chest, looking at Paddy and shaking her head, Paddy storming out into the night.

And Davie. He had been so gentle, so kind. She had never forgotten the feel of his arms around her when he sheltered her from the storm the day of the tornado. Isa was so lucky to have a man like him.

She had tried to be a good wife to Paddy, cooked and cleaned, even strived to have a conversation, but that was difficult as she could never think of anything to say. For a long time he had turned from her as if she disgusted him and for a long time, she had disgusted herself.

With a sigh, she lifted her hair and let it fall so that it tumbled down her back. Then she crossed to the bench where she slept and removed the flat box from underneath. She opened the lid and pulled out the baby clothes she had altered to fit a new born, the baby clothes she had received from Isa, Annie's cast-offs. Below that was a small bag of coins. What little she managed to squirrel away over the years, the money she planned to use to make her escape some day; except that she feared she would never find the courage. If only there was some way she could find work in the town. But she had no training, nowhere to live, little knowledge of anything beyond this shack and the land it stood on. Her only contact with the outside world was an occasional trip to the store with Paddy and an even more occasional visit to the church service. The church put on activities, but Paddy never offered to take her and she had never asked to go.

The wheels of the cart made a crunching noise outside. Paddy was returning. She stuffed the money and the garments back into the box and shoved it once more under the bench.

'Are ye in there, me girl?' He pushed the door open. 'Come on, we need to go to the store. It's clean out of ammunition I am.'

There was no knowing when Paddy would turn up needing her to help him with the supplies, the traps, or whatever else he had in his mind to do at that moment. He expected her to be prepared as if he had arranged it with her beforehand. She tied her hair up. 'Yes, I'm ready,' she said.

Left alone outside while Paddy did business in the store, Sarah strained her ears to hear the words of three young women standing on the decking chatting about going across the seas as nurses. Interested, Sarah moved ever closer in an effort to catch every word.

One of them turned and looked at her. 'Do you want something?' she asked.

Realising she had been staring, Sarah's immediate instinct was to turn and run. She began to shake her head, but then, with a sudden burst of courage, she took a deep breath. 'You're going overseas?'

They stared at her for a beat.

'Yes,' said one. 'They need nurses for the hospitals. Why should the men have all the fun?' The others laughed.

'I'd like to go too,' said Sarah in a small voice.

'Are you a nurse?' asked the other.

Sarah's face grew hot. Of course she wasn't. How could she have been so foolish? She lowered her head and backed away, her legs suddenly weak as if they belonged to someone else who didn't know how to work them properly. She tripped on the hem of her skirt and staggered back before the hitching rail saved her from falling over.

'They're taking volunteers, too. Just to help. Everyone's going to be needed,' said another girl quickly. Sarah grasped the rail behind her. She thought of how she must look. Her shapeless shift, her straggly hair, her rough hands with broken nails, her red face and clumsy movements. 'Would… would they take…me?' She hadn't meant to speak, but the words had rushed from her as if her tongue had a mind of its own. Now she felt more foolish than ever. Of course they wouldn't. What had she been thinking?

'Yes. I'm sure they would,' said the woman, startling Sarah. She looked kind.

'They…they would?' A sudden spurt of hope lightened her heart.

Just then Paddy came out. 'Come away, girl. No time to stand around gawpin.'

'My name's Ida McLean.' The woman who had spoken last smiled. 'I help out at the school sometimes. Ask for me there.' Glancing at Paddy, she nodded, a brief nod of acknowledgment and she moved away with a smile of farewell to Sarah.

'What did she want?' asked Paddy.

'Being neighbourly, I suppose.' Sarah suppressed the urge to hug herself. Perhaps they would take her, perhaps she could really be of some use.

'Aye, well, some women have high ideas. You'd best not be listening to them.' He cracked the whip and the horse took off at a trot.

From then on, the idea of leaving spun in her head until it gave her no peace, until she knew that she would rather die than spend the rest of her life in this half existence.

The following day, after Paddy left, she brushed her hair and pulled on her best blouse and skirt, at the same time glancing out of the window. He could be gone all day, or he could return at any minute. She didn't know how he would react if he came back and found her gone, it had never happened.

With her heart beating a staccato, she pulled on her only footwear, a pair of winter boots, and with her pouch of money tied to her belt, set out to walk to the schoolhouse.

Two hours later, a weary and footsore Sarah stood outside the school and waited until the children tumbled into the yard, followed by a slim young woman, her hair rolled neatly behind her ears.

'You take care now,' she called, then noticed Sarah. 'Hello,' she said.

'I was looking for Ida McLean.' Sarah began to wish she had never come. What if Paddy had returned to find her gone? What excuse could she use?

'Nurse McLean? She comes here to check the children on her day off. But I'm sorry, she'll not be here till tomorrow.'

Sarah almost felt relief. She had tried. She checked the buttons on her blouse, her shabby clothes embarrassing her before this smartly-dressed young lady. She walked backwards. 'Thanks. Tomorrow. Right.' She bent down and removed the boots, which were hurting, then she turned and ran as fast as her blistered feet would let her.

'Who will I say called,' shouted the schoolmistress, her voice dying as the distance between them lengthened.

Sarah kept running. Finally, exhausted, she stopped and sat by the side of the road, tears of frustration streaming down her face. What had she thought? That someone would take her under their wing? Give her food and shelter and arrange for her to go overseas? That would never happen. If she were to break free, she would have to find the courage to see it through herself. And what was out there? After all this time, would the world overwhelm her, would she make a laughing stock of herself? And what of Paddy? He had been kind to her in his fashion. Did he deserve to be abandoned this way? Maybe she was better off where she was. These questions plagued her, turned over in her mind, but now that the possibility of escape had presented itself, her life had become intolerable.

How she wished she could talk to Paddy, tell him what was in her heart. Yet if she did and he forbade her to speak to those women again, she would be worse off than she was now. As she walked home, she decided to keep quiet and prayed that he would not find out she had been to the village.

As luck would have it, Paddy did not return until late that night, and had no knowledge that she had been away.

Chapter Twenty

Donald

Donald had been called to the trenches to minister to those too fatally wounded to be transported to hospital before they departed this earth, and to assist in bringing the bodies and injured back to the holding base. He arrived just before dawn as the last ambulance was leaving, it being too dangerous to travel in daylight.

'We've been joined by a platoon of Canadians,' said the sergeant who accompanied Donald to the front line. 'They're grand fighters.'

Bullets whizzed over their heads, shells burst in the heavy clouds.

'Keep your head down,' shouted the sergeant as Donald straightened up to see the way ahead. Underfoot was muddy and slippy. It had been raining for several days and they found the soldiers in the trenches up to their knees in muddy, stinking water.

'You're stationed with the doctor in the regimental aid post just behind the trenches,' the sergeant told him. 'Here.'

He led him down into a sandbagged dugout. The first thing that struck Donald was the cold and damp permeating the air. A brazier sat against one wall and there was a couch of sorts and a paraffin stove with a kettle, mugs and a box of tea.

The doctor, a young man with a sad face, wiped the blood from his fingers before offering Donald his hand. 'Good to have you on board, Padre,' he said. 'Usually I have two dressers as well, but they've gone to the front to bring in more injured. We've just shipped out the last batch of poor fellows. Has everything been explained to you?'

'I'm aware that this is the first place that the wounded are brought to,' he replied, 'To be treated before being taken to the dressing station.'

The doctor gave a short laugh. 'Treated? All we've time to do is to wrap up their injuries as best we can.'

'At least we have a little warmth.' Donald looked hopefully at the dying embers in the brazier, as if somehow heat might keep life within the expected wave of shattered bodies.

'There's a ruined building in no-man's-land,' said the sergeant. 'The cellar is full of coal. Some of the lads have been sneaking over in the dark and bringing back what they can. For now there's none left.' Eyes that held a world of tragedy met Donald's. 'Here a man has no time to think, thankfully so, otherwise we would go mad.'

Donald knew what he meant. Thoughts, dreams, memories of home floated above the realm of reality. Here there was no sense of time, just a desperation to do what had to be done without question.

Then came a lull when the guns were quiet, but almost at once, noise exploded through the silence, the rattle of rifles, machine guns and bursting shells. Donald walked to the door of the dugout. The countryside was alight with Very lights and blinding flashes of explosives, the air filled with flying lead and steel. Within minutes of the assault, the injured began to arrive, many walking, even more on stretchers.

The two dressers introduced themselves briefly while they worked.

'What can I do?' asked Donald, wishing he knew more than basic first-aid.

'Pray with them. Give them a cigarette, wipe the sweat from their faces. We can't get them to better facilities until the ambulance arrives once it's dark. We do our best here, but...' The doctor shook his head.

Donald knelt on the floor and gave what comfort he could. His prayers were a despairing and futile plea to his God to intervene, to somehow stop this carnage. One man exhaled his last breath as Donald grasped his hand, desperately trying to sustain him with his own life force. The lad's leg was missing, and half his face gone.

The air within the bunker grew thick with the smell of blood and death, and the crying and moaning from the men ripped at Donald's heart. A confident rat waited in the corner, its eyes fixed on the reverend as if daring him to chase it away. A shiver ran up Donald's spine. 'Get, scat,' he shouted, waving his hand, but the rodent simply fixed him with a beady, devilish stare.

'He'd be in a pot of stew if I could catch him,' came the angry voice of a stretcher bearer as the two men brought in a muddy, blood-splattered young man and rested him in the last available space. One foot dangled from a bloody trouser leg and lay at an impossible angle.

Donald straightened up and rubbed his cold hands together. Something about the soldier stirred a memory. The lad was openly staring at him, his eyes bright blue in the mud splashed face.

'Reverend Charleston.' The soldier gasped allowing his head to fall back.

'Doctor will be with you in a moment.' Donald, knelt beside him. He raised the man's head and gently wiped some of the mud from his face.

'Davie?' he said. 'Is it Davie Reid?'

The soldier smiled, his teeth a flash of white in the blackened face. He grabbed Donald by the wrist. 'My...but it's grand to see you. Are there others? I mean...from Raumsey?' His voice was hoarse and pain-filled.

'I came over with a couple of lads, but we were separated. I haven't bumped into any others, but all the young men have left the island. Most went to the navy.'

'Aye, they would.' Davie's face twisted and he squeezed his eyes shut. 'God, it hurts.'

One of the dressers, a man too old for active fighting, came over and ripped away Davie's trouser leg. 'By, lad, thee'd be losing that leg if'n we don't get thee to a hospital.' He shook his head. 'The bone's broke. We'll need to put it in a splint.'

Davie's eyes, filled with a desperate plea, met Donald's. 'Don't let them take my leg.'

'We'll do us best.' The dresser forced a wedge of cotton between Davie's teeth. 'Bite down on this, lad. Over here, Doc.'

The doctor came up, took one look at his injuries and gave him a shot of morphine.

Davie pressed his eyelids together, his face twisted in pain and he bit on the wad until the drug took effect. The dresser roughly aligned the bones in his leg and bandaged the wound. 'All done.' He stood up.

Davie relaxed, turned his head and looked at the corpse on the stretcher next to his. 'Mac. Oh God, is that you, Mac?' He raised his eyes to Donald's. 'We…we came over together, an immigrant, Scottish…like me. Were you in time, Minister? Did you say the words for him?'

'I was in time.' Donald walked to the stove and filled the kettle from a container. Somehow he had slipped into the island way of making tea when there was nothing left to say.

'Tell me, Minister, is hell worse than this?' whispered Davie. He had started to shake. 'Guess it'll be warmer, eh?'

Donald tried to smile but only managed a grim stretching of the mouth. 'How is Isa?' he asked, lowering himself to the floor, hands clasped round a steaming tin mug which he held to Davie's lips.

'Grand. Likes the life better…than me.' His voice broke, his body tensed. The morphine must be wearing off, Donald thought, but there was no more to spare. What little they had was reserved for the most extreme levels of pain. Davie stared ahead, his eyes fixed on some distant point, each breath shaking its way to his lungs.

'How long have you been here?' Donald asked.

Davie blinked. 'Just arrived…last week. Guess we're not going…to get home for Christmas, then?' He eased himself onto one elbow so he could take another sip of tea. 'What day is it?' He fell back as if exhausted.

'Seventeenth of December.' Donald stood up. 'They'll get you somewhere more comfortable soon.' Once night had squeezed out the last of the daylight, the bodies and the wounded could be shipped out.

'More than a week, then,' whispered Davie as the stretcher

137

bearers came for him. 'Will you still be here if I'm fit to return?'

'I don't know. Like everyone else, I have to be ready to move on when I get the order.'

They shook hands and parted.

Donald had grown used to the noises around him, used to lying on a damp ground under canvas, used to blanking out the misery of the day to catch a few precious hours of oblivion. But tonight, he dreamed of Isa, her black hair, her flashing eyes, the way she had looked at him with absolute trust. The words she had said to him, when he had offered to take her away; *'It would never be right. I could never forget Davie, and you could never forget God.'* He woke with a start, her name on his lips, and realised he was still in hell.

The next day he was moved several miles south along the trenches, and he wondered if he would ever see Davie Reid again.

Chapter Twenty-One

Sarah

It was another month before Sarah and Paddy went to the store again. A group of women stood around the counter and the talk was all about the war. Recognising Isa among them, Sarah caught her eye and gave a small, nervous smile. The two women hadn't seen much of each other in the last few years. Sarah missed her friend and envied her strength and the way she was making a success of the farm, the loneliness of her own life exacerbated by Isa's achievements.

'It's grand to see you, Sarah,' Isa said. 'Jess here was telling me how the Red Cross are looking for volunteers to make bandages.'

'Red Cross?' Sarah had never heard the term before.

'Sure, they need willing workers. It'll be hard with the men gone and many folks with farms to run, but we all need to do our bit,' said Jess.

'There's more work than ever to do on the land, but we all can spare a few hours,' said another woman.

'I...I *could* make bandages.' Sarah's nervousness caused her breath to speed up. A tingle started in the pit of her stomach. Here was a chance to get away from the cabin, to mix with others, to make friends. 'But... I wouldn't know how.'

Isa gave a light laugh. 'I'm sure it's easy enough. Come with me. I'll call for you tomorrow.'

Then a new thought struck her. Would Paddy allow it? 'I...I don't know...'

Isa shrugged. 'I'll call for you anyway. Take you with me. Tomorrow.'

'We need as many hands as we can get,' said Jess. 'You'll be made very welcome, Sarah.'

Her voice was kind, warm. What would it be like to work

along with these women, make some real friends? This was her chance. She suddenly knew she wanted this so much she could taste it.

'Yes, thanks. I want to.' She hugged herself, her eyes darting round the other faces. 'Thank you,' she said again and backed away.

'What's up with ye, girl?' asked Paddy coming up behind her. 'There's a fine sparkle in yer een I've not seen before.' He eyed her suspiciously.

'I…I was speaking to women here.' She twisted her fingers together. 'The Red Cross needs women to make bandages and pack stuff. I..I could help.'

'What? I'll no have ye doin a thing to help the English.'

'But it's not the English. It's our own soldiers who are wounded and dying.' Isa spoke with a catch in her voice. 'It could be Davie or Hector or any of the young lads you traded with, Paddy.'

'All the other women are helping.' The woman called Jess added.

'I want to do it. Please.' Sarah suddenly found a passion that had been lacking before and realised that she didn't want to join the Red Cross simply to get out from her life of solitude, but that she genuinely wanted to help.

Paddy narrowed his eyes and stared at her. 'It'll no give ye fancy ideas, now?'

'What fancy ideas? Isa's going to do it.' She knew Paddy held Isa in high regard, saw his hesitation and threw the other women a glance that said, *help me here*.

Isa laid a hand on Paddy's arm. 'Let her be. This war's a terrible thing. Any little I can do, I'm going to do it, and Sarah here is fit and able. I'll call for her tomorrow.'

Paddy grunted and relinquished. 'If ye're sure she'll be home in time to make my supper.'

Unbidden, Sarah felt the smile spread across a face so unused to smiling that the muscles ached. She could have hugged him at that moment.

***

That night she washed her shift and polished her boots. For the first time since she had come to Canada, she had something to look forward to.

She waited by the window the following morning, her fingers gripping the sill until they hurt. When she saw Isa's trap approaching, she ran out and clambered up beside her.

'My,' said Isa, 'Ye look like a wee girl going to her first party.'

Sarah laughed and the laugh filled her up. That was exactly how she felt.

On the way to the village, they sang together, old songs they had learned when they had been children.

'My ma used to sing with us,' said Sarah. 'Ee, she had a lovely voice. Could've sung in a music hall, I've heard folks say.'

'Ye have a good voice and all.' Isa sounded surprised.

Sarah fell silent. She hadn't thought about her mother for a long time, now the memory came back at her with enough force to bring tears to her eyes. 'I'm proud of ye, Sarah,' she used to say. 'You're such a help with the wee ones.'

What would she think if she could see her now?

When they reached the village, Isa tied the pony to a hitching post and they joined a group of women of all ages filing into the school. Two ladies in Red Cross uniforms greeted them by the door. 'Nice to see you all, take a seat.'

Sarah sat between Isa and Connie Fisher, an unmarried lass from Stony Plains. There was a general shuffling and settling as the two Red Cross officers climbed onto the platform. One remained standing and welcomed them to the meeting. 'Women aren't just needed to make bandages,' she said, looking around. 'We need them to produce and conserve food; raise funds to finance hospitals, ambulances, hostels, and aircraft. If you can't leave your home for whatever reason, we need you to knit socks and scarfs to keep our poor boys warm. There's plenty to do on your own doorstep. With the men gone, women are needed to fill the workplaces. So whether you have family or are free to leave, we need volunteers inside and outside the country.

The second woman stepped up. She held a letter in her hand. 'Yesterday I received this from a nursing colleague of mine. She's in France. For those who choose to go, it's as well that you know what to expect.' She proceeded to read part of the letter aloud.

Despite all the tragedy, we have a healthy life here. When our work is over we sleep. We wash in cold water (no bath-tubs here), and we have eau de cologne to rub down in the morning. We walk to and from the hospital. It is bitter cold and misty and half-dark in the morning. We often get glimpses of regiments on their way to the front, and white-capped old French-women. At night the stars are wonderful, and every day and night there is the boom of the guns and flashes in the sky. Food is hard to get, and we only occasionally have meat. We live mostly on a soup made from beans and potatoes. But I am glad I am here doing what I can for the effort. It is a wonderful feeling to be part of it.

Sarah listened to every word, her excitement growing. No, she didn't want to stay here and make bandages or knit socks. She wanted to go to Europe, be part of something more, be important at last, leave her life of nothingness behind, be closer to her siblings, perhaps even see them again. All at once it seemed possible and she was swept away on a wave of optimism.

Summoning all of her new-found courage, she approached one of the Red Cross officers when the talk was over.

'I want to be a nurse,' she said. 'But I've not got the training.'

'We need both trained nurses and helpers.' The woman handed her a leaflet. 'We'll be back here tomorrow if you're serious.'

That night, for the first time, she had something of significance to tell Paddy. He stared at her, surprise on his face. 'Ye look different, lass. Sure it's done ye a power of good. I have no objection at all to ye making bandages for the poor fellows.'

Sarah fiddled with a button on her blouse. 'I want to do more, Paddy. I want to be a nurse, go to Europe.' She trembled. Her words shook as she grabbed what morsel of courage she possessed and allowed it to grow within her.

There, it was said. Out in the open, hanging between them like a tangible accusation. As the words twisted in the air, filling the spaces in the shack, she held her breath, waiting for the onslaught, prepared to deflect any argument.

Paddy's first reaction was anger. 'Damn, woman, what fanciful notions have ye got in yer head now?' As his eyes met hers, he saw something there that he'd never seen before. Behind the demure, passive exterior, there was a new and gritty determination. For the first time he saw, not just a faint-hearted girl without an opinion of her own, but a woman with needs and wants like any other.

'Making bandages is one thing, but this! It's lost yer head ye have. Sure didn't I take ye in and give ye respectability and a roof over yer head? And now ye want to go and help the British army? Ye might as well take a knife to me heart.'

'I'm forever grateful for all ye've done for me. But my life here is lonely. Sometimes I want to run into the woods and let a wolf or a coyote eat me, for I have no existence at all.' Red dots appeared on her cheeks, her lip set in a determined line.

Horrified and shocked at this thought, Paddy grabbed her hand, felt the bones beneath the rough skin. And he looked at her, really looked at her. Her eyes were round, angry, her shoulders squared, her nostrils flaring slightly with every breath. He wanted to say something, to seize control again, but words failed him. It was true, all these years he had taken her for granted, enjoyed the fact that a hot meal was waiting for him every night, that his clothes were clean and folded when he needed a shift, that he had a confidante when he wanted to get things off his chest, and she hadn't complained, not once. He had never stopped to consider her needs. However he acted now, he feared he was going to lose her.

He backed down under her glare, surprised by the ferocity of it, surprised too, by his own sudden insight. 'Sure it's the eejit I've been. I never knew what I had here, right under my roof, for I know that if ye go, I'll miss ye sorely.' And he meant every word.

'I'm sorry, Paddy, but they will take me.' She cleared her throat and met his eye. 'And I'm going, with or without yer blessing.'

Suddenly he saw the emptiness of his life without her, yet knew by the set of her mouth and the determination in her eyes, that he had no longer the power to command her. 'Stay with me, lass. Not because I order ye to, but because, I ...' the word he was about to say stuck in his throat. 'I love ye.' He turned away to hide his face. 'Not like...not like my Nikota, no not like that at all.' He faced her again, coughed and fought to find the words. 'I know I have to let ye go. It's the least I can do for ye. I'm not a man to pray, but I will. I'll pray that ye'll see fit to come back to me... because ye want to.' To his horror, he felt his eyes fill with tears.

'Paddy?' she said, coming up to him.

'Ye shoulda told me, lass. Said what ye wanted. I've been a real eejit. I thought ye were content cooking and cleaning and I know ye never wanted me to lay a finger on ye. I shouldn't have married ye, for I've come to look on ye like a daughter, not a wife. When I said I loved ye, and mind, it's not a word that comes easy, I meant...I meant it, like ye were my own flesh and blood. Ye go and do what ye must, but I wish ye'd stay.'

Sarah leaned forward and kissed his cheek. It was the first physical contact she had ever made with him, and she, too, realised that this gruff, untidy man meant a lot more to her than she had believed. In spite of her longing for a child, she was suddenly very glad that he had never laid a hand on her.

She said, 'I will come back, when all this is over. I promise, for you've been a far better father to me than the one I left behind.'

Chapter Twenty-Two

Donald

'Time to be moving on,' said the colonel. 'Bad business up at Vimy Ridge. The padre there was hit by a piece of shrapnel and had to be sent to hospital. They can't hold off the funerals for long. They did well, though, those Canadians. Captured most of the ridge and the town of Thélus. If we ride all night we should be there by daybreak.'

Donald went to collect his kit. He was growing used to this, packing up at a moment's notice, riding to wherever he was needed. But he doubted whether he would ever become hardened to the horror and madness that seemed to escalate with every new day.

Dull with exhaustion, they entered the camp in the early morning, just as the fog was rising. The Canadian burial officer met them, a tired-faced man, droplets of mist outlining his head and shoulders in a silvery sheen.

'We've got fifty-three bodies.' He didn't wait for introductions. 'We've got the Boche on the run and we need to press on to keep the advantage. There's no time for individual burials. I've ordered that a bomb crater be used as a mass grave.'

Donald's hands tightened on the horse's reins. It was unthinkable that the dead be shown so little respect, yet he knew the practicalities of war. He slid from his mount and secured his pack across his shoulders. 'Take me to them.'

His heart sank when he looked at the bodies piled one on the other in the bottom of the crater. The oxygen seemed to have been sucked out of the air and his head spun. 'Oh, dear God, give me strength to carry on,' he said beneath his breath.

'They were brave men, all of them.' The officer joined Donald, removed his hat and stared down into the hole.

'Have they been identified?' asked Donald as the world collected itself around him.

'Impossible with some of them. But we have their dog tags. Fifty of them were Canadians. Are you ready to say the words, padre?'

Donald moistened his lips. At this moment he didn't want to say kind words, he wanted to curse and scream, berate the God he believed in for allowing this to happen. All these young men, each one someone's son, father, sweetheart. He wanted more time to write his sermon, to give these lads the send-off they deserved. He clenched his fists and closed his eyes as the mist prickled his skin and he gave himself up to a silent prayer without words.

The steady rat-a-tat-tat of machine guns and the exploding shells, distant now but still fierce, told him that time was not on his side. He suffered the dreadful sensation that there would be many more bodies by nightfall.

'We have a list of those in the regiment. Can I ask you to write to the next of kin?' the burial officer's voice was flat, emotionless.

'Of course.' His own voice was no different. He knew the words he was expected to write by heart. Yet no words he could imagine would salve the pain that his letters would bring to the families.

That night he sat with the Sergeant going through the dog tags, each one all that was left of a brave and promising young life. When he set the last tag down he sighed with relief. He had not come upon the name he had been in dread of finding, David Reid.

'Try to get some sleep, my man,' said the sergeant. 'You're to be moved to the military hospital in Caux Seine Auf, tomorrow. A bit of mean respite for a while, what? You can write the letters there.'

Donald nodded, but they both knew that he would get no rest that night. His head was too full of recent images to leave him in peace.

The next day, after a difficult train voyage, he was faced with a scene that he considered closer to Hell than anything he had seen before. A consignment of wounded had been drawn from three distributing stations instead of one. He arrived almost at the same time as these men and the smell of death, blood and putrefaction thickened the air. Cries for help and screams of pain rising above the rumble of the jeep engines were the first sounds that assaulted his ears. This was not new, he had helped with the seriously wounded before, but here he was met by the devastation in a much larger scale. Most of these patients were amputees and medication for pain relief was scant and had to be rationed. The hospital was no more than several large tents with beds lining both sides. Storm lanterns hung at intervals down the makeshift street.

He was met by a woman about his own age in a sister's uniform.

'Good day, minister.' She grasped his hand in a firm, dry handshake. 'I'm Sister McBeth. It's good to have you aboard.' Her wide welcoming smile lit up an otherwise plain face, but her deep blue eyes held a depth of both pain and acceptance.

He liked the fact that she called him 'minister' and not 'padre' the term to which he had become accustomed, and he recognised the soft lilt in her voice at once.

'You're from Scotland,' he said, as she withdrew her hand from his.

'Yes. Paisley. Before I show you your quarters, you have to see someone. Both his legs have gone. He lay in a shell hole for six days with nothing to eat and the hole was filled with water. He had to drink that water to keep alive. It's a wonder he made it this far.'

Donald followed her, imagining the muddy, disease-filled liquid.

'That's not all.' The sister lowered her voice as they reached the tent entrance. 'Beside him in that water was decaying the body of his best friend.'

As soon as Donald saw the man, he knew that he had arrived just in time. The shadow of death which he had come to recognise on so many faces was poised to steal his soul. Donald narrowed his eyes and summoned his willpower. *You will not have him yet,* the unspoken words were directed at the unseen spectre.

'Are you alright, minister?' asked Sister McBeth.

'Yes, of course.' He realised he was shaking. 'What's his name?'

'Private White. James.'

Donald grasped the soldier's hand. When Donald spoke his name, the eyelids flickered, the lips parted slightly and a sense of peace settled on his features.

'Mary?' His eyes flitted to the sister.

She glanced at Donald before sinking to her knees. 'I'm here,' she whispered.

'Padre…padre…' The words choked from him and he fought to say more.

'Hush.' Sister McBeth stroked his head. 'Don't try to talk. I'll stay with you.'

The body stiffened. 'Pray…for…me…' the words sat on a rush of outward breath, his head fell slack, then he lay still.

Donald prayed fervently to a God in whom he no longer had any faith as the last breath rattled from James' lungs.

'I think he was holding out for your words,' whispered Sister McBeth as she rose. 'They often think we nurses are their sweethearts or their mothers. It's a kindness not to disillusion them.' She pulled the sheet over his face.

'Are there others I need to see?'

'Not as near death as this soldier. Some didn't make the journey. I've got to go now. One of the volunteers will show you where to stash your kit.'

He was quartered in what had once been a farmhouse, but most of it had been demolished. However, the kitchen and a good part of the main room had been preserved and although there was a stove, there was little fuel. He shared with the surgeon, a solemn old man from Wales who had come out of retirement to help the cause. The rest of the camp was made up by tents and hastily erected wooden huts. Darkness had already fallen. The oil lamp on the windowsill reflected in the glass, and beyond it, the room where he was to sleep. The pallets on the floor, the scarred walls, a rickety table, a dead fireplace and in the midst of it all, he saw himself. He was almost startled by the pale, haggard face staring back at him. In the yellow light every crease and shadow on his face seemed darker and more deeply etched. 'Oh God, is there no end to this?' he muttered, as he dragged his hand over his eyes and turned away.

Later that night, when the crickets and tree frogs were once more heard and the twilight was soft, he sat on a bench outside the hospital watching newly-patched-up soldiers enjoy a game of football before they were shipped back to the front the next day.

'Turn your back on the devastation in there and it's hard to believe there's a war on,' said a voice at his elbow. Sister McBeth lowered herself onto the seat beside him. She brought out a cigarette, lit it and blew smoke into the air. She handed the cigarette to him.

Donald had only begun to smoke again since he had come to France. The taste of tobacco helped to kill the bitter air of war that found its way into a man's lungs and seeped through his pores. He thanked her and drew deeply before passing it back. 'Aye,' he said.

For several minutes they shared the smoke in silence, a companionable silence that needed no words.

'I need to get back.' She rose and handed the still-lit stub to him.

'You've never stopped working.' He had noticed the dark rings shadowing her eyes.

'Tiredness is nothing compared to what those poor souls are going through.' She smoothed her hands down her uniform and nodded towards the men, still kicking the ball, laughing and shouting. 'I wonder how many we'll see back here. I wonder how many will ever go home. War is evil.'

'Aye, the devil's work, Sister McBeth.'

She looked at him steadily. 'My name is Margaret. And we're officially off duty.'

'Donald.' He smiled.

'But then we never really are – off duty, I mean, Donald.' Her body exuded weariness and he wondered how many hours' sleep she had had the night before. 'Maybe you would ask your God to end this madness,' she said as she left.

Donald nodded and stared grimly at the empty sky as the distant booming began again.

Day after day he worked alongside Margaret. She was kind but firm with the nurses under her charge and she was everything to her patients. One night as he took his evening stroll, he saw her come out of the hospital tent. She walked slowly, her shoulders bent. Suddenly she staggered and collapsed against a light pole. He ran over and caught her as she fell. Shouting to the doctor, he carried her to her quarters. Ten minutes later, the doctor came out to find Donald waiting beyond the door. 'She's exhausted,' he said. 'She admitted that she has not had any sleep for three nights. I've given her something to make sure she sleeps at least for eight hours.'

It was several nights later before they met up again and shared a cigarette. She looked better, rested. 'You'll be no use to your patients if you've run yourself into the ground.' He passed the cigarette back to her.

She said nothing, but their eyes met and held, and at that moment he knew his admiration for her was something much more. As if driven by an unseen force, they simultaneously leaned towards each other until their lips touched, gently, chastely at first.

In the distance bombs fell from a rumbling sky. When the kiss became more demanding, Margaret pulled back. 'This is madness.'

'I know.' He remained where he was and clasped her hand, holding the palm against his mouth, allowing his eyes to roam over her face, now flushed in the pale light.

'After the war,' she said.

Donald nodded and closed his eyes. He did nothing to hide the fact that he was aroused by her. If she had been willing, he knew his vow of chastity before marriage would not have stopped him seizing the moment. There was a possibility that neither would come through this war alive. Surely God would forgive them for grasping at whatever pleasure they could. Realising he was shaking, he dropped her hand. 'You're right of course.'

She fumbled in her pocket and brought out another cigarette, lit it with a trembling hand and offered it to him. 'Me smoking. My mother would be horrified,' she said.

Chapter Twenty-Three

Sarah and Isa

There was a general air of excitement among the volunteers as they filed down the street and shuffled into the building, finding seats on the long wooden benches. A woman in a matron's uniform stood on the platform, flanked by an army sergeant and a priest.

'Good evening, volunteers.' The woman had a loud booming voice, and the general hubbub in the room fell silent. She held up a sheaf of papers. 'We have our orders. We are to depart in December for Quebec City to receive military training.'

The women cheered.

'We hope you will be ready to sail for England by February,' she continued. 'Congratulations on joining the Canadian Overseas Expeditionary Force as part of the Canadian Army Medical Corps.'

Now that her imaginings were taking shape and becoming a reality, Sarah's nerve shook and threatened to desert her. She looked around at the other excited faces and ran her tongue over dry lips. She, Sarah McAfferty, for she never thought of herself as O'Brien, was going to be part of something, be someone of importance.

'Frightened?' said a voice at her elbow. She turned around to see Maureen, a quiet girl, with whom she had formed an attachment, but knew little about.

'I am a bit,' admitted Sarah. 'You?'

Maureen nodded. 'I've never been away from home before. My folks are real worried, but my dad and brother have gone already. I wouldn't go if I didn't have two sisters at home. How are your folks about it?'

Sarah thought of Paddy. 'I've only got my dad. He doesn't want me to go, but he'll not stop me.' She said it proudly, pleased with her new-found identity. Yes she would remain O'Brien, but now for different reasons.

The official-looking woman and two of her helpers were going around taking names. When they stopped at Sarah, her pen poised above the clip board, the woman looked at her enquiringly.

'Sarah O'Brien.' Her heart thundered, her stomach roiled, but there was no going back now. She would talk to Paddy tonight. Ask him about a divorce. The Catholic church did not allow divorce, but when had Paddy ever had much time for the confines of religion? The marriage had been unconsummated. Would an annulment be allowed so many years later? She did not know. In any case, she would offer to keep his name and live with him as a daughter. Yes, that's what she would do. He had been kind to her in his way, he was her only security and she had to admit that the thought of breaking all ties with him scared her.

***

The following day, as Isa rolled her last bandage, she smiled her goodbyes to her workmates. Here in this warehouse, converted for the war effort, she had found the fellowship reminiscent of her days working for the Floating Shops of Orkney as a young, single lassie. However, the harvest was looming. Work still had to be done on the farm, and now, with most of the young men gone and labour more difficult to find, it was harder than ever.

As she made for the door, she felt a hand on her arm and turned around to see Sarah, her eyes shining.

'I'm going back to England.' She looked more alive than Isa had ever seen her. Since she had started working for the war effort, there had been a transformation in the girl. She was changing from a frightened waif into a woman with opinions of her own. Today she almost looked animated.

'England?' Isa could hardly conceal her surprise.

'Me and some of the other girls. We've enlisted. We're volunteers – going to work in a hospital. Maybe in England – but we want to go to Europe. Oh Isa, I want to be a nurse.'

'What does Paddy say about this?' asked Isa, doing nothing to conceal her surprise. It had always appeared that he dominated her, told her what to do, what to think.

Sarah's face fell a little. 'I haven't told him. Well, not that I'm actually going. But he'll not stop me. We've spoken. And...I will miss him. He's been good to me.' She stopped for a minute. 'I'm hoping they'll let me go to Liverpool before...well, I want to see my sisters and brothers again.'

Isa felt a frisson of envy. If not for the bairns she would have joined them. 'I wish you every luck,' she said. 'I hope you see your family.'

'I wanted to say goodbye.' Sarah's voice was smaller.

'Will ye come back?'

'If the Boche don't get me.'

'Don't even joke about that.'

'I'm sorry.'

'It's fine. Good luck.' Isa smiled, squeezed the other woman's arm then hurried out the door. She climbed onto her bicycle and jolted over the rough track towards the homestead. She was glad for Sarah. Glad the girl was finally getting out of a nothing existence; but, for herself, every day had become a monotonous round of work from morning to night. She was grateful to have her mother at home and for Pierre for his help on the land. The man was old, his back bent, but his loyalty was absolute.

Then she had Dan, old enough and strong enough to do the work of a man, and he loved the farm. She looked up at the endless sky, the evening sunlight casting a golden glow over the prairies, the dark scars of forests, the few scattered cabins and sizable barns, indistinct in the distance and she thought of the war. So far away, yet impacting so much on their lives. And what of Raumsey? How were they faring now?

In her mind the waving grasslands became an ocean and she imagined the roar of the waves, the yelp of the seagull and the lonely three-note call of the sandpiper. She wondered whether Davie would be able to go home for a visit during his leave and imagined his welcome, wondered how many of his friends would survive this war, and silently prayed that it would be over soon.

When the cabin came into view, she stopped. A plume of smoke as straight as a pencil reached high up before dispersing. At least the fire had been lit. Tilting her head back, she closed her eyes, the tiredness that had dogged her for days finally reaching a peak. She batted a mosquito from her hand, remounted her bicycle and rode towards home.

***

Meanwhile, Sarah tidied up her workplace, dreading the night ahead. The volunteers had to prepare and she had to face Paddy with the news that she was actually going. Although he had given her his blessing, she believed he had never faced the possibility that she would really leave.

She had cooked a stew the night before, and she now pulled it over the flames to warm it up. Setting the table with slices of bread and boiled corn cobs, she waited for Paddy to appear, her speech ready. On hearing the dog bark in the distance, she rubbed her hands down her skirt and gave a little cough to dispel the dryness in her throat.

'It's grand to come home to the warm smell of stew, so it is.' Paddy swung in through the door and dumped a sack on the floor. 'A couple of rabbits and a squirrel for tomorrow.'

Losing her courage, she turned away from him and ladled the stew into plates.

He wiped his mouth, rubbed his hands together, took a seat and prepared to eat. 'Any news for me the day? What's the word in that warehouse ye work in?' he asked as he scooped the stew up with his bread.

Sarah took a sip of water from her tin mug. Her mouth was so dry she doubted she could form the words otherwise. 'You know you said you didn't mind me going away,' she began.

He stopped chewing and lifted his eyes, fork poised midway between his mouth and his plate. 'Aye.'

'It's … it's going to happen. I've signed the forms.'

He swallowed and faced her for a full minute without speaking. 'But ye'll not be going for a while yet.' His voice was guarded, anxious.

'Tomorrow.' There it was. It was said. She twisted her hands in her apron, knowing that, no matter what happened now, she was leaving with the others.

He blinked twice. She waited, realising for the first time how old he had grown. His crinkled hair was now pure white, the furrows round his eyes and mouth much deeper, his skin more florid. He did not shave often, and tonight the stubble on his chin rasped as he ran his hand across his face. He took a deep breath, his face reddened, his jaw clenched and he trapped her with his gaze.

Maybe it was something in the determined way she stared back at him, but she saw the anger die in his eyes, to be replaced by a deep sadness that tore at her heart. 'If that's what you want. I'll speak to the priest about ending this marriage.' Without eating another bite, he stood up. 'And if he can't do it, I'm sure the courts will.'

'I don't want to leave ye forever, for you're the one thing that's been constant in my life.' She reached out to grasp his sleeve, but she didn't quite reach and her hand hung in the air.

'Just come back to me, queen. I would be honoured to call ye my daughter.' He blinked quickly, turned away and stumbled into his bedroom.

***

Three months later, Sarah walked along the streets of Liverpool, suffering the wind that sighed among the soot-blackened buildings. She clutched her bag tightly and turned away from the Mersey River, travelling inland. Women appeared in doorways in long aprons, some with rags in their hair, some with cigarettes dangling from their lips, their eyes following her as she passed. Children ran in the street, laughing, kicking stones, rolling hoops, their clothes threadbare, their faces and hands dirty, shafts of sunlight creeping over buildings and brightening one side of the street.

Here in this Irish-Catholic immigrant community, so different from the clean open spaces of northern Alberta, memories dribbled in like a heavy smog. Memories of growing up in these streets, her father's cruelty and most of all, that one dark night when she had been forced to walk home alone. It was there, up that very close, just across the way, where three youths had chased her, had tripped her up, knocked her down on the hard ground.

The breath caught in her throat and she clutched her nurse's cape more tightly around her. For a long moment the desire to turn and run gripped her so strongly that she was incapable of taking one more step.

'Are ye alright, pet?'

She started at the sound of the voice. An old woman, steel grey hair pulled back in a knot, shoulders covered by a black woollen shawl, one solitary tooth protruding from her gums, leaned towards her, eyes narrowing as she peered into Sarah's face.

'Are ye lost?'

Recognition came slowly at first, and then with a sudden rush. 'Brigit?' she said. 'Brigit O'Leary?'

The old crone shrank back, her pale blue eyes opening as wide as the wrinkled folds would allow. 'Who are ye that knows my name?'

'I'm Sarah. Michael McAfferty's daughter.'

'Oh, sweet Mother o' God.' The crone covered her mouth with her hand and stood still for a moment. Her eyes scanned Sarah's face. 'Come away wi' me. Come away in.' She took Sarah's arm and led her along the cobbles and through a doorway, a doorway Sarah knew well. This was the door to which she had come many a time looking for refuge, her hands frozen, her body bruised and her stomach empty. The years rolled away and she was back there again dreading the hoot that signalled the end of her da's shift, feeling the fear, the desperation to stay in this warm, homely environment. Brigit had been the grandmother she never knew, setting her before a warm fire, feeding her on hot, thin soups and home-baked bread. With these memories crowding her mind, Sarah crouched before the well-remembered iron stove.

So little had changed in this room. The wax-cloth on the table was a different colour, the old dog no longer lay in the corner, instead a large ginger cat had pride of place, but the same pendulum clock struck the hour, the same circular mirror hung above the stove. The chairs – she couldn't remember them anyway, only that she had sat here, wordlessly, while Brigit had railed against her father's brutality.

'I don't expect ye've come back for yer dad.' Brigit stoked up the fire and pulled the kettle directly over the flames.

Sarah shook her head. 'My sisters and brothers. Are they still here?'

'Young Michael was, married a Protestant.' She spat out the word as if it left a bad taste in her mouth. 'But he's been called up. His wife went too – no bairns ye see. It's like that with Protestants. Connor stayed in yer da's old house until he was called up. Drank too much, no lass would have him. Maybe the army'll make a man of him. Pat's in London, or was. He'll be away at the war too.'

'What about our Eileen and Bridie?'

'Eileen lives in a nice house along the street. Her man works at the docks. Got two bonnie bairns and all. Bridie, well, sorry lass.' Brigit stopped and her face became sad. 'She died of diphtheria when she was twelve.'

Sarah's heart clenched. She closed her eyes against the surge of pain. Poor Bridie, only two when her mam died and always catching colds. 'I've thought of them often, of them all. My poor little Bridie.' How had she fared without Sarah to take care of her?

But Eileen was still here. At least she could see one of her siblings.

Then she asked the question she'd dreaded. 'Me da'?'

Brigit opened the hob and spat into the fire. 'Gone with the bad chest six years ago. There was none but Michael and Connor to put him in the ground.' She poured the tea.

Sarah thanked her. She should not be sorry to hear about her father, for he was nothing to her. And yet hearing of his death

opened a chasm, removing any chance there might have been of…
of what? A face-to-face confrontation? A chance for him to
apologise? A reconciliation? She didn't know. For some unknown
reason, she was filled with an impenetrable sadness.

'Tell me about Canada and what brings ye back – and a nurse
no less.'

Sarah cleared her throat and wiped her eyes, turning her mind
to brighter things. 'I lived in Alberta, way out west. It was a better
life than here.' Yes, she thought, it had been. 'I came to Quebec
City, that's in the east, with the nurses and volunteers to get my
army training. It was hard, but fun.' Excitement once more crept
into her voice.

For an hour she and Brigit sat together while Sarah poured out
amusing stories of her time in training camp. She had no wish to
talk about Paddy.

The mist had drifted in from the Mersey and the long, sad call
of a ship's horn sounded across the waters when Sarah knocked
at the door of a terraced house in slightly better condition than the
one she'd just left. From inside she heard a child cry and a woman
shouted, 'Kian, will you get the door.'

The sound of running feet on stairs and seconds later the door
was flung open.

'Yes?' A gangly youth of about twelve or thirteen stood on the
threshold, his reddish hair fell over his brow, freckles covered the
rest of his face.

'Is yer ma in?' asked Sarah, her heart quickening. This could
have been her brother, Connor, at the time she left.

The youth looked behind him. 'Ma, are ye in?'

'Who's askin?'

He turned back and raised his eyebrows.

'Tell her it's Sarah.'

'Aunt Sarah?' he asked, taking in her nurse's uniform. 'Her
that went to Canada?'

A pretty woman with green eyes and soft reddish hair
suddenly appeared behind him, a small child in her arms. 'Sarah?
Oh my Lord, Sarah.' She handed the baby to Kian and pushed

them both out of the way. For a moment the two women faced each other, before Eileen gave a little cry and wrapped her arms around her sister.

Tears welled and burst from Sarah's eyes as the sisters clung together on the doorstep, both trembling and sobbing.

When they moved apart, holding hands, Eileen's eyes roamed over Sarah's face. 'Ye're the image of Mam,' then her voice faltered. 'Oh, Sarah, I couldn't remember her face till now.' Recovering, Eileen stumbled over words full of tears. At last she became more in control and, still clinging to Sarah's hand, led her into the house.

Sarah glanced around the small hallway as the years rolled away. This house was identical to the one in Dock Street, where she had grown up, two up, two down. Only in this one could she sense the love. This one was clean and in as good a state of repair as meagre funding would allow. 'Can I use your outhouse?' she asked, taking off her cape. She knew where the outhouse would be, in the small, square courtyard in the back yard.

'The lav? Aye. I'll put the kettle on.' Eileen sniffed and wiped her nose on the back of her hand. 'My, our Sarah, it's great to see ye. Just look at ye, a nurse and all.'

After tea and a slice of lardy bread, Sarah sat with the baby, Inish, on her knee, enjoying the slight weight, the milky smell. The child stared at her, large green-blue eyes that hardly blinked. With chubby, sticky fingers, she reached out and touched Sarah's nose. Sarah hugged the warm body, pain of her own childless state striking her anew. The child squirmed and gave a little cry. Realising she had been holding too tightly, Sarah relaxed her hold. 'Sorry, pet.' She kissed the damp cheek, her heart full.

'I wrote to you, often,' she said to Eileen.

'We never got a letter.' Eileen sniffed. 'If only I'd known yer address, but I was too afraid to ask Dad. After he died, I looked, but I couldn't find any trace of where ye had gone.'

'Don't feel bad. I guessed as much.' In spite of everything, it still stung that he could wipe her from his life so totally.

Kian shoved his head round the door, 'I'm off to work now, Mam. Bye Aunt Sarah.'

'Kian,' shouted his mother after him. 'Ye'll sleep down here when ye come off yer shift. Yer Aunt Sarah is to have yer room.'

'Aw, Mam, can't she sleep with ye?'

'No. After coming all this way, she deserves a bed of her own.'

'I don't mind, really,' said Sarah. 'It'll be like when we were little. I don't want to put the hard-working lad out of his bed. Please, I'd like that.' Now that she'd found her sister, she didn't want separation, not even for the hours of sleep. Tomorrow she would be gone and who knew when they'd meet up again.

'Aye, it would be like old times, though we don't want to dwell on them, do we? Are ye sure ye can't stay longer? With Nichol away at the war and Kian working at the docks, there's plenty room.'

'I'm sorry, but I only got a couple of days' leave. I was lucky to get that. We'll be away to France soon.'

'France? My. When did ye arrive in England?'

'We sailed in February, women from all over Canada. I'm stationed in Mount Vernon Hospital near Hampstead. It's been taken over by the War Office as a military hospital. They reckon we'll be there close to a month then sent to hospitals in France.'

'A whole month? And ye can't come back?'

'I was lucky to get this time off.'

Eileen picked up baby Inish and wrapped her in a multi-coloured blanket, knitted with scraps of wool. 'Let's get this one ready for bed, then we'll catch up good and proper. Eee, but it was bad when Dad sent ye away. I was next in line to be dog's body.' Tears spilled from her eyes once more. 'The wee ones cried for ye for months.' With another lingering look at her sister, Eileen left the room.

Without the baby in them, Sarah's arms felt heartbreakingly empty. Here, in this small room with the ticking clock and the hiss of flames in the stove, the rush of a kettle not yet boiling, the wooden chairs and rag rugs, she felt comfortable, but displaced, as if she was no longer part of it. She had spent almost as many years in Alberta as she had in this street and despite her solitary existence, Canada with its fresh air and clean wide vistas had bled into her soul.

That night, in the creaky, iron double bed in the room above the kitchen, by the gas light thrown in from the street, they talked, and when the first grey streaks of morning lit the pane, they were still talking.

After a breakfast of lardy cake and tea, Sarah had to head back to London. With a tearful goodbye and a promise to keep in touch, the sisters bade farewell to each other. Sarah felt more confident this time as she boarded the train. Both happiness at finding her sister, sorrow at leaving her, and excitement about the adventure ahead, mingled in her heart. The train was full of soldiers returning from leave or young men going to join up and the air was one of joviality. She soon found herself laughing at the ready wit as the miles passed in a haze of anticipation.

***

It was March before Sarah sailed to France to begin her active service. Along with the other nurses and volunteers, she spent one week at Le Tréport and then was posted at Wimereux, near Boulogne-sur Mer. There a 300-bed tent hospital had been erected. They arrived in the rain.

Another tent had been set up as the nurses' quarters. Inside, as well as rows of beds, there was a little oil stove, teapot, kettle, cups and a box of Ridgeway's tea brought in from London.

A young woman who had been over for a while introduced herself as Jean Whitely from Devon, England. 'Welcome to paradise,' she said. She had a cheery face and a wide smile. She spoke as she directed them to the unoccupied beds. 'The French like their coffee, but we can't do without our tea. The water tastes like tar, the milk's condensed and the cups are granite.' She gave a laugh. 'But we don't care. None of us would miss our tea for the world. The meals are different from what you'll be used to, but the French are anxious to give us everything we want, so there's no chance of going hungry.'

Sarah set her pack on her bed. The other nurses were friendly and by now she felt one of them, all working together for a common cause.

'Follow me,' said Jean. 'You've got your normal uniforms, but you'll need a sou'wester, raincoat and rubber boots.' She looked up at the rain drumming on the tent roof. 'Hitch your skirts up around your knees whenever you go outside.'

'And the patients?' asked Sarah.

'Your job right now is to prepare for them. This is a new hospital.' Her smiling face grew solemn. 'Once they start coming, you won't have a minute to call your own.'

'I'm ready.' Sarah had seen some dreadful wounds in England, comforted men who couldn't sleep for the nightmares and she thought she was ready for anything.

It was April before everything was ready for the first batch of wounded from the front line. The matron called all the nursing staff into the mess tent to explain what they were to expect. She was a stern-faced woman and now stood to attention as she looked around the faces, silent and eager, turned towards her. She clasped her hands and spoke in a loud, clear voice.

'This is no picnic, so don't expect it to be. The men you nursed in England were healthy specimens compared to what you will encounter here.' She stopped and let her eyes scan the room again before continuing. 'Not only do the men suffer from horrendous wounds, they are also struck with infections and illnesses. There's trench mouth, trench fever, but the most common is trench foot. Because of the hours spent in the flooded trenches, a soldier's foot will swell up and become physically disfigured. Some soldiers have to have their feet amputated while others have to lose their entire leg.' She stopped again for a few seconds. There was a general shuffling, a few discrete coughs. 'Most shave their heads as otherwise lice would continuously infect them. Some are as pale as milk. That is Weil's disease and other rat infections. The rats urinate on the trench water that men have to drink.'

Sarah shuddered. The thought of wounds and shattered limbs were not as repulsive as rats and lice.

The matron's voice continued. 'The symptoms are a high fever, severe headaches, chills, muscle aches, vomiting and rash developments. Then there's typhoid fever, which also causes diarrhoea, abdominal pain and nose bleeds. Some men have large blisters which caused excruciating pain. These are the victims of mustard gas.' She lowered her eyes. 'But it is a worthwhile job you are doing. Work hard, laugh when you can, and do what you have to do. That's all.'

After the talk, the women filed out of the tent in silence, each lost in their own thoughts. A steely determination had filled Sarah. She couldn't wait to do her bit to help those poor fellows back to health and as she and her colleagues waited for the first batch of wounded, an air of excited fear permeated the camp.

'Are you scared?' asked Jean Whitely, as they sipped their cup of tea.

'A bit,' said Sarah.

'You'll be fine,' said Jean and winked.

All too soon the wounded began to arrive by the truckload.

Although the nurses had already been primed on what to expect, nothing in their training prepared the inexperienced such as Sarah for the horror of the actual carnage and human suffering this close to the front.

The nurses and volunteers worked together to make the men as comfortable as possible and to administer pain-relieving drugs where needed, before attending to their wounds. The stench was strong enough to take the breath away. As well as gangrenous wounds and fevers, many of the soldiers had not been out of their clothes for up to eight months.

It was an exhausted, bone-weary Sarah who fell into bed each night, too drained even for the much-longed-for cup of tea. She had no time to think, no time to pray.

After barely four hours' sleep, the nurses were roused again and relinquished their beds to the night-shift workers.

After eating a hurried breakfast, they presented themselves in the ward ready for another round of trying to patch up broken bodies to be churned back out to the front.

***

They had been there for over two months when someone came in with a wild yell that there was tons of mail. The girls leapt up and danced around hugging each other with excitement. Along with the others, Sarah ran to the mail house, waiting in anticipation as the names were read out. She had three letters, one from Canada, one from Liverpool, and another posted right here in France. She ripped that one open first and her eyes flew to the name at the bottom of the page. 'Connor,' she said out loud. Her little brother, Connor, and he was here, in France, somewhere not too far away. The second one was from Eileen, giving her news of the children and the goings on in the streets of Liverpool. The final letter was from Paddy, telling her how much he missed her and giving her news of the homestead. She read this one twice, visualising the peace and quiet of her cabin, not overly surprised to discover that in the few quiet moments afforded her, she had actually thought about it and Paddy and his stories, with nostalgia.

Chapter Twenty-Four

Isa

In Canada, as the harvest approached, Isa sat at the edge of a field of shrivelled crops. The rain had failed to come again and one more drought would finish them. If it had not been for the winter wheat, everything would have been lost already. She stood up slowly and dusted her hands together. Above her the sun shone without mercy. Ants gathered around her, climbing onto her sandaled feet. She dusted them off. A fair amount of her savings had been used up to see the family through the winter last year and she feared she would have to sell what remained of the livestock to see them through another.

She looked at the hard, blue, cloudless sky. Surely there could not be a drought for three consecutive years. The wheat had been her idea, her dream, and now it seemed it would be the downfall of them all.

She turned to look at the expressionless face of Pierre. 'Will the rain come?' she asked hopelessly.

'Perhaps not.'

She had been told about droughts, but in her early enthusiasm, had refused to face the possibility of it ever being this bad. Most of her savings had gone, the cattle were lean, and the parched grass of the prairies did not give them the sustenance they needed. Once more the family were relying on trapping and shooting wildlife for food. But money was needed for other things. Oil for the lamps, material for clothes, boots for the winter, seed for the winter grain. But even if she had enough money, supplies in the store were minimal since the war.

She no longer had help on the farm. Even if she could pay a wage, the young men were away to the war, a war that surely could not last much longer. Her thoughts turned once more to

McArthy, one of the few who still seemed to prosper.

'The news from Europe's hopeful. Once the war is over, Davie'll go back to the paddle steamers and get a wage. If only we can survive for one more year things'll get better again, it will.' She was trying to convince herself as much as her son and Pierre. She refused to look into the face of failure.

'Don't worry, Mam,' said Dan. 'The rain can't stay away forever. I'll check the traps and water the vegetables.'

'Bless you,' she said, but nothing could erase the worry from her mind. Summer was almost over and the crop barely reached her knees.

A week later it did rain, a vicious storm that lashed the country. Isa watched the clouds gather, almost forgetting to breathe. When the first fat drops hit her face, she laughed and held out her arms as it soaked her clothes and turned the dusty ground to a quagmire.

For the next two weeks, the wheat grew quickly. Without men to help, Isa gave up her voluntary work again and prepared for the harvest, but she could barely afford the seed for the winter sowing. Once again she thought of McArthy. A small loan was all she needed to tide them over. Once this crop was harvested and sold, she would be able to pay him back right away. He had been fair with them before and she could see no reason why he wouldn't be again. Her only other option was to give up on the winter wheat, something she did not want to do, as it grew better than the summer crop. She looked with satisfaction over the waving acres of gold and grabbed Dan's arm. 'It'll be a grand harvest after all. It's going to be all right, it is.'

'Aye, Ma, it sure looks that way.' Dan smiled, his skin golden, his eyes as blue as his father's, his hair as black as her own and reaching his shoulders in loose curls.

'Are you sure we can afford to grow the winter wheat this year?' he asked.

'We can. I'm away to the store for some supplies.'

She wouldn't tell Dan that she intended to see McArthy. This was her decision, her gamble and she couldn't contemplate it not paying off. With the war on, the government could no longer be relied upon to help, especially in such a dry area.

'I'll need to lend it to you from my own pocket,' McArthy said dusting his hands on his trousers.

'Please,' replied Isa. 'I reckon I can pay you off once I sell the crops.'

'With the price of wheat rising, I reckon you can.' He grinned. But I'll need to hold the farm as collateral.'

'Of course.' With the promise of a bumper crop, Isa could see no risk attached.

***

It was early in the morning and dawn had barely broken. Isa had bought the winter seed and the harvesting was due to begin in two days' time. She was making her way to the byre to milk the cow when she saw it. A great black cloud in the distance, low on the ground. It moved towards them, rising and blocking out the sun, blocking the air with a whirring of wings that grew louder until it filled her head like a nightmare. Dragonflies, thousands of them. They hovered, then settled over the fields of wheat, turning the gold into a dark mass.

Isa screamed and ran into the field lashing out in all directions, but as soon as she'd cleared them away, they resettled, feasting on her livelihood. They had come before, if not them it was the grasshoppers, but never like this, in such large numbers.

Before long, her family had joined her, even Annie and Martha, but finally, exhausted, they gave up, all except Annie who continued to slap the insects away, tears running down her cheeks.

'It's no use, lass,' called Isa. 'There's too many of them.'

By the time they left, the field had been stripped bare. No one spoke as they trailed back to the house. Annie wept softly, Martha made coffee, Dan retreated to his room.

'It'll be okay,' said Isa, drained and as empty as the bare stalks left in the fields and doubting her own words. 'So we won't be able to pay McArthy back this year. We've still got the seed for the winter grain and some money left over. Come spring I'll start the repayments. It'll take a bit longer, that's all.'

Her family looked more at ease. They trusted her to make it all right, she always had in the past. She left them, walked outside and, blurry-eyed, she saddled her pony and rode across the plains, around the acres of ruined crops, not only hers but the whole area. She was tired, weary of trying. She wouldn't cry, for what good would that do? In anguish, she dashed a rebellious tear away. Perhaps she had been wrong. Perhaps she should have moved to Prince Rupert when Davie had wanted to go. All she could do now was pray to a God in whom she had no faith, that the war would soon be over and Davie would come back unscathed. She could pretend to be strong, hide her black moments, but the truth was, she needed him and she needed him now.

***

Isa returned to her voluntary work after the first fall of snow. She enjoyed helping with the war effort and the companionship it offered. For a few hours every day, she could laugh with the other women and push her worries to another place. But the debt to McArthy wasn't the only thing on her mind. Annie had been spending more and more time away from the ranch. As a child, Isa did not have too many concerns about her playing with the native children, but now she was a young woman and should be showing an interest in boys of her own race.

Isa often referred to her 'bairns'. Eva, a second generation Canadian, whose family originated from Poland, had laughed at Isa's Scottish words at first.

'But surely they're not children anymore,' said Eva as they walked towards the paddock after work. With snow on the ground, riding was easier than cycling. Isa climbed over the fence, caught and saddled her gelding.

'Dan's a good lad, a real help on the land, but Annie's a right wee besom. I think she's got her eye on a boy.'

'I guess she's coming of age. Is it a nice boy though?'

'I'm worried. She spends most of her time in the Indian village.'

'You think it's a boy from there, a Red Indian?' Eva looked horrified.

Isa wished she had said nothing. 'I don't know.'

'I understand your concerns.'

'She was a real wee daddy's girl. She's never been the same since he left. It's almost like she blames me.' Isa gave a sharp, unhappy laugh.

'It's difficult being left to cope,' said her friend. 'My two are similar. They sure need a man's firm hand.'

Feeling no easier, Isa bade her friend goodbye and mounted her pony.

Riding home she glanced at the sky. Thunderclouds gathering over the distant treetops heralded a storm. She urged her gelding on, cantering over the flat plains and through the forest, a rutted path, impossible on a bicycle but easy enough on horseback, which she had discovered cut at least a mile off her journey. Hoping to reach shelter before the elements overtook her, she ducked below overhead branches. The howl of wolves resounded from somewhere behind her, and she took no comfort in the fact that, in her years in Canada, no one she knew of had been killed by a wolf. The horse whinnied and stumbled backwards, ears flush with his head. It was dark here, and Isa wondered at the wisdom of taking the shorter route. She tightened her hands on the reins and dug her heels into the animal's sides. He shied away from a shadow to her left, almost unseating her. It was with a great deal of relief that she broke free of the towering spruce trees and found herself once more on open land. A wind had sprung up whipping her face, a crack of lightning lit the sky, followed by the loud roll of air pockets crashing together. Rain began drumming into her face and soaking her clothes within minutes. From the east the remembered black funnel began to form, growing in velocity and travelling across the earth at an amazing speed. She watched in horror, knowing there was nothing she could do. Ever since the shack had been destroyed, tornados had petrified her and left her gasping for air.

Suddenly the inky column changed direction, raced towards the forest, flung several trees into the air, then just as abruptly faded into a smoky column, dissolving before her eyes. Isa loosened the horse's reins and clung onto his mane as he plunged into a frantic gallop towards the homestead.

Dan ran to meet her. 'Mam, I saw the twister. I was worried.'

Isa dismounted and stood for a minute, holding on to the paddock fence to remain upright, her heart thundering, the breath squeezing from her lungs. Dan took the horse from her, led the trembling beast into the paddock and untacked him. He whinnied, shook his head and galloped around the enclosure as if pleased to be home. Isa stared into the distance, at the fading funnel and caught her breath. This was the second tornado in two months. The last, she heard, wiped out a few outlying houses near Edmonton. *Everything happens in threes. The third one is never forbidden*, her mother always said. Isa shuddered at the thought.

Dan took her arm and led her into the house. 'It's over. You're alright.' He eased her onto a chair where she struggled to regain her breath.

'Has Annie come home?' she asked, once she was able.

'I haven't seen her all day and she's not in the native village. Pierre just came from there.' Dan piled some logs onto the fire.

Isa rubbed her hand over her face and studied her son. He leaned forward, his shirt straining over muscle. The curve of his cheek was still rounded with the remnants of boyhood, the slant of his nose turned slightly up at the end, and her heart swelled. Thank God her older child gave her little worry.

Martha, hands bent by arthritis, sat rocking slowly in the arm chair. Her eyes were closed and her head hung to the side. She didn't do much work anymore, spending a lot of her time dozing, but as her body weakened, her tongue grew sharper.

'I need coffee, Dan,' said Isa.

'Why d'you worry about Annie? She knows her way as well as any Indian.' Dan reached for the kettle.

'Aye, but she's not an Indian.' Brought up among the natives, Isa thought, what did she expect? Pulling the sodden jacket from her shoulders, she threw it over the back of a kitchen chair. 'She likes an Indian boy, doesn't she? I'm worried.'

Dan spooned the ground coffee beans into the percolator and set the pot on the stove. 'Aye. Maybe Annie'll marry him. She'll be Missus Muraco, or maybe she'll use Missus White Moon – she prefers the translation.'

'What's that?' Martha sprung awake. 'Annie can't marry an Indian. She'll be a squaw with a string of papooses running after her. You have to stop this, Isa. I always said you were too soft with her, letting her play with Red Indians!' She spat out the last words.

You're old-fashioned, Granny. No one uses words like that anymore. Anyway, Annie wouldn't have a hard life.' Dan gave a laugh. 'Annie would end up as the first white woman chief of the Cree.'

'Aye, well. Yer granny's right about one thing. Annie's just a bairn. She doesn't know her own mind yet,' said Isa.

'What've you got against Muraco? He's a good guy.' Dan picked some plates from the dresser and put them on the table.

'They live in poverty…' What was the use? Since the first time she had held her in her arms, she'd had dreams of a better life for her daughter. Perhaps the life she had dreamed of herself as a child.

Dan loved this land and he loved the work. He knew the drawbacks of farming as well as anyone, but it was what he wanted for his future. But Annie – her only hope to escape the trap of poverty was to marry well.

'I always said it,' muttered Martha, 'The apple doesn't fall far from the tree. You were just the same, a wilful besom.'

Isa sighed and turned away. She had learned not to let her mother's tirades affect her.

Isa's years in Canada had changed her, sharpened her round edges, hardened her tender heart. In her few trips to Stony Plains and her one trip to Edmonton, she had seen glimpses of a different life, a soft life, A life she might have lived in other circumstances, a life where she could imagine her daughter, maybe married to a banker, or even a store keeper.

Now she turned and stared at a window blank with night. She tried not to listen to the rising wind that battered the gables and rattled the windowpanes in their frames. She tried not to remember the tornado. Annie would come back when she was ready; she always did.

Just then the door swung open and curtains, tablecloth, deerskin rug, flames from the oil lamp, pages from the journals lying atop the bureau, all rose and fell in the blast as if flicked by an invisible hand. Annie, as wild as the wind following her, blustered into the room.

Dark curls tousled round her face, droplets of rainwater shimmered on her skin and her eyes glistened. Her fingers clutched at the sodden wrap around her throat. The wind-stung blush on her cheeks enhanced her looks.

'Where have you been?' Isa rose to her feet. Annie sniffled, cocked her head and swept past, throwing her buckskin jacket over a chair.

In spite of her anger, Isa never failed to feel her heart lurch at the sight of her daughter. She knew Annie favoured her in looks – same dark hair and flashing eyes, yet the girl had a voluptuousness about her that Isa had never possessed. For a instant she wavered, then caught herself.

Before Annie could answer, Martha's hands clutched at the arms of the chair. 'You listen to me, Annie Reid, we've all been sick with worry. Is it not bad enough with your father deserting us and clearing off back to Europe when there's so much work to be done? Do you have to break my heart too?'

'Mam, I'll deal with my daughter.' Isa held up her hand, but Martha wasn't to be placated.

'You're old enough to be helping out. I'm left here all day with your mother working in the town and your dad gone.'

'Mam, I'll speak to her.' Isa's voice sharpened.

Annie's chin pressed into her chest. A single tear trickled down her cheek. She gave a snort, sniffed hard and lifted her head.

'Annie, yer granny's right about one thing, we need to know where you were.' Isa spoke more softly.

'I've been helping at the hospital. It's the diphtheria epidemic – it's getting worse. Another three bairns died today.' Silent tears sparkled on her eyelashes.

'Hospital – you?' Dan spoke with a snort.

'Yes, me. The Indians are the worst hit and nobody cares.'

'I can't believe you,' snapped Martha.

Isa wished she'd be quiet. This wasn't helping, but it was unlike Annie to be so selfless. Words of accusation hung in the air. For a moment mother and daughter held each other's gaze and Isa recognised truth and hurt in Annie's eyes. The anger ran out of her, to be replaced by fear. She could not lose this child. 'Mother, be quiet.'

She turned to Annie. 'I'm glad – honestly. We didn't think … but … what if you catch diphtheria?'

'I wear a mask. They make me wear a mask.'

'Diphtheria? Have we not had enough to put up with?' Martha's breath came in short gasps as she sat upright in her chair, her rheumy eyes wide open.

'But why didn't you tell us?' Isa covered the distance between herself and Annie and gently touched her shoulder.

Annie shrugged the hand off. 'Because you don't listen. None of you. You'll never understand Muraco. He wouldn't leave me the way Dad left us.'

'Your dad went to fight for his country. He had to go, you know he did.'

'Canada's his country, not Scotland.'

'We're still part of the British Empire…' But her words faded with the sharp click of Annie's closing bedroom door.

Isa stared after her.

'Annie'll settle eventually, Mam.' The gentle voice of Dan interrupted her thoughts. And helping at the hospital – surely that's good?'

'Good? Aye, you'll not be saying that when she brings diphtheria into this house.' Martha sank back in her chair. 'I warned you. Don't say I didn't.'

Ignoring her mother, Isa turned to look at her son, at the

young-old eyes, at the creased forehead, Dan, the sensible one, the worker, the one who would not let her down. She wanted to hug him, but her Scottish roots held her back from what she saw as an excess of physical affection.

She opened the door of the stove and stared into the flames and her daughter's words came back at her. 'You'll never understand,' Annie had flung. But she did, she understood the strength of passion that drove the young couple into each other's arms against all opposition. She understood only too well. She had been no different at the same age. Back then she too had believed that love was enough. But an impoverished Indian was quite another matter from a whisky runner of her own race.

'I'll go and check on the animals,' said Dan, 'and I'll chop some more logs for tonight.'

She walked to the window and watched as he lifted the lantern from the deck and carried it into the barn. Behind her Martha had settled and was snoring gently, her head on her shoulder, a line of dribble trickling down her cheek.

No stars were visible tonight. No moon in which she could find comfort, knowing that Davie was possibly looking up at that same sky. Wondering what it was like in Europe at this moment, she went to the desk and took out the bundle of letters he had sent from the front. She thought of him now, mud to the knees, bullets passing above his head. Oh, he had talked of football matches and dances where there were only other soldiers as partners, of concerts and the occasional dram, but she knew he was making light of it for her sake. Some of the women she worked with had already received the dreaded telegram. They did not even have the comfort of burying their loved ones, men condemned forever to lie in foreign soil. But she could not think like that, she had to remain optimistic, otherwise she would go mad. She leafed through the pages, rereading them as she went. Then there was the last one.

Dear Isa,

I am lying here in the field hospital. It's no more than a tent, and I can hear the guns blasting away in the distance. I've been

*injured, but you're not to worry. Just a bit of shrapnel in my leg.
It hurts right enough, but while I'm in here I'm safe from the
bullets.*

*You'll never guess who is the chaplain here. None other than
the minister from Raumsey! We had a good talk about old times
and he asks for you. He came over with a couple of other lads,
but so far I've not met anyone else from the island.*

*Give the bairns my love and don't let them forget me. I miss
you all so much. I even miss Canada – imagine that!*

*I so look forward to mail from home. Sometimes we don't
get any for ages and then we get piles at once....*

The rest went on to tell her about his day, describing the hospital,
men he'd met and fought beside, the countryside of France.

Much as she loved and missed Davie, how she wished for
Donald Charleston's common sense and calming influence now.
Thinking of him brought back memories of Raumsey, of soft, long
rollers running up a sandy beach, of the sad, unearthly song of the
seals and the distance between herself and her homeland had
never felt so vast.

Chapter Twenty-Five

Davie

Several weeks later, Davie lay in a hospital bed in England to where he had been transported from France. After his leg had healed, he had been sent back to the front, but within a month, he was carried back on a stretcher. He suffered from painful blisters all over his body, he could hardly swallow and he had lost half his mind. He found himself unable to lie still. He had barely remembered the journey through France and over the channel.

Although he had felt chilly earlier, now he could hardly breathe for the heat that rose from his body. He reached over to his locker and found what he was looking for. Because his hands shook so badly, he lit a cigarette with difficulty. Pulling in a lungful of smoke, he tried to calm himself by concentrating on the soft swish of the water from somewhere outside and the distant hoot of an owl. The ward was quiet with only the sounds of sleep. A night light glowed from the nurses' station. His eyelids began to droop. The cigarette fell from his fingers and he drifted down a soft dark void. And suddenly the sounds changed. The night birds' call became the screams of dying men. The slightly disinfected air changed to the stench of smoke and human waste and the sharp cold from the open window was the cold of mud and clinging wet clothes. And then someone shouted 'gas' and they were piling up the dead and climbing on the bodies to escape the trenches.

'Davie, Davie,' he could hear a voice. His friend, his companion calling to him and when he looked around, that same friend suddenly disintegrated, the green face exploding in a mess of blood and bone and brain. And his dead hand reached out and closed on Davie's shoulder.

'Davie, wake up.'

He opened his eyes and for a beat saw nothing, then he gasped and sucked on air as his stomach rose. He swallowed, trapping the bile in his throat. 'Isa,' he whispered peering at the figure before him.

'You were dreaming,' she said.

His vision cleared and he looked up into the face of Nurse Collins, who had been taking care of him and he began to sob, his hands covering his face. 'It's like this whenever I close my eyes. God knows if I'll ever find peace.'

'It'll take time to forget,' said the nurse. 'But you're in England. You're safe. We'll make you well again.'

'I was due leave. I was going to go to Raumsey.'

'You will get there.' Nurse Collins laid her hand on his brow. 'Hush now, try to get some rest. I'll get you something to help you sleep.'

When Nurse Collins returned with the medication, Davie's bed was empty. She ran outside, but could see no trace of him. She shouted to another nurse who was attending a patient at the far end of the ward. 'Did you see Private Reid?' the nurse lifted her head. 'No, I've been busy. Maybe he's gone to the lav.'

But somehow Nurse Collins doubted that. He had been hardly able to walk, verging on delirium and in a great deal of pain. She went to the lavatory door and knocked. When there was no answer she opened the door. The stall was empty.

Outside, Davie limped forward, ever drawn towards the sound of the sea, trying to escape the fiendish concert playing out in his mind. His one aim had been to get out of there, away from the hospital smells, from the devils in his head, somewhere he could breathe. A light wind blew high clouds across an black sky and stars, fixed luminous dots, sparkled in the inky dome. The sound of the ocean, a slow steady breath, filled him with a sense of eternity. A pale moon appeared and flooded the scene with a colourless, silvery light.

When he reached the dunes he stumbled, falling on the sand. Picking up a handful he allowed it to trickle through his fingers. Sand. He had not seen sand since he left Raumsey. He rubbed it on his face and the grains stuck to his damp cheeks. Before him the sea rolled in with a dull thunder and the moon threw pebbles of light across the water. Cool water. He could almost taste the salt on his lips. Pulling himself to his feet, he lurched, fell forward and dragged himself along the beach until his hand touched the trickle of incoming tide. He rose to his knees, moving ever forward until a cold wave settled around him, cooling his excruciating blisters. But it wasn't until the sea closed over his head, filling his mouth and his eyes and above him the stars blinked and the moon smiled and he tasted the salt and he floated away free from pain, that he finally found peace.

When his lungs expelled the air in them for the last time, Isa knew. Her heartbeat quickened and, colder than the winter chill which still claimed the land, a sudden wave of ice passed over her like a shadow that stopped her breath. She gasped and dropped the bucket of water she had been carrying. He stood before her, his uniform torn, his face smeared with mud, his blond hair shaved to an inch from his scalp and his blue eyes holding an impenetrable sorrow. But something was wrong. She only saw him from the waist up. I'm sorry, Isa, she felt the words rather than heard them, and then, like a dissolving mist, he had gone. The whole thing happened in a flash, in the time it took for the bucket to hit the ground and the water to spill across her feet.

'Davie,' she called, his name falling unbidden from her mouth. She spun around, but only saw the cotton woods, the pines and the flutter of some bird high in the branches. She ran indoors to where her mother bent over the range, preparing the evening meal.

'Oh Mam,' she cried, 'I saw Davie.'

Martha's face lost its colour. She pushed a lock of hair from her forehead, a look of horror flashing in her eyes.

'He came to me, as clear as day.' Isa's legs shook like saplings in the wind, the room swirled around her and she sank to her knees.

'You're over-tired. You've been worrying too much, maybe it's not true,' said Martha, kneeling beside her.

'I hope to God you're right,' cried Isa, 'But you know as well as I do, what the vision means.' It was a deep-held belief among the highlands and islands of Scotland, that when someone passed over, he or she would appear to the person they were thinking of at that moment. She willed strength into her body and holding onto a chair, forced herself to rise.

Chapter Twenty-Six

Sarah

Sister Meekson turned to Sarah. 'Nurse O'Brien, could you bathe and change the patient in the second bed. He had to have a leg amputated last night.'

'Of course sister.' Rubbing the sleep from her eyes, Sarah went willingly. First in England and now here, she had embraced the work wholeheartedly. This was the job she had been born for. As she approached the bed, her stomach clenched and she stopped, frozen. Slowly the head turned towards her and the coal black eyes fastened on her face. Time stood still. His tight curls had been cropped close to his head. Her fists tightened, the breath fled from her lungs. The patient was black. All the feelings of panic, all the memories she had buried in the back of her mind returned in a rush.

'What's the matter?' the sister came up behind her.

Sarah shook her head, stared at the floor. 'I can't … I can't attend to a black man.'

The sister's face hardened. 'He is a soldier. He and his fellow Negroes are fighting alongside our men. We'll have no prejudice here.'

'It's not that…I'm…just… so tired.' Her voice trailed away. How could she explain?

'If you want to be a nurse, you will wash this man. We're all tired, for God's sake.'

'I'm sorry.' Sarah turned and as if her legs had a mind of their own, she ran out of the tent. Outside she pressed her hands to her head and breathed deeply, fighting the panic that grew and swelled inside her.

Sister Meekson followed her out. 'Are you up to the job or not, O'Brien?' Her voice was icy.

'I am. I'm just… I can't explain…'

'Then I will arrange for your transfer home immediately. A nurse cannot pick and choose whom she treats.' She turned and marched towards the office.

'No, no,' Sarah ran after her. 'Please no.'

'Then are you going to tell me exactly why you cannot tend to a brave soldier who's risking his life for the better good?'

The palms of her hands were damp. She rubbed them on the side of her skirt and tried to swallow, but her mouth was dry. 'I'm sorry, I can't.'

'Then get back in there and attend to Private Smith. We have no time for petty hysterics. You've been a good nurse up till now, I don't want to lose you, but I can't have this.'

'Yes, Sister.' Sarah respected Sister Meekson. She was strict but fair. For a minute she hesitated, wondering whether she could confide.

'Well?' The sister's brow screwed down, her eyes fixed Sarah with an angry stare.

'At once, Sister.' Fighting the memory of the black face above hers, the thick hand over her mouth, suffocating her, the pain of her back on the rough road, hands holding her down, the things he'd made her do, the musky odour of his sweat, of old oil and cigarettes. Sarah turned back to the ward and closed her fists to control the shake. She forced her unwilling legs to carry her forward. Whatever she had to do, she couldn't be sent home, she just couldn't.

She approached Private Smith's bed, a basin with water, soap and towels in her hands, saw the face dripping sweat, the head twisting in pain. Her stomach roiled. Her knees were jelly. 'I...I have to wash you.' Keeping her eyes averted, she knelt by the bed and pulled the blanket down. Maybe if she didn't look at his face. Didn't think of the colour of his skin.

'Thank you, nurse,' he said. 'The pain's mighty bad.'

She looked at the stump where his leg should be, at the bloody bandage hurriedly applied last night. She swallowed and allowed her training to take over. She forced herself to imagine this was Connor, tried to bathe him with the tenderness she would have given to her brother.

Once she had made him as comfortable as she could, she rose to go. He reached out and grabbed her hand. She inhaled, fighting the urge to snatch her hand away.

'Nurse,' he whispered hoarsely.

'Yes?' she said without turning round.

'Why won't you look at my face? Please look at my face.' His accent was not British.

She forced her head around, took in the young, smooth skin. No, no, this wasn't him. 'Where do you come from?' she asked.

'Pennsylvania, USA,' he said. 'I guess it's hard for you white girls to nurse someone like me.'

Shame filled her up. Had she been that obvious? 'It's not that. I have to go.' She pulled her hand from his, hurried from the tent and, choking back vomit, went to wash out the basin. In the laundry room, she scrubbed her hands until they were in danger of bleeding.

'What's the matter?' asked Megan, a nurse she had befriended and who slept in the next bed.

Sarah searched her mind for a reason. 'I didn't expect it to be so bad,' she said, fighting the tears which had been threatening since she had first seen Private Smith.

'But we're doing good, aren't we? We're making a difference?' Megan looked tired but content. She pulled a pile of fresh sheets from the shelf. 'Could you help me with the beds?'

'Yes, yes, sure.' Sarah smoothed her hair and wiped her hands on her apron. 'I'll be fine,' she said, noticing Megan's worried face.

As gently as possible they began to remove sheets stained with sweat, blood and other bodily fluids from under seriously damaged young men, chatting to them as they did so, offering them cigarettes, giving them sips of water.

And then they came to Private Smith's bed. In spite of his earlier wash, his sheets were already soaked, his head twisting on the pillow. When he saw the nurses he smiled through his pain showing strong white teeth.

Sarah turned away. She caught Megan's confused glance, breathed deeply and stood back as Megan treated the soldier as she would any other patient, speaking perhaps a bit too much to compensate for Sarah's strange behaviour.

As soon as they were finished Sarah spun around and almost ran from the ward. Megan came after her. 'What's wrong with you?' Her voice was angry.

Sister Meekson was right behind them. 'I've been watching you, O'Brien. You don't treat patients like that,' she snapped. 'I'm warning you, you're not going to last long here. Now take that man a glass of water, and you,' she looked at Megan, 'get on with your duties.'

'Yes, sister,' said Megan, shooting an unsympathetic glance at Sarah before hurrying away.

Sarah lifted the glass of water and forced herself to return to Private Smith's bedside. 'Would you like a drink,' she said stiffly.

'You'll have to help me, I can't sit up.'

Aware that the sister's eyes was on her, Sarah knelt by the bed. She slipped her arm beneath the pillow supporting his head, so that she wouldn't have to actually touch him, and held the glass to his lips.

He took a sip. 'Thank you, nurse,' he said as she lowered him back.

Grateful the ordeal was over, she rose to go.

'I guess they'll move me on real soon. I know you hate helping me.'

She turned fully around, feeling a desperate need to explain. 'I'm sorry. It's...it's...one of your race hurt me badly once, that's all, and for a moment I thought..,' Her eyes met his and she forced herself to hold the gaze. For the first time she realised how young he was, no more than a boy. Not much older than...the thought struck her from nowhere with a force that took her breath away... her own child would have been now.

'I apologise for one of my race,' he said. 'My name is Eugene.' He extended a hand.

She swallowed and grasped the hand lightly. 'Nurse O'Brien, Sarah.'

'We're not all bad and white men are not all good.'

'I know, I'm sorry.'

'You're going to get many more of my race. We're fighting alongside the French, as equals.'

A lump rose in her throat. It wasn't the lad's fault, in her heart she knew it, but the shock of seeing him and confronting her nightmares had been too sudden. If only she had had prior warning, she would have been prepared.

Determined to be professional, Sarah did the best she could, pleased that as they chatted, she began to see beyond the colour of his skin. He told her about his childhood, about his life in America and the prejudice he had been forced to live with until he came here. 'Here we're equals,' he said. 'Our blood all runs red.'

'It's dreadful that you've been treated like that,' said Sarah, and meant every word.

That night, in spite of her fatigue, Sarah could not sleep. She lay staring at the white walls of the tent, ghostly through the darkness. She could not get Eugene out of her thoughts, his young, handsome face, his coffee-coloured skin, his sad liquid eyes. And with him returned the memories of her own child, the child she had not been able to bring herself to look at longer than a fleeting glance, which was all it took to know which of her attackers had fathered him. What would he have been now? Who would he have been? Would she have been able to love him if she'd had a chance? In a few years' time, if this dreadful war still dragged on, would he too have ended up in Europe fighting for a cause he did not understand? She should have at least studied him, carried that precious memory in her heart. Eugene was a fine young man, the kind any mother could be proud of. For some reason, she could hardly wait to see him again.

Next morning, when the bell sounded to raise the nurses, she had not slept at all. She entered the ward and was surprised to find his bed empty. 'What happened to the soldier in that bed?' She asked of the nurse who was just going off duty.

'Private Smith died last night.' The nurse hesitated, as if noticing Sarah's stricken face. 'He…he asked for you.'

'Why didn't you come for me?' Sarah was overwhelmed by a

sense of loss greater than she had felt for any other soldier who had died in her care.

'I didn't want to disturb you.' It often happened that a young soldier asked for a particular nurse, but seconds later asked for their mothers or sweethearts. Many of the dying were delirious.

'What...what happened?'

'The gangrene had spread through his body. We got him too late.'

Sarah swallowed and the tears came. Tears for Eugene, tears for the child she had lost and what he might have been. She silently swore that the next black soldier to enter this ward would receive her best attention.

Chapter Twenty-Seven

Isa

Meanwhile in Alberta, Isa rode around their acres and turned her pony towards the homestead. The spring harvest was almost upon them and the winter wheat had grown well, but by the time she paid McArthy, there would be barely enough for the next batch of seed. She didn't notice Martha at first, standing at the edge of the yard, shoulders slumped, waiting, and the sight of her filled Isa with dread.

She flung herself from the pony and stood, afraid to take step closer, afraid of the tragedy she saw in her mother's eyes, afraid of what she already knew.

Martha's hand lifted in a slow, wooden movement and held something out towards her. At first Isa failed to recognise the paper in her hand. Her mouth grew dry. A telegram. The final nail in the coffin of hope.

'No,' she said backing away. She didn't want to see it. Without written proof, she had held onto the improbable likelihood that several nights with little sleep had addled her brain, that she had been hallucinating, experiencing a nightmare in the middle of the day. Davie had not appeared to her. All that was superstitious nonsense. Pushing aside her mother's hand which held the cruel proof of her worst fears, she walked into the cabin. Annie's arms were across the table, her head resting on them. She lifted her head. Her curls tangled around her face, tendrils sticking to the red cheeks.

'Annie, go and untack Smoky,' ordered Isa.

'Yes, Mam,' Annie said wetly, and rose, knocking the chair backwards so that it fell to the ground.

Isa didn't want to see the telegram, didn't want to read the words that she knew would slam into her brain and make it real.

He had gone. This time there was no coming back. 'Oh my God,' she whispered to no-one, 'It can't be true.'

Martha returned, each footstep slow, dragging, as if she had aged overnight. She set the telegram on the table, where it lay and screamed out its devilish news. 'I'll make coffee,' she said.

Isa looked out of the window. Annie had her arms around Smoky's neck, her face buried into the old horse's warmth, the animal providing comfort she had been unable to give.

When Dan returned, the telegram still lay on the table. He walked into the silence of the house and glanced at the telegram, not long enough to digest all the words, but long enough for his face to lose all colour. Without a word he wrapped his mother in his arms. Isa stiffened, but something in his embrace released the tension inside her, making it possible to feel the raw pain. She hiccupped and gasped but she wouldn't cry. Crying indicated a kind of acceptance and she wasn't ready for that.

***

Finally in bed in the quiet of the night, Isa lay staring at the dark wood of the ceiling. Every creak of the timbers, crack of the burning logs, every patter of feet as a creature of the dark ran across the shingles of the roof made her pulse increase and her stomach knot. She still clung to the notion that some mistake had been made and Davie was at this minute on his way home. Sometime before dawn, she drifted into a restless slumber, in which she heard a door open and quiet footsteps in the room beyond. 'Davie,' she said, springing awake, ears straining, listening to nothing more than the sounds of a farmyard coming to life. Fully awake, she realised it had only been a dream.

Overtaken by a sudden desire to hold her daughter, to reach out to her in a way she had not been able to the previous day, she rose, crossed to Annie's bedroom and pushed the door open. The room was empty. Annie's bed had not been slept in. 'Dear God, Annie.' Her voice broke the silence in the house. Why had she not offered comfort last night? Why had she been so wrapped up in her own pain that she forgot about this child, this child who worshipped her father? She and Dan had sat long into the night while she drew on his strength, and Annie had turned to the cold comfort of her grandmother. Isa ran outside to the paddock. Smoky had gone.

Dan had been up since dawn and had taken his own horse to God knew where. Back indoors, she grabbed her jacket and prepared to walk the ten miles to the Indian reservation, to the boy to whom she was sure Annie would have run.

'Where are you going?' Martha had dragged herself out of bed and now stood, her hair straggling around her shoulders, puffy eyes dark-rimmed and sunken, sad testament that she, too, hadn't slept all night.

'Is Annie with you?' asked Isa, hoping Annie had climbed into her grandmother's bed like she had often done when she was small.

Martha shook her head.

'If you could see to the hens, Ma, I'll do the rest when I get back.'

'Wait, wait...' The thin voice floated after her, but Isa was already though the door. Although early, the sky was clear blue with not a stir of wind to disturb the dust beneath her feet. Where the sky and land became one, a puff of grey cloud rose and gathered in density. She squinted into the early light and realised a horse and rider were galloping towards her, dust trailing behind them like a voile curtain. Closer up she recognised Muraco, or Luke White Moon, as the nuns at the mission school had named him, his hair tied back in a single braid, one feather in his headband and dressed like most natives, part traditional buckskin and part western. His trousers and jacket were the Indian fringed skins, but his shirt and boots had been bought in the general store. He reined the spotted pony, and the beast snorted and pranced on the spot.

'Come quick,' the boy said. 'Annie's hurt.'

'Annie – what's wrong – where is she?'

'I take her to hospital. She will not wake up.' Bending forward, he offered her his arm. At first she hesitated; looked at the sharp angles of his face, at the light sliding over his ebony hair, at the coal black eyes pleading for trust, and gave him her hand. With a strength belied by the slimness of his body, he pulled her up and she scrabbled behind him and onto the pony.

'She try to break in a mustang,' he said.

'What–what? Get me there.'

They did not talk again as they galloped to Stony Plains. Her hair tore free of its knot and blew back from her face. She clung to the young man in front of her; felt his youthful strength against her body. Her knees fitted behind his as she clamped her legs around the belly of the saddleless pony, aware of the powerful muscles rippling beneath her.

The university hospital was a large, forbidding building, two storeys high, built just before the war. Inside was clean and smelt of paint and antiseptic. Nurses bustled about in neat uniforms, doctors came in and out of doors, stethoscopes hanging around open-necked shirts.

Luke Muraco stepped into the vestibule, stopped and self-consciously moved from one foot to the other.

'Wait here,' Isa said, and ran to the front desk where a plain young woman with pale eyes looked up from a ledger in which she was writing.

'My daughter, Anne Reid, she was just brought in.' Isa leaned forward, her arms resting on the desktop, a pulse hammering at the base of her throat.

The young woman traced her finger down the list of names and the finger appeared to move unnaturally slowly. 'The horse accident. Yes, ward 10, first corridor to the left. The doctor is with her now.'

Isa ran to the ward almost colliding with a young man as he exited. 'Annie Reid. I'm her mother,' she gasped, still trying to catch her breath.

'Mrs Reid? I am Doctor Evans.' He was young – too young. He looked pale, as if he had spent too many hours without sleep. Taking her arm, he led her a little way along the corridor. 'Anne's had a nasty bump on the head and her shoulder bone is broken.'

'How is she?'

'She's badly concussed.'

'Can I see her?'

The doctor hesitated.

'What is it? What's wrong?'

'She's unconscious.'

'Unconscious?' Isa wanted to shake him. Wanted to tell him to go away. Bring back someone older, more experienced – someone she could trust. 'What do you mean – unconscious?'

'We have every confidence that she will not remain in this state.'

'What? How long – I mean unconscious…!'

'We'll know more when she wakes up. As I said before, we can see no sign of a fracture or any internal bleeding in the head. Don't worry – we'll keep a very close eye on her.' His voice was solid, confident.

Isa hesitated, not sure what to say next. 'I'm going in.'

'Yes. Don't worry, I'm sure she'll be fine. Talk to her – could be she can hear you.'

Without waiting to say more, Isa rushed to the ward.

'She's behind the screen,' the doctor called after her.

Annie lay still; her head wrapped in a bandage. A web of thread-like veins turned her eyelids mauve. Her lashes lay against her cheek, her nostrils flared slightly with each breath. Isa sank onto the chair beside the bed and clutched the limp hand that lay on top of the covers. The bones beneath the cold skin felt delicate, as if they would break if she held on too tightly.

'Annie – Annie, can you hear me?'

There was no movement.

A nurse walked in and lifted her wrist. She smiled at Isa. 'Her pulse is strong,' she said. 'She'll probably sleep until morning. Why don't you go home for a while?'

'No,' said Isa. I'll stay here until she wakes up.' Then she remembered Luke Muraco waiting outside.

'I'll be back.' Rising, she returned Annie's hand to the bed and patted it. The corridor echoed with the click of heels, the rasp of trolley wheels and muted voices. A couple walked past her clinging to each other, the woman crying and the man's eyes staring and unfocused.

Doctor Evans stood by an open door, talking to a colleague. He laughed at something, caught Isa's eye and nodded. She forced a smile of acknowledgement, knowing that speaking to him would be pointless; she would only get the same answers. Outside the door, a cold sharp blast of spring air slapped her skin.

Luke Muraco was pacing the length of the sidewalk. He stopped, his gaze met Isa's, his eyes mirroring her own fear. Isa had the impression that the boy was a coiled spring, ready to snap.

'She'll be fine.' She answered his unspoken question and watched the tight lines on his face relax slightly. She would not tell him her concerns. She wanted him gone.

'Can I see her?' he asked.

'They wouldn't let you in – not outside visiting hours.'

His face tightened, but he seemed to accept her explanation.

'My grandfather is preparing good medicine for Annie.'

'Thank you for taking Annie to hospital.' Isa's voice trembled. 'But we won't need your grandfather's medicine.'

'But it is good – better maybe than here.' He waved at the hospital doorway.

'Maybe,' she said, remembering Pierre's concoctions and how they had helped her in the past. 'But I don't think they'll approve, not in a hospital.'

Luke's eyes narrowed and burned.

'If she still needs help when she comes out...' her hollow words floated in the space between them. 'Luke,' she called after him as he turned away. He stopped and stared at her, his head leaning to one side, his lips a tight line.

'I'm staying with her. Could... could you tell Dan and my mother?'

He nodded briefly and veered away to where his pony was tethered.

'And Pierre...' she called after him.

Back in the ward, Isa settled down to watch her daughter. Annie, her skin almost as white as the pillow beneath her head, didn't move. This was the baby she had carried from Scotland all the way to Canada. The child Isa had one day hoped to take back to Raumsey to meet her paternal grandparents, her aunts, her cousins. A nurse came in often to check on her, but the soft smile to Isa gave nothing away.

The sounds of the hospital night fell around them; gentle snores and the occasional moan from other patients in the ward, the click of the nurses' heels on the linoleum floor, the clatter of a trolley in the corridor outside, whispered voices, the occasional rattle of a motor car or the clack of horses' hooves on the road outside.

'Talk to her,' the young doctor had said.

Isa leaned forward and lowered her voice. 'Annie can you hear me?' The figure on the bed did not stir.

'You won't remember, but I was so full of hope when we sailed up the St Lawrence. You were just a baby then and you wouldn't let me out of your sight.' She leaned closer and laid her head on the pillow. 'I was exhausted and you were so heavy my arms ached and your dad offered to take you, but I wouldn't let you go and I won't let you go now.

'You're called after my sister, the other Annie.' She eased herself into a more comfortable position and talked of her sister, of the games they had played back in Orkney. Then she dozed for a while. She blinked, straightened her stiff spine, and began to talk again, telling her tales she had never tired of hearing when she was a little girl.

The rattle of a trolley in the corridor jerked Isa from her dream. She moved, finding her bones stiff and her neck painful where it had cricked.

The runners on the rail above her hissed as the curtain moved aside and a nurse entered and stooped over the bed. Isa glanced up at her. At her expression Isa sat upright, fully awake. Annie's eyelids fluttered slightly. The nurse patted her hand. 'Anne, Anne, can you hear me?'

Her eyes half opened. With her lips barely parted, she breathed the word, 'Mam.'

'Thank God… thank God. I'm here – don't worry – you're going to be alright.' Isa clutched her daughter's hand. The fingers moved, barely perceptible, but movement none the less.

'One moment,' said the nurse.

Within a few minutes, she returned followed by the doctor.

'Ah, Anne, you've decided to join us.' He smiled as he spoke. 'Go get yourself a coffee,' he said to Isa. 'We'll be a little while with this young lady.'

The hospital coffee was surprisingly good and in spite of her broken night, Isa returned feeling awake and almost refreshed.

'How are you feeling?' Isa slid into the chair.

Annie ran the tip of her tongue over her lips. 'Thirsty,' she answered, her voice grating.

'I'll get her some fresh water.' The nurse left.

'What happened?' Annie turned away and stared at the green folds of the screen.

'You were riding an unbroken horse. You might have been killed.'

'Was I… could I?' Her voice was a low monotone. Her vague, unfocused eyes did not move.

'Annie…'

Her eyelids fluttered and shut. Her head rolled to one side.

'Doctor Evans would like a word with you.' The nurse had returned with a glass. She laid her fingers against Annie's neck. 'She sleeping naturally.'

Isa found the doctor in the corridor. He led her to a seating area. 'Anne's confused,' he said. 'Don't expect too much right now. We'll have to wait a while – see if her mind clears.'

'And if it doesn't?'

'I don't think there's any permanent damage.'

The words 'think' and 'permanent' chased each other round in Isa's brain. 'But there might be?'

'Her vital signs are good. She's responding well.'

'That's not what I asked you.'

'It's all anyone can tell you at this stage. You look exhausted. Your daughter will sleep for a while. Why don't you come back later?'

Didn't these people ever give you a straight answer? Without another word Isa trailed back to the ward. She was tired. There was work to do at home. She hadn't eaten since…she couldn't remember. Annie would sleep for most of the day – the doctor had said.

She opened the door and stopped. Martha was sitting by the bed. She looked up as Isa entered. 'I had to come,' she whispered.

'Thank you.' Isa stared down at the silent figure of her daughter. 'I'm leaving now Annie,' she said. 'But Granny's here. I'll be back later.'

'Yes. Please go home and get some rest.' The nurse moved to Annie's side and placed her fingers on the girl's wrist, glancing up at Isa in a way that told her the statement had been an order, not a request. 'Your mother will sit for a while.'

'Annie,' said Isa again.

Annie's eyes remained closed.

The nurse gave Isa a small smile. 'Later.' She mouthed the word.

With a nod of gratitude to Martha, Isa left, moving automatically as if her mind and body were no longer connected.

The morning air filled her lungs, fresh and clear. Isa blinked away the tiredness and the sudden rush of tears that threatened to overwhelm her. The sun shone from a clear blue sky but with little heat. Luke Muraco sat on the hospital step. 'How long have you been here?' she asked.

'I come in the dark.' His eyes pleaded for answers.

'Annie's been awake. She's sleeping now. I have to get home. Where's my pony?'

'Your pony over there.' Luke indicated the paddock where two horses scratched each other's necks, teeth bared, eyes closed as if in ecstasy.

In the space of two days, Isa's whole life had been turned inside out.

Back home, the ranch was deserted. A pile of wood lay waiting to be cut into usable chunks. The chickens raced at her wanting fed. Her milk cow bellowed from the paddock.

Four hours later, with a few of the most urgent chores already finished, Isa lay on the bed, meaning only to have a few minutes rest, but when she next opened her eyes, it was morning. Martha and Dan were in the kitchen drinking coffee.

'You should have wakened me.' Isa looked in horror at the clock.

'What good would it do?' said Dan. 'She's fine. You get some breakfast, and we'll see to the chores.'

Unable to eat more than a mouthful, Isa changed into clean clothes, mounted her gelding and rode the ten miles to Stony Plains where she hitched the horse to a post outside the hospital.

Annie had a good night, the nurse told her, but they intended to keep her in another night – to be on the safe side.

She found Annie sitting up looking a lot brighter than she had the day before. Her face lit when she saw her mother then slipped past her as if searching for someone else, and her smile wavered and died.

'Hello, Mam,' she said in a defeated voice.

'Annie, how do you feel?' Isa knelt by the bed and clutched her daughter's hand. The fingers were warm and limp.

Tears gathered in Annie's eyes and she blinked them away.

'Luke was waiting on the step this morning. They only let family in. He'd be here if he could,' said Isa, guessing the reason for her disappointment.

Annie shrugged and winced. She laid her head back on the pillow and stared at the ceiling.

'Do you remember what happened?'

'Not falling off the horse; not getting here.'

'You were riding an unbroken horse, why?'

'I want to ride in the rodeo at the Calgary stampede. I need to practise.'

'For God's sake, Annie. You're a girl.' Indignant irritation rose.

196

'A woman in America rides the rodeos. I can do it too. This is just a little setback.'

'What am I to do with you?'

'Let me be what I want to be.'

Isa sighed. 'Did you spend the other night with Luke?' She immediately regretted her words. In spite of her worries, this was not the time.

Annie's eyelids drooped. 'I'm tired now. I need to sleep.' She turned her head away.

'Annie,' Isa tried again, but the girl did not answer.

A nurse had come into the room and was hovering behind her. 'The doctor will be a couple of hours yet,' she said. 'But Anne's fine. She is a real little fighter.'

Annie's face remained angled away, the eyes closed, lashes fluttering against her skin.

Isa watched her, torn. There was so much work to be done back home. Her mother was unfit and Dan needed her, too. She wanted to stay, but what good could she do?

'I'll be back later, then.' She left, slowly.

Outside, something was going on. A sense of excitement filled the air. Doors were opening, people running into the street. 'Did you hear, did you hear,' a young lad shouted to Isa as she reached for her horse.

'Hear what?'

'The war's over,' shouted the lad. He didn't stop, but ran on, telling everyone who would listen.

'Is it true,' she asked a group of women who had gathered on the sidewalk.

'It's true,' said one. 'The Germans have accepted the British terms. Our boys will be coming home.' She covered her mouth and began to cry.

Isa retied her horse and ran back into the hospital. The news had filtered through, moving from mouth to mouth with the speed of a tornado. Without stopping at the desk she ran to Annie's bedside. 'Annie,' she sank beside her bed. 'The war's over.'

Annie turned to face her. 'Maybe Dad...maybe they made a mistake.'

'Aye, he's a real survivor.'

Annie had voiced her own hopes, her own reluctance to accept the words written on the telegram, the vision she had seen.

Annie's eyes filled with tears. Isa felt her own fill also and, clutching each other, they finally cried together.

Chapter Twenty-Eight

Sarah

As the train drew into Victoria Station, London, Sarah all but pressed her nose against the glass. Crowds of cheering people crowded the platform, men waving hats in the air, women with children in their arms wielding banners. The train drew to a stop and the carriage doors slid open. Soldiers stepped out to be swept up by sobbing wives and mothers and shy children, their fathers strangers to them. She suddenly heard a shout. 'Sarah, over here.'

Her sister Eileen was waving to her, a young soldier by her side.

She took two steps towards them before she recognized her brother, Connor. Apart from being over a foot taller than the last time she had seen him, he had the same cheery face, same button nose and clear blue eyes as the lad she had left behind.

He hugged her, then he held her at arm's length. 'Sarah. By. And ye've been in Europe all this time? Ye look well.'

This time she hugged him, the roughness of his unshaven face against hers, the soldier smell still around him, and she didn't want to let go.

'Just the last three years,' she said as they were jostled by the surging crowd.

'Let's go and grab a cup of tea somewhere,' said Eileen.

Sarah looked around again. 'I've lost the girls I travelled with.'

'It's impossible to find anyone in this. Over here, they serve tea in the station. We'll not leave until they find us.'

As they walked he lurched against her, and she realised he was limping badly.

'You've been injured,' she said.

'Shrapnel in the hip. Others had a lot worse.'

'And the others, Pat and Michael?' Sarah asked. 'And yer man, Eileen?'

'Nichol's fine. Was injured not long after ye left and was sent home.' For a moment a shadow crossed her face. 'Nothing'll be the same again.' A forced air of brightness lightened her eye as she dashed a tear from her cheek. 'I've heard no word of Pat and Mike but that surely means they must have made it through the war. They'll be right glad to hear we're back in touch with ye.'

They found a table by the window and sat down, sipping tea and swopping stories. Connor's staying in London overnight,' said Eileen, What about you?'

'Yes, the nurses are as well.'

'Great. There'll be a dram and music laid on for us. To be honest, most of us just need a bath and a good night's sleep,' said Connor.

'Are ye going back to Canada?' asked Eileen.

'I am. I miss Alberta if truth be known.' As she spoke she realised just how much she looked forward to the enormous skies, the empty plains and the solitude, the peace. 'You should all come. Paddy's not a bad fellow really. I should have stood up to him sooner.'

'I've been thinking seriously on it,' said Connor. 'Britain's in a poor way with the war and all.'

Sarah clasped his hand. 'Come, please come.'

'Hey, our Sarah, we'll all be over, lock, stock and barrel!' They laughed together.

'Ah, there you are.' Two nurses Sarah had served with came through the door. 'There are street parties everywhere. Come on Sarah. We've got to celebrate. Who's this?'

Sarah introduced her brother and sister and stood up. The sense of relief, the desire to relax, the exultation of knowing it was over and yet the inability to truly believe the world was free, was as strong within her as it was in her colleagues. She reached towards her siblings. 'Come on,' she said, 'come with us.'

'I have to go,' said Eileen, 'Nichol's watching Inish, but he gets stressed.' Once more a shadow crossed her features, making her blink.

'What is it, lass?' asked Sarah.

'We're fine. We'll stay in touch.' They hugged each other. Connor kissed her cheek. 'It's been grand seeing you, our Sarah. I'm meeting up with some lads from my regiment now, but I'll be over to Canada before you know it.' They hugged once more before the surging crowds drove them apart.

***

Reverend Donald Charleston stood in the courtyard of the French farm house where he had been finally billeted. He stubbed out his cigarette and gazed up at the clear moonlit skies. A perfect night for bombing. It seemed strange, almost surreal that there was no drone of zeppelins, no longer any boom of guns, no more flashes in the sky. He walked as far as the road, his breath misty before him. His head was full of the young men whose hands he had held as they drew their last breath, of the letters he'd written to bereaved mothers, wives, sweethearts; of the silent fields of wooden crosses, bearing testimony to the bravery of soldiers and the foolishness of politicians; of the emotion he had felt when entering the ruined city of Ypres, with the skeletal remains of buildings reaching into a pewter sky, the rubble piled into the streets, the silence. He remembered the one emaciated mongrel slinking away from him and how he had given the beast his last chunk of bread and cheese.

Placing his elbows on the top of a stone wall, he clasped his hands together. He knew he should give thanks to his God for peace, but the images were too vivid in his mind, memories too raw. What would he find on his return to Scotland, how many widows and fatherless children among the people he knew?

And yet there was a bright star on his horizon. Before he had parted with Sister Margaret MacBeth, he had asked her to marry him and she had agreed wholeheartedly. His feelings for her was not the rush of blood that Isa Reid had stirred in him, but a deep understanding born of shared experiences, a love that had grown from admiration and respect. Margaret was a strong, non-judgemental woman of high ideals and he loved her totally. She would make an excellent minister's wife. Their love would be all the stronger for not having been consummated although the temptation had been intense for both of them. Whether or not she would follow him to Raumsey or whether they would remain in the south was a matter for discussion, options they were both willing to consider. She had gone on ahead with the other nurses and should by now be waiting for him and celebrating in her family home in Paisley.

He returned to the farmhouse kitchen and joined his companions who had already packed their gear and were having a final cup of coffee before the trucks that would transport them to Calais arrived.

Chapter Twenty-Nine

Sarah

The nurses and soldiers returning to Canada were welcomed with no less celebration than they had received in London. As the train appeared on the track, its bell clanging, a mighty cheer rose from the crowds on the platform. Then, with a hissing of steam, the great monster pulled into the station and the doors slid open. Underweight soldiers, tragic eyes revealing the sights they had seen, spilled onto the platform. The masses surged forward, each waiting family claiming its own.

The snow was already solid on the ground. Shy and awkward, Paddy stood on the platform, grasping the rim of his Stetson, his hair plastered down with some kind of grease, an unruly curl escaping and standing out from his head like a horn, his clothes were unsoiled, albeit crumpled. Clean-shaven, with a few nicks on his skin, he stepped forward, his face brightening, as if, upon seeing her, a light had come on in his head. They faced each other awkwardly.

'Aye, Sarah, lass. It's a fine sight ye are.' His eyes never left her face.

'I'm glad to see you, Paddy.' Nervously she clutched her bag to her stomach, both hands closed tightly on the flap.

'Well,' he hesitated. 'Come, come.' He turned, led the way to the sleigh and took her hand clumsily helping her onto the seat. He wrapped a blanket round her shoulders, then rocked the sleigh to free the ice-bound runners before climbing in beside her.

D'ye like this fine sleigh?' he asked, slapping the reins against the horse's sides. The beast strained in the harness, his breath steaming before him, until the sleigh jolted forward. 'Would have made a covered cabin for ye, but there's not the money for it. There's been a drought in the land these last few summers. Dragonflies and all, thousands of them. The cattle are thin and there's surely not enough feed for them to see them through to spring.' He turned towards her and tucked the blanket more securely around her legs. 'Ah but here I am, giving ye all the bad news. Sure it's a grand thing to have ye back again in one piece.'

Sarah was glad he did not ask about Europe. That was another life. Her other life, one that she had no desire to share at the moment. She looked up at the blue expanse of the sky, at the miles of flat country, darkly scarred by forests. The air was frigid and silent save for the swish of the runners on the snow, the occasional snorting of the horse and the steady muffled clop of his feet. Once they saw a herd of caribou in the distance.

'What happened to the last horse?' asked Sarah, for the first time realising that this was a younger heavier beast than the one Paddy used to own.

'He grew old, worn out. I still have him, though I can ill afford his feed. He might do ye. He's only good as a woman's mount.'

When they reached the shack, Sarah drew in a sharp breath of surprise. The place had been cleaned up. Inside was even more of a shock. Paddy took the blanket from her shoulders and held his hand out for her coat. The stove glowed warmly. Her eyes fell on the bench, the bench that used to serve her as a bed, and with a start she realised that there were no blankets or skins. Surely he did not expect her to share his bed? She thought they understood each other as far as that was concerned.

'Paddy,' she said, turning to him. 'Where am I to sleep?'

'Ah, queen, I have a surprise for ye.' He took her hand and led her to the bedroom door.

'No Paddy,' she said. 'I'm not...' The door swung open to reveal a small square landing. 'I've added another room.' He pushed open the nearest door. There was a wooden bed with a table by the side which held an oil lamp. Against one wall sat a chest of drawers and a jug and basin on top. A deerskin rug lay on the wooden floor.

'I built a room for ye. I didn't put up curtains. Ye can choose them yerself.' He gave an embarrassed laugh. 'What do I know about curtains?'

'Oh Paddy!' Without thought, she threw her arms around him and kissed his cheek.

He stepped back, his face red. 'D'ye like it, queen?'

'I love it.' Sarah had not been totally sure about her decision to return to Canada until this moment. 'Isn't it strange how things work out,' she said, more to herself than Paddy.

'You know, my brother might come over. How do you feel about that?'

He gave a loud laugh. 'Sarah, my queen, if they're fit to build themselves other rooms, ye can take the whole family as far as I'm concerned.'

'Thank you,' she whispered. 'It's good to be home.'

Chapter Thirty

Donald

Donald Charleston's first stop after leaving his father's house in Glasgow had been the barber's shop for a haircut and shave. Now, dressed in his only suit, he stepped from the train in Paisley railway station and checked the address on the slip of paper in his hand. He took a deep breath. 'You can walk it from there,' Margaret had said. He read the directions again. In spite of the poverty brought about by war, there was an air of exhilaration in the town. The conflict was over and the world was rejoicing. Slipping the folded page into his pocket, his heart speeded up and his mouth dried. Torn between feelings of anticipation and schoolboy nervousness, he quickened his step. The last time he had seen her was before he had been moved south, one week before peace was declared, and it was then they had pledged themselves to each other. Now that the situation had changed, would the feelings between them still be the same? He had never seen her out of uniform and imagined her in a dress, her hair, always so severely pulled back, loose and tumbling round her face.

He read the street signs as he passed until at last he came to Baron's Walk. The houses were stone buildings, three storeys high and small neglected gardens in front surrounded by iron railings in what had once been an affluent part of town. He went up the two steps that led to the front door. The brass knocker was tarnished, paint was peeling from the door. He lifted the knocker and let it fall, twice. After what seemed like an eternity, he heard footsteps. He removed his hat and cleared his throat. The door opened. An elderly woman, tall and slightly stooped, with thick white hair and a high forehead stood before him.

He turned his hat round, feeding the rim through his fingers. 'Good day. I've come to see Margaret, if I may.'

'Reverend Charleston?' The woman asked.

He nodded.

'I am Margaret's mother. Mrs McBeth.' She held out her hand. It was limp and cold. 'You'd better come in.'

He followed her through a narrow hallway and into a dark room with heavy furniture. It was then he realised what he had failed to notice from the outside. The curtains were drawn despite it being midmorning. The only light was provided by a shaded lamp and reflected from the surfaces of the polished mahogany furniture. Around the room were photos of whom he assumed was Margaret at various ages. A sepia baby on a large basket chair, a little girl in a school uniform, as a nurse with her parents, then a group of nurses on a platform, waving, a train behind them.

'She told me about you,' Mrs McBeth said stiffly. 'If you take a seat, I'll make tea. Things were hard during the war. I had to let the maid go.'

'Mrs McBeth,' said Donald, 'Never mind the tea. Where's Margaret?' A feeling of dread had crept into his heart and tightened in his stomach.

The woman pulled a handkerchief from the sleeve of her cardigan. 'She had a cold when she returned. We thought it was a cold.'

The blood drained to Donald's feet. An icy finger traced itself up his spine. 'Tell me.' He lowered himself into the couch.

She took a seat directly across from him and cleared her throat. 'It was flu. First her and then her father. I prayed it would take me as well. It was all very sudden.' Her voice caught and she twisted the handkerchief on her lap. For a long moment, the stillness of the room was broken only by the ticking of the clock, the wind whistling around the windows and a mother sobbing quietly for her lost family. At last Mrs McBeth patted her eyes, blew her nose and rose. 'I'll get the tea.' She left abruptly.

Donald was as cold as the room around him. Before his vision blurred, he saw her solemn and posed, in the photos on the wall, a happy family come to an abrupt end. The ticking clock filled the silence. A child shouted somewhere outside and running feet and young laughter passed in the street and faded into distance. Donald pressed his eyes firmly shut. This couldn't be true.

Chapter Thirty-One

Isa

McArthy's motor car stood at the door, the wheels and paintwork scarred with mud. Isa swung from the trap and unyoked the horse. McArthy strode towards her. In spite of his advancing years, his body remained slim, his shoulders broad. Normally she would be pleased to see him, but something made her scalp prickle today. He stopped, removed the Stetson from his greying hair. 'I'm sorry, Isa, but things are tough. I need to call in the loan.'

A heat filled her up. 'But you can't, you said you'd wait...'

He studied his feet before meeting her eye again. 'Because of the droughts, a man needs a hell of a lot more land than you've got just to survive. Hell, we all need more land, me included. Sure doesn't look set to get much better.' He nodded towards the horizon. 'Many farmers are leaving. I can't risk losing everything, and if I wait another year...' He lifted his hands in a gesture of helplessness.

'If you'll give us time,' Isa pleaded.

'I'm sorry for your loss, but without your man, you're not going to be able to pay off the loan.' He gave a deep sigh. 'You have to face facts. Folks are starving, moving further south to the cities, America even.'

'But we don't know any other life.'

'God knows, I don't want to put you out, Isa. Things are hard for us all. But I'm a reasonable man. I'll give your lad a job and you can stay in the house meantime, that's the best I can do.'

'Excuse me.' Isa squeezed past him, pressing herself against the door-jamb to minimise body contact. Once inside, she turned to face him. 'Give us time to get on our feet. You'll get your money. The rains might come next year, and I hear the price of grain has never been so high. Now is hard, that's all. I can do it.'

'You have to grow the grain first, and there's no guarantee that the rain'll come.' He scratched his head. 'There is another solution.'

'What?' Isa looked at him.

'You could marry me.'

The air rushed from her lungs. 'What!'

'Think about it. I've a fine big house in Stony Plains. You can have a real comfortable life. You, your children and your mother.'

Speechless, Isa stared at him, at the folds in his skin, his square jaw, his pale eyes.

'I need the ranch. I know I'm older than you, but I can give you comfort, security and I'd treat you real good. Don't say no right away, think on my offer.' He cleared his throat, nodded, then spun on his heel and strode over the yard.

Isa watched him go. Marry him? She had never once thought of him in that way and the offer had shocked her. Shaken, she marched into the cabin.

Dan looked up from where he sat on the bench mending boots. 'What did he want?'

'Money.' She had tried to shield her children, but now the time had come to tell them the truth. She dropped into the chair, defeated. 'The war's brought the country down and drought's near finished us off. I borrowed money from him and I can't pay him back.'

Dan sat up. 'You did what? Why didn't you talk to me first? What did he have to say?'

'He needs the money or he'll take the farm, but he'll give you a job.'

'Work for him on land that should be mine?'

'It may be time for us to move to town. Maybe we'll both get jobs.' She no longer had the fire for farming. Dan was but a boy, Martha was ailing and Pierre did his best, but he was very old. There was no money to pay workers. Even if the droughts were over, they were already broken.

Dan threw down his tools. 'There are no jobs in town even for the soldiers who have come back. They say this drought could go on for years. Farmers are abandoning their land and moving south. McArthy's right, we're finished.' He rose and slammed out the door.

Expecting Martha to be upset, she prepared herself for her mother's acid remarks, but her reaction was a surprise.

'I'm glad,' she said. 'My sister in Vancouver invited me to come and stay with her. I didn't know how to tell you.'

'Do you want to go?' asked Isa, amazed.

'Yes. I'm too old for this life and I'm tired.'

'Oh, Ma, why didn't you say?'

'I couldn't leave you. Not with the bairns to watch. Now I'm free to go. If you want security, marry McArthy. He seems like a decent man and I won't have to worry about you any more.'

Marry McArthy? How could she even consider it? Yet what was the alternative? The money had gone, Davie had gone, the life she had dreamed of had gone and that was hard to accept. When her mother left, she would have one less responsibility and Dan would have a job. There was only herself and Annie. She could work, but there were few jobs, even in the cities, so she had heard. Marrying McArthy was a way out and no doubt many widows in her position would accept it as a means of survival. It would mean money in her pocket, good food, an easy life and he wasn't an unattractive man.

Once the house was quiet and the family in bed, Isa collapsed into Davie's chair her body aching with a deep sadness. They could remain in the house for now, McArthy didn't need it, but with only one wage and no acreage, they could not survive here. Once more she wondered whether, if she had gone to Prince Rupert with Davie when he wanted, would things have been any different. But looking backwards never solved anything. She had learned that many years ago.

A week before they had to vacate the farm, the letter arrived.

'It's from Raumsey.' Dan handed it to Isa.

'Not before time. It's been well nigh on a year since I had the last word from Chrissie.' Isa unfolded the paper. She read a few lines. 'Oh, my,' she exclaimed. 'Your Uncle Jack is dead.' She harboured no love for Davie's violent brother, Jack, but the death of a young man was always a tragedy.

'Does it say what happened?'

Isa had often spoken about the family in Raumsey, so that her children would know their roots.

'An accident. That's all it says.'

Chrissie had written that she was moving her family to the mainland. Only Bel, Isa's niece, was to remain behind.

Britain is hungry and there's more call for the herring than ever before. Our boats are not big enough to take in fish in sufficient amount, so we're going to where the work is.

Isa read aloud.

Bel won't come with us. She says she'll never leave the island. But she's unmarried and I worry for her. Jimmy is the heir to Scartongarth, but he is not at all interested. That leaves Dan as next in line to take over the tenancy. I don't know your situation, but Scartongarth would welcome you home.

Isa looked up from the page. 'Chrissie wants us to come home, run the farm.'

'Would you really want to go back to Raumsey?' asked Dan.

'I don't know.' Isa shrugged. She did not regret her years in Canada, but now that her dream had been crushed, her thoughts had strayed more and more often to the past, to Raumsey, to the place where she had belonged a long time ago. Raumsey with its fields of gold and solidly built wee houses standing defiantly against the bitter north winds. Raumsey of the lashing gales and roaring seas and mourning seals, of the frozen hands and warm hearts, of sunlit days and soft musical nights, of back-breaking toil and moments of wonder. 'Would you come back with me? Have a place of your own to run?' she asked.

'No. I'm happy here as long as McArthy keeps me on. He's

always been fair with us, and I believe him when he says he had no other option. And I can support you. You don't have to go anywhere.'

'You'll take a wife soon enough, Dan. Then you won't want me around.' Isa would never forget her own difficulties with her mother-in-law when she first went to Scartongarth, and how would Dan support a family of his own as well? She could see how tired he was already.

He grabbed his jacket from the back of the chair. 'You do what's best for you, Ma. I have to go. Work'll not wait.'

Isa re-read the letter. But going back was an impossible dream.

'Now you've got another option,' said Martha when she told her.

'It's not worth thinking about,' Isa said. 'Even if I chose to, I've not got the money for the fare.'

Martha rubbed her hands together as if they pained her. She cleared her throat. 'I've a wee bit put by. It was my insurance for my old age.' She looked at Isa almost guiltily.

'You mean, you've had money all this time?' Isa thought of the drought, of the hard years, of having to go cap in hand to McArthy.

'It's not a lot,' Martha declared, 'Not enough to keep this place going and it's as well, isn't it, for I would have lost it all. I had hoped I would never be forced to part with it, but times have never been this bad. Furthermore, you never asked me, did you? You were as bad as all the rest, only thought a man's opinion was what counted.'

Isa lowered her head. Her mother was right. She had never considered the possibility that her mother would have money. However, it was her hard-earned nest egg and she had the right to do with it what she wanted.

'All I need is enough for my fare to Calgary, then my sister will see me alright. If you really don't want to marry McArthy, it's yours, whatever you choose to do with it.'

Isa swallowed. 'It's your independence,' she said, covering her mother's hand with hers. 'I can't take it.'

'My life is almost over. This is the last thing I can do for you. Please. I can't see you married to a man you don't love. But, if my opinion's worth anything, he seems like a decent sort.'

Isa could no longer hold back the tears. 'Thank you, Mam,' and she hugged her mother for the second time in her adult life.

As she lay in bed that night, Isa's thoughts took her back through the years to when she was a happy young bride, very much in love. She thought of her mother-in-law, Tyna of the bitter words and kind heart, her sister-in-law, Mary-Jane of the doe eyes and quiet depth, of her friend, Jessie, buxom, kind, slovenly, homely Jessie of the whisky breath and the gigantic heart.

For a moment she considered what going back would mean. Annie away from danger, a farm of their own, support from loving friends and family. No more uncertain future.

Bel was one year older than Annie and was being left to run a croft on her own with not a man to fish for her. But the British Isles were struggling in poverty after the war, probably harder than in Canada. Yet the sea was full of fish, the silver darlings, whereas the prosperity of the prairies depended on rain, rain that might never come.

With her mother's money, she might get a small place in town, but how long would that last with little chance of a job? And Annie, Isa needed to take her far away from here, from rodeos, from the diphtheria, from the Indian boy. In Raumsey they could be self-sufficient. But could she live without the son she loved?

It was morning before she had a chance to speak to Dan again and harboured the hope of persuading him to come with her. 'If we went back, wouldn't you consider coming too? The farming life is easier, no droughts or dragonflies or grasshoppers. And there's the sea. The herring.'

Dan shook his head. 'No, Ma. Canada's my home.' He lowered himself into the chair. 'Seems to me there's a lot of folk who wish they had a reason to go back home, but they have no option. Don't worry about me, I'll be just fine and I will come and see you one day when I've made my fortune.'

She reached out and grabbed his hand. 'Are you sure?'

'I might not stay here. With just myself to think about, I'll go where the money is.'

'I love you, Dan,' she whispered, realising she had not said these words to him since he was a little boy.

Now she had to speak to Annie, already knowing what her answer would be. She wouldn't tell her about McArthy's offer. She couldn't. Not now she had an alternative.

***

'No,' said Annie. 'You go. I'll stay with Dan.'

'We will come back one day. But come with me now. Get to know your dad's family.'

'All the family I need is right here.'

'We've lost everything. Do you want us to live like paupers?'

'The natives have less than us, yet they're happy,' she flung back.

'I'll not go without you,' said Isa.

'Then we'll have to find a way to survive here.'

Isa covered her face with her hands. She couldn't forcibly drag her daughter back to Raumsey, yet the very reasons that held the girl to this land were the very reasons she had to take her away. Within her daughter was the same determined streak that she, herself, possessed as a young lassie in love with an unsuitable boy. She knew by the set of the jaw, the flash of her eyes, that nothing she could say would change Annie's mind.

If she didn't want her family to fracture, marrying McArthy was her only choice. She was thirty-five years old, threads of grey already beaded her hair and fine lines spidered around her eyes. She was tired. Tired of the land, tired of the constant struggle. And back in Raumsey would be no different. McArthy offered a life of relative comfort for her and her family and freedom to pursue her own interests. So what if he was twenty years her senior? So what if he had never made her tremble? Some might say he was still an attractive man in his way and possessed a strength missing in Davie. Perhaps she could grow to love him. But would the price be too high to pay?

Chapter Thirty-Two

Annie

That night Annie could not sleep. She lay staring at the oblong of pale moonlight that was her window, suffering the ever-present pain which throbbed in her heart. She had to talk to Muraco, had to see him, tell him of her mother's plans. She missed her dad dreadfully and needed Muraco, needed his comfort; nothing else would placate her now. If he asked her to come with him and be his woman, she would go willingly. But in spite of all her efforts to attract him, he continued to be aloof, holding himself away from her. If only she could have remained on the mustang – proved to him she was as fit as any of the dark-skinned girls on the reservation to embrace the native way of life, as fit as Minola, the girl his parents wanted him to take as a wife, maybe then he would see her as more than just a childhood playmate. She knew he found her attractive, saw it in his eyes when they met hers and she couldn't understand why he turned from her whenever they got too close.

She waited until her mother and Dan had gone and her grandmother had fallen asleep in the fireside chair. After wrapping up some bread and cheese to take with her, she left the house. She would ride – all along the boundaries of the ranch – all along the land that should be her inheritance, the inheritance that was being wrenched from her family, forcing them backwards into a past she felt no part of. Galloping across the plains with the wind in her hair was the only way to ease the angst that swelled within her until she felt she would burst. When she tired, she would go to the native village and find Muraco.

Annie dug her heels into the pony's side. The sharp air cooled her burning cheeks. Cattle scattered before her as she rode towards the trees. Several hours later she found herself in the forest, the air was still and strong with the scent of pine. Snow clung to hollows and animal tracks criss-crossed before her. A hare darted from its hiding place and the pony started, breath clouding before him.

'How dare her mother decide her future? Stay away from sick children; stay home and do some work; stay away from the woods. Cougars, bears, wolves. Her mother's words rang in her ears. Stay away from the Indians. Drunkenness, poverty, no prospects – what did she know? When did she ever take the time to find out what was really going on? If she'd had her way, Annie would go to school in the city, meet a bank manager or someone of that ilk, attend tea parties and go to music halls and eat in fancy restaurants. Just as well they never had the money for it. Annie never hankered after the finer things in life, she was happier with the natives, the sense of danger driving her ever forward.

Annie knew why Isa really wanted to go back to Raumsey. To get her away from Muraco. Hot tears trickled down her face tickling like ants. She steadied the horse with her legs and wiped her nose on her gloved hand. It wasn't that she didn't want to go to Scotland, she had always wanted to see the homeland of her parents, but she had the terrible sensation that once she went there she would lose Muraco forever.

Smoky whinnied and tossed his head. 'Go on,' she commanded, digging her heels into his sides. He reared and backed away. A low branch smacked the back of her head. 'Stop this, Smoky,' she shouted, kicking him to urge him forward. Now more branches were digging into her back. Smoky suddenly reared and leapt forward. The branch had snagged on the hood of her jacket and suddenly she was off balance.

Screaming, she tried to grab at the pony's mane, but with her damaged arm, she was unable to get enough purchase and found herself falling. She hit the ground on her elbow and the pain jolted up and through her body and into the shoulder, not yet fully healed.

'Smoky,' she called uselessly. The horse galloped down the track and was soon out of sight.

For a long time she lay like that, the pain in her arm and shoulder so severe she could not move. When the sharpness of it blunted, she pulled herself into a sitting position. She must be miles from home, but there was no choice, she would have to walk. First she needed to get her breath back.

She leaned against a cradle of branches and trees brought down by the last tornado. The snow still clung to this hollow, the wind had vanished and the approaching night was sharp with a cold that found her bones. She would have to move soon.

Looking around, she gasped. Just a few feet from her was a wolf, grey and matted, his head lowered. A wolf on his own. A lone wolf. Separated from their pack, they were dangerous. But her native friends had taught her well. Stay still. Do not panic. Roll over on your back – show submission. The wolf can smell your fear. She tried not to breathe. The wolf padded silently around her, his yellow eyes never leaving her face. Was she bleeding? She did not think so, but if she was, the wolf would smell it, and she would be in greater danger. Eventually he passed by and slunk into the forest.

Annie waited for what seemed like hours. She wanted her mam now, she would tell her what to do, like she always did. Crawling from her shelter, she looked upwards. The sky was beginning to darken. If she didn't get out of here while she could still see the trail, she would be lost. She stood up and rubbed her aching shoulder.

All of a sudden the wolf came bounding out of the trees snarling. He leapt at her sending her to the ground, knocking the wind from her lungs. She rolled on her back and closed her eyes. The wolf's stinking breath stiffened in her nostrils making her gag. For a brief second she wondered whether they would find her body, or would the wolf devour everything. Would her bones be buried and left to rot before being chewed by a hungry pack. 'I'm sorry, Mam,' she whispered, and counting each second, she waited for the sharp teeth to close on her throat.

As suddenly as he had appeared the weight lifted from her and the wolf moved away. After a period of silence she opened her eyes. He sat at a short distance, watching her. She turned her head slowly; saw the twisted branches that formed a cavern just behind her. If she could get in there, she might have a chance. Surely Smoky would be home by now and someone would come looking for her. They would go to the native village first, and Luke Muraco would track her through the forest. All she had to do was remain safe until then.

She began to edge backwards. The wolf stopped panting. His ears shot forward, but he remained still. Gaining confidence, Annie shifted first her hips, then her shoulders, stopping in between each movement to gauge the animal's reaction. Still as a statue, he stared at her.

Once she had reached the relative safety of the cradle, she lay still, regaining her breath. The wolf lay down, his head between his front paws, his eyes still on her. It occurred to her that this was what he wanted, her in this cage. But why? Was this his store-cupboard for when he grew hungry?

She waited – either for sleep or death, for even if the wolf did not touch her, the cold would get through her in the coming night and she would die anyway.

How she longed for the comfort of the cabin, for the large iron range and crackling logs, for her mother scolding, her grandmother bringing her coffee. She allowed her mind to drift and saw her own funeral; her mother and brother crying, blaming themselves for the way they had treated her. She saw herself lying in her coffin, dressed in white. She was always beautiful in white. And then she remembered. The wolf. She would lie in no coffin. There would be nothing left of her.

At that moment she was filled with a new determination to survive at any cost. She dragged herself upright and felt around until she managed to locate a stout branch. Holding it tightly in her good hand she crawled into the open and rose to her feet at the same time lashing out at the animal with the branch. 'Get out of here you brute. Leave me alone,' she screamed.

The wolf sprang upright and snarled. For a minute he backed away, growling. Spurred on by her success, she continued forward, swinging the branch and screaming. He crouched. He wrinkled his nose. His body tensed and he sprang forward, grabbing her weapon between his teeth, wrenching it from her hands. Taken by surprise, she screamed, this time from fear, and retreated back into the cradle, rolling on her back, submissive. The snapping jaws drew near her face until she could smell his breath, strong and rancid. He continued growling while she lay prone, tears damp on her cheeks. He retreated a bit, then lay down again, his watchful eyes on her until her limbs grew stiff with cold. She would not be alive by morning.

Where were they? Her rescuers. The wolf stood up, lifted his head and howled. Far in the distance his cry was answered, not by one but by many. So that was it. He was not a lone wolf as she had thought. He was going to share his dinner with his pack. She edged a fallen stick across the opening and felt behind her for another. It took a long time but eventually she had built a barrier trapping herself in a wooden cage. She might die this night, but the wolves would not get her body.

Gradually the cold claimed her, freezing out the will to live, and in her mind she was back in the shack, cuddled in the crook of her father's arm. He was telling her a story about Raumsey, about when he was a boy, about the seals and how they changed into men and women in the night and danced and sang on the shore. And as he spoke he tickled her and made her laugh. And then she saw it, the sea rolling on the shingle beach, the sun warm on her face, the seals dancing and singing their mournful songs. And she smiled and drifted and she wasn't cold any more. And the dream changed, and dad was telling them he was going to war. Her mother was crying, and then she was crying too. How could he go and leave them?

'Annie, Annie,' she heard the voices a long way off. She was still dreaming. The voices grew louder. As if she was being dragged from a deep dark well she opened her eyes. Moonlight dappled through the trees and fell on the empty space where the wolf had been. Memory rushed at her and she tried to shout but her voice was hoarse and frozen. Lights danced among the trees.

At first she thought fireflies, but they grew, and the voices grew. 'This is where she fell,' the voice of Luke Muraco. And then it stopped.

'What is it, what's wrong?' Dan's voice.

'Wolf tracks.'

She tried to move, strike out, anything to make a noise, but her body would not respond. And then she grunted. She couldn't be sure. Had that been her or something else?

Luke Muraco heard it. She could see his feet, inches from the cage she had made. The lantern swung towards her, the light falling on the twisted huddle of branches.

'Over here,' he called.

Suddenly hands were pulling the branches away. 'She's in here.' Hands lifted her from her freezing bed, held her close to a warm chest.

'Let's get her home.'

'Quickly,' said Luke. 'More tracks here. Mountain lion.'

'Thank God you didn't try to walk home,' said Dan.

Mountain lion, thought Annie, her blood running colder still. Dan swung her up before him onto his pony and held her tightly against him. His warmth thawed her frozen body and, finally feeling safe, the tears began to trickle down her cheeks.

'Thank you, Luke,' said Dan. 'You saved my sister's life.'

Had he? It was a belief among the Indians that once you saved a life, that life belonged to you. Now her life belonged to Muraco. As their eyes met in the silver swathe of light, he gave a brief nod. He did not smile. The Cree seldom did.

From behind him in the darkness of the trees, she saw it. A movement – little more than a shadow. And then the shape crept forward until a shaft of broken moonlight settled on the grey coat and lit up the eyes.

At the same time Pierre reacted, swinging his rifle to his shoulder.

'No,' Annie cried as the shot rent the deep silence of the forest, but the space where the animal had been a moment before was empty. Annie breathed deeply, relieved. If it hadn't been for the wolf, she would have no doubt been dead. A mountain lion was far more dangerous. She wondered if, perhaps, he had been trying to protect her by herding her into the wooden cage. She turned to look into the forest where the wolf had melted into the night and said a silent thank-you.

Back at the ranch, Isa ran outside to meet them. 'Annie! Where were you? We've been out of our minds with worry.'

Dan slid from the horse and lifted Annie down. Isa grabbed her daughter, crushing her in an embrace. 'I decided, while I was waiting,' she released Annie and turned to look at Dan. 'I am going back to Raumsey and I'm taking Annie with me.'

Annie heard the determination in her mother's voice, said nothing, but stiffened and drew away. She would not go. Her life belonged to Luke Muraco now and there was nothing anyone could do about it.

Isa led her into the house and wrapped a blanket around her, poured a coffee with a tot of whisky and set it in her cold hands.

'You really are going?' asked Dan.

'I have to. What happened tonight made me realise. If I stay here, one way or another, I'm going to lose my daughter.'

'You do what you have to do, Ma,' said Dan.

I'm not going, thought Annie, but she was too exhausted to argue tonight.

***

Much later, as Isa lay in her bed chasing sleep, she spoke to Davie in her mind. 'I'm going back,' she said. 'I'll feel you beside me when I walk on the road to nowhere.' She reached up and imagined his hand in hers and concentrated on feeling the solidity, but her fingers clutched at air. 'I'm going back for both of us, for our daughter. Let me find you there.'

Her heart had been so full of happiness the day they sailed up the St Lawrence River and the smell of the new land had come out to meet them, the smell of strong scented pine. She had snuggled against Davie for warmth and he had placed an arm around her and kissed the top of her head.

As she drifted into the sea of sleep, she was back there, Annie in her arms, Davie's arm around her, Wee Dan clutching her skirt.

'It's beautiful,' she breathed as the sunlight hit the surface of the water, sending diamonds to welcome them to Canada. Lifting her head, her eyes met his and he smiled his lop-sided smile. His fair curls fell across his forehead soft against her face as he bent to kiss her lips.

'Everything's going to be fine, I'll make it fine,' he had said, with enough force that she had believed him without question. She was willing to believe anything he said back then.

The dream shifted and they were sitting in front of the shack by the cottonwoods watching the glorious display of the northern lights as they danced across the sky. She felt his arms around her, felt his breath on her cheek. 'I'll never leave you again,' he whispered, 'I promise.'

When she woke in the morning, the dream was still with her. She lifted her hand and wiped her cheeks, finding them wet. 'Why did you have to go?' she whispered, hugging her pillow. 'Where will I find you?'

Chapter Thirty-Three

Annie

Three days later, Annie padded from her bedroom into the empty kitchen. She picked up a basin from the sideboard and filled it from the kettle on the stove. After carrying it back to her bedroom, she stripped and washed, taking care to avoid her injured arm which still pained her badly. Slowly she pulled on her vest, bodice, thick woollen jumper, knickers, socks and trousers. Muraco had not come for her as she had hoped he would so she would have to go to him; her life was his and his alone. Now he would have to take her to be his woman. After all, it was not as if she was a stranger to the native ways. As a child she had attended the missionary school and played with the children of the Cree and the Blackfoot. Went to their villages, scratched letters in the mud, sat around their campfires, listened to the stories of the old men, picked up a little of their language and dreamed of being part of the once-proud race as they rode after the herds of bison roaming the prairies.

Outside she heard the thud of axe on wood and glanced through the window. Her mother, clad in a long skirt and buckskin jacket, with a red woollen scarf around her head bent down and picked up another log, placed it upright on the old tree stump, and expertly hewed it in half.

Annie took a pitcher of milk from the cupboard, filled a cup and helped herself to a bannock and butter. That done, she picked up her jacket and went outside to where her mother was gathering an armful of logs. As Annie approached, Isa lifted her head. Her hair lay in curls around her shoulders, her face was flushed from exertion.

'I'm taking Smoky out,' Annie said.

Isa straightened her spine. Her forehead crinkled. 'Are you

sure?' The voice was careful, guarded, the way it had been ever since the night of the wolf.

'Just a short ride round the ranch.'

Isa hesitated and for a heartbeat, woman and girl held each other's gaze. 'You won't go near the forest?' said Isa at last.

'Don't worry. I'll never go back there again.'

'Be careful of your arm.'

'I will.' Annie mounted and walked the horse slowly from the yard. She didn't want to hurt her mother, but what she felt for Muraco was too important.

She rode to the point where the trees hid her from view, then she turned the pony and headed for the native village. Once there, the horse picked his way to the middle of a stream over grey and brown pebbles as he had done many times. There he stopped and drank, only lifting his head when the other horses whinnied to him. He whinnied back, water dropping from his mouth. In the creek bed were hides, held down by stones. Others were pegged to the ground in the encampment or stretched upon wicker frames, women scraping them clean. She urged the horse forward and into the enclosure to where the odour of burning wood filled the early air. No smoke came from the cabins, but a fire crumbled to ash before her, a haze of blue ribboning upwards. Men sat outside the lodges, smoking, watching the women work. No one except one old man paid any attention to her. He wore only skins, his greying braids hung on either side of his face and around his head was a band sporting one feather. Grinning with a toothless mouth, he raised his hand in a customary sign of greeting, the empty palm turned up to indicate that he held no weapon and Annie answered using the same gesture. A naked child with a dirty face and sucking its thumb watched her from the lodge door.

Further along, a group of young men sat on the decking drinking beer from bottles. Muraco rose as she approached and her breath caught at the sight of him. He was easily as tall as her brother and head and shoulders taller than her own five feet four inches. His face was chiselled with the same proud lines as his ancestors, broad cheekbones, high forehead and eyes as dark as the midnight sky.

She swung from the saddle and they faced each other.

'Annie,' he said at last. 'What do you want?' The air around him carried the familiar scent of wood-smoke and home-cured buckskin.

'My mother's going to take me away. I have to stay with you. My life is yours now.' As she spoke her throat ached and her breath came fast and short. She felt his eyes, heavy with denial, burning into her soul.

The other youths grew silent, waiting.

'No, you do not belong.' His words twisted in the air before her.

'I do. You saved my life.' She wound the reins around her hands. 'I belong to you.'

'You belong to another world. You must go back.'

She watched his Adam's apple bob in his throat and his eyes slip past hers.

'No.' Her vision grew blurry.

'I have a woman. We will have a child in the spring.' He turned from her and disappeared into the lodge. The other young men continued to watch her. One whispered something she did not understand. His companion nodded and gave a mocking twist to his mouth that might have been amusement.

Her stomach churned and as if she held the sun in her mouth, her face and throat grew hot.

Minola, the girl betrothed to Muraco, the girl Annie was sure he did not love, rose from where she had been crouched over a skin and she stared at Annie. The sun washed over the girl's face and her eyes narrowed. Her lips parted, but not in a smile of friendship. The mound of her belly pushed out the front of her loose shift. Two other girls joined her. Girls Annie had once played with in the dirt. They all stared at Annie and for the first time, she felt she did not belong here.

'What is wrong?' she asked, looking from one to the other.

'He is not your man,' said Minola.

Hot with shame, Annie turned her horse, dug her heels into his flanks and drove him through the sour, damp wind that had sprung from nowhere and rode back to the cabin slowly. How dare they treat her like this, as if she was never one of them? How dare Muraco reject her so completely? At that moment she hated him.

She dismounted and struggled to remove the saddle with one arm. Suddenly her mother was behind her, taking the saddle from her hand, easing it off.

'Thank you,' said Annie.

'Why didn't you ask for help?'

Annie shrugged her shoulders.

'Go inside. I'll rub him down.' Smoky snorted and stroked his nose against Isa's shoulder.

Inside, Annie poured herself a coffee and lowered herself onto the couch, tucking her legs beneath her, her heart so heavy it seemed to weigh her down. She couldn't forget the way Muraco's eyes had burned with the heat of stoked coal. He should have stood up for her, told his father he would choose his own woman. Yet there was no denying that Minola was carrying a child, his child. The rejection was too much to bear.

'Mam,' she said as Isa entered. 'I want to come with you to Raumsey.'

Chapter Thirty-Four

Isa

The decision had been made. The passages were booked, the kist packed ready for the departure. Martha had already left to stay with the sister she hadn't seen in years. Isa sat in the swing on the decking under the light of a lantern, suffering both sorrow at leaving and excitement at the thought of once again seeing her homeland. Life on the prairies had been hard, but there had been moments of wonder, too. She could still hear her dad's laughter as he and Paddy played a game of gin rummy, hear Paddy's deep, beautiful voice as he sang a sad lament for his homeland accompanied by Davie on the mouth organ, hear her mother's scolding and the children's chuckles.

She thought of the girls who had made bandages beside her, how they would laugh and joke in the face of worry and dwindling supplies. Many, like her, had had to move away in order to survive.

A shadow moved behind a tree. An upright shadow too small to be a bear or a moose. Isa reached for the gun from the wall. She remembered the early years in the shack when she had been afraid to go outside alone. Those days were gone. She stood up. 'Who's there?' she shouted levelling the gun. 'Come out or I'll shoot.' To prove she was sincere, she fired a warning shot high into the trees.

'Don't shoot, please don't shoot.' A slight figure scuttled from the cover of the cottonwoods.

'Come here, into the light,' called Isa, squinting over the gun sights.

His shoulders were hunched and he was shaking. Isa stared. The lad had Negroid features, but his tight curly hair was soft brown and his skin the colour of milky coffee. She had not seen a black person since she had come to Canada. She lowered the rifle and stepped forward, grabbing him by the shoulder.

'I didn't mean no harm.' He looked scared.

'I'm not going to hurt you. Who are you?'

'Wynono. Means first born son.'

'Come on.' She led him into the cabin and studied him in the light from the lamp, surprised to see that his eyes were green. 'Are you hungry?'

He nodded.

'Why are you watching my house?'

'Papa Pierre watches over you. He sometimes comes at night to check you are safe. But he is ill. I think it is his time to die. He said I must go to the white people.'

'Pierre? Pierre watches my house? He's ill? I have to go to him.' She had not seen Pierre since McArthy had taken over the ranch.

'No. He wants to be alone. He sent me away.'

Isa set the boy down at the table and served him corn bread and syrup.

'Now Wynono, where did you grow up?'

'In the mission school. They called me Adam. That means first born too, but I don't go there any more.'

'Do ye know where ye came from?'

'I was coughed up by a fire mountain.' Wynono stared at her. 'Are you my earth mother?'

'No, what makes you think that?'

Papa Pierre told me my earth mother was a white woman. He worries for you. I thought...'

'Where is this mission school?' Isa wondered why he had not been seen around before.

'Many days to the west. They sent me there to live with the nuns. But now I am a man.' He puffed out his chest. 'I must learn to be a brave.'

So the child didn't die. Sarah and Paddy had been lying. Isa knelt down before the boy. 'What else did Pierre say?'

'That it was time my mother met me.'

'I'm not your mother, Wynono, but I think I know who is. You can stay here tonight. Tomorrow I have someone I want you to meet.'

The next morning she rode over to Paddy's shack. She meant to confront Sarah, shame her into taking responsibility for the son she had rejected and at the same time wondering what she would do if Sarah refused to acknowledge him. She couldn't go back to Scotland and leave him here alone.

Sarah was in the yard, feeding chickens. When she saw Isa, she ran forward and enfolded her in a hug. 'I heard about you leaving. I'm so sorry things have turned out this way for you.' she said.

Isa drew away. 'The way things are, it's for the best. Sarah, come inside, there's something I have to tell you.'

Sarah's brows screwed down. 'What? Tell me now.'

Isa breathed in. There was no easy way. 'Your son's looking for you.'

Sarah stepped backwards and gave a sharp laugh. Anger flashed in her eyes. 'How can you be so cruel? My son's dead.'

'You really didn't know? You really thought he had died?'

'You mean…' Sarah's face drained of colour. 'What are you saying?'

'His name is Wynono, or Adam, if you prefer. He's been staying with the nuns in some mission school out west.'

'I can't believe this.' Sarah's hands shot to her mouth. 'It can't be true.' Her fingers remained across her lips as she staggered against the wall and sank to her knees. 'For years I blamed myself for his death. Are you sure?'

'I'm sure. He has your green eyes.' Isa walked over and knelt beside her. 'He didn't die.'

Sarah raised her face to the sky. 'Oh, Blessed Virgin, you have answered my prayers.' Her hands folded together, tears flowed down her cheeks. After a few minutes like that, she turned around and threw her arms around Isa, crying and shaking against her shoulder.

'It's fine,' said Isa eventually when Sarah's howls turned into sniffles. 'You have him back where he belongs.'

'Does…does he hate me?'

'No. He doesn't hate you.'

'Where is he? I want to see him.' Sarah wiped at her nose, her eyes.

Wynono was helping Dan to load Isa's belongings into the cart. She hadn't given Dan any explanations this morning, just that she would tell him later.

'Could you leave us, Dan,' said Isa.

He glanced from her to Sarah, and he went back into the cabin leaving the two women alone with Wynono.

Sarah leapt from her horse, ran to the boy and crouched before him. For a long minute she studied him, then reached tentative fingers to touch his cheek. 'Oh my dear Mother of God,' she whispered. 'I thought you were dead.'

Surprise crossed the child's face as she pulled him to her in an embrace, once more dissolving into tears. Finally, she released him, but with her hands still on his shoulders, said, 'Has Pierre been watching over you all this time?'

Wynono nodded. 'But it is his time to die. He sent me to the white homesteads. Are you my mother?'

'Yes I am.' She laughed and hugged him again. 'Now you must come home with me and meet your grandfather.'

'Come on, Ma,' said Dan, as he and Annie came out of the cabin. 'We need to get moving if we're going to catch that train.'

'I'm ready,' said Isa.

'Thank you so much,' Sarah said. 'I can never explain what this means to me.' She grabbed Wynono's hand again and pressed it to her chest as if she would never let him go.

Isa watched Sarah and her son ride away, happy for them, but sad for Pierre, sad she didn't get to say goodbye, but the natives had their own customs and he would prefer it this way.

She glanced back at the cabin that held so many memories, her heart once more looking forward to an unknown future.

Chapter Thirty-Five

Isa

Since she had arrived in Britain, fragments of a hundred memories Isa had tucked away had grown, falling into her mind like gentle rain. She had watched her daughter's depression deepen since they left Edmonton. None of the new things she saw lifted her spirits, and she had silently stared from the train window, watching the same landscape day after day. Isa tried to engage her in conversation, but she answered in grunts or single words. On the ship she leaned on the rail, tears leaving trails down her cheeks, until Isa despaired.

When then they arrived in Wick, Isa took her to the harbour, disappointed that so few of the herring fleet were in port. They walked past the rows of herring gutters, women whose hands moved so fast it was impossible to see what the knife did, their fingers wrapped with rags, their aprons spotted with silver scales.

She felt the memories shift like shadows in her heart, the smell of the sea, of fish, of old rope, the clattering of the cooper's hammer as he built his barrels, the yammering of the gulls hungry for fish guts, the singing of the gutters and packers, the bark of a dog, the grind of wheels against the cobbles, the clomp of horses' hooves and a new sound, the idling of a motor engine.

'Is it like this in Raumsey?' Annie asked.

'No, lass, nothing like this.' She took her daughter's arm, glad that something had prompted a response, a flutter of interest, and she led her away towards the main part of town where they would catch a bus for Huna, where the boat for the islands would pick them up.

***

More than an hour later, they stood on the shore watching the yole bobbing towards them in the misty cold sunlight.

'Are we going to sail on that?' Annie asked. 'It's just like the one Dad made.' Her voice caught and she fell silent.

'I've sailed in such a boat on many a rough sea,' said Isa, remembering.

The yole pulled up alongside the slipway used for launching the lifeboat, which was housed in a large stone structure higher up the shore.

'How are we going to get down?' asked Annie.

'We have to climb down the slip. I hated it when I lived here, always scared I'd fall through the spaces.'

They watched as the small craft bobbed under a soft grey sky. A bearded fisherman leapt ashore, ran up to Isa and swept her into his arms, spinning her around.

Catching her breath, she pushed him to arm's length and looked full into his round, simple face and pale eyes. 'Larry,' she breathed, recognising the soft lad.

'Behave yourself, man,' said his companion as he joined them and picked up Isa's kist, 'and help the lasgies into the boat. We're that glad to see ye, lass. It's been far too long. And is this yer bairn? My, she's right bonny.'

Annie's lip twitched with the beginning of a smile that failed to materialise. She showed no fear as she walked down the slip and accepted Larry's help to board the boat.

It was a calm crossing. Porpoises raced each other in the distance, seabirds floated on the surface of the water, gulls swooped and cried, a large liner appeared in the distance.

'You'll be glad to be home, then?' said Larry, his smile broad, his eyes never leaving Isa's face making her squirm.

'I am,' she said, and stared ahead at the blue hills of Flotta, the mounds of the Skerries, the sharp rise of Swona, the green fields of Stroma. And in the far distance the outline of mainland Orkney, a place she would have to visit soon.

The sharp tang of the sea, the yelps of the gulls, the sudden splash of spray were all full of their own special memories. As the cliffs of Raumsey grew higher and the land grew greener, she could see figures on the quayside. The sun appeared from behind a cloud and sent sparkles across the water, welcoming her home. She didn't speak again, her throat was too full, her eyes too misty. Annie, too, had fallen silent.

The boat rose and fell on the swell. One of the men threw out the line of corks that served as buffers, daft Larry threw the rope ashore and a young lad on the quay grabbed it and secured it to an iron ring embedded in the concrete. Larry sprang ashore and offered Isa his hand.

On the pier stood a painfully-slim girl holding the reins of a heavy workhorse yoked to a cart. The girl's fine, pale hair rose in the wind. As they approached, the oval face became clearer and sharply reminded Isa of someone else.

Isa walked towards her. 'Bel,' she said, recognising her at once. 'You are so like your mam.'

Bel's large, almond-shaped eyes, deep grey, fringed by dark lashes, enhanced an otherwise plain face and made her almost beautiful. A flash of pain caused the smile to fade a fraction, then she seemed to catch herself. 'Aunt Isa, I'm right glad to see ye.'

Isa opened her arms and Bel moved awkwardly into them, her body stiff and unresponsive to Isa's embrace. Isa stepped back. She had forgotten how reserved the islanders could be.

'It'll be grand having ye here,' said Bel. Her voice was soft, a little breathless.

Annie said nothing, but reached up and patted the horse's nose. The animal stamped his feet and tossed his head.

'Jimmy, that's my brother, says Teddy's the craziest Clydesdale ever to put a foot on Raumsey.' Bel gave a laugh. 'The men'll put your luggage on the cart, come on, sit up front with me.'

As the cart trundled along the road, Isa remained silent, bittersweet memories crowding her head. Her gaze flicked over the countryside to where the low, stone-built houses of the crofters and fishermen, with their assortment of outbuildings and thatched roofs, spread haphazardly over both green fields and heather-clad moors. Beyond that, the ribbon of rip-tide split the expanse of the Pentland Firth. As they approached the kirk, she turned to Bel. 'Who's the minister here now?' she asked.

'Donald Charleston came back after the war,' said Bel.

'Is…is he alone?' she asked, surprised. Chrissie had written to say he had left. Isa had not expected him to be here.

Bel shrugged. 'The schoolteacher told us he'd met a woman in France and they were going to be wed. She's not come with him though, unless she's coming later.'

Isa felt a twinge of disappointment which surprised her. For many years he had been no more than a soft shadow on her heart.

They passed the schoolhouse and then Lottie's wee shop, the young folk who habitually gathered outside, sadly missing. 'Is Lottie still in the shop?' she asked.

'Na, her daughter runs it now. Lottie's still alive, though she seldom gets out of bed.'

They reached the brow of the hill, and there, before her, beside the shore, was Scartongarth, a low, long thatched-roof cottage welded between rock and moor, just like she remembered it, defiant of the strong winds which swept from the Pentland Firth.

They climbed from the cart and Bel looped the horse's reins over a fence post.

'I've thought of this place so often.' Isa rested her hand on the rough grey stonework warmed by the sun. 'And the scent of burning peat – my goodness I missed that.'

Her gaze swept across the fields to the high rise and the row of similar houses along the road; to the lighthouse sitting on the most northerly outcrop and to the beach at the far side of Scartongarth. The air was full. The cry of the seagulls, the waft of salt in the breeze, and most of all, the memory of Davie. It was almost as if he would walk from the cottage at any minute, looking as he did back then; his hair as blond as ever, tumbling over his forehead, his smile lop-sided, sleeves rolled up, arms muscular and weather-beaten brown.

Along the base of the wall, daffodils waved in the breeze. Back in northern Alberta, the seeds would not yet have germinated. 'I missed the sea, the sounds – the smells,' Isa said. A black and white collie came to greet them, tail wagging and he pushed his nose into her hand.

'Come in. I told Jimmy to have the kettle on. He's staying to help out until ye get settled. Ye'll be dying for that cup o' tea.'

'Aye, I am. They only drink coffee in Canada.'

'Why do you keep your cows and sheep on ropes?' Annie's voice cut across.

'We tether them,' said Bel, 'for we've no' the money to buy fencing. Ye'll not find much changed,' she said to Isa, and headed through the narrow, wood-lined hallway bulging with coats on hooks, and into the kitchen.

A young man sat at the white-wood table, his fingers clasped around a tin mug. Rising, he rubbed his hands down the sides of his dungarees. His hair was blond and his eyes like the sea under a clear sky. He looked so like Davie at that age that time stood still. 'Jimmy!' Isa edged between the kitchen chairs and the box bed, which was set in the recess of the wall. To go anywhere in this room she would have to go sideways; no different from the small shack where she had first lived, back in Canada.

'You're so like your dad,' she whispered, thinking of Davie's older brother, Jamsie, who died at sea not long after his son was born.

Jimmy's cheeks coloured. A polite smile flickered across his face.

'Och Jimmy, yer face is like a boiled lobster,' Bel said with a laugh. 'Get out and tend to the horse and bring in yer aunt's kist.'

The boy glared at her.

'Ah – stop teasing him,' said Isa.

'She never stops,' he said, but his eyes were on Annie.

'Come on.' Bel indicated to her cousin. 'I'll show ye where ye're to sleep.'

'Sure,' said Annie, and followed Bel past the box-bed and up stairs so steep they were almost vertical.

'I'll see ye in a wee while,' said Jimmy, as he went to the door. He turned to Isa and smiled again, this time a wide, easy smile, showing his perfect teeth.

'I believe you've a lass on the mainland,' said Isa.

'Aye. Bessie MacGuire. She's a herring gutter. I'm learning to be a cooper – making the barrels – you know?'

'Yes, I know.'

He glanced again at Annie's retreating back before making his exit.

Bel returned and began to bustle about making the tea. 'I baked bannocks especially. Do ye bake in Canada? Of course ye do.'

A black cat jumped on the table, stretched, sat and began to lick his paws.

Bel shooed the cat away, lifted a pan of potatoes from the hearth and set it on top of the range.

Isa studied the room. The once-white walls and beams were now smoke-blackened, the plates and cups on the dresser chipped and cracked, the screen across the bed recess faded and so ripe that a sharp glance would tear it apart. Broken many years ago, the globe on the oil lamp, mended with paste and brown paper, had never been replaced. The floor was black flagstone. The smell was of peats, wax polish, baking and fish. Light from the small window shafted into the room. Isa suddenly felt more at home than she had done since the day she left Raumsey, as if she'd never been gone.

The door opened and Jimmy treated Isa to another one of his heart-breaking smiles. 'I've put yer things in the ben-end. I'll get back to the net.' He pulled a chair to the side of the fireplace where a half-knitted net hung from a hook in the wall. Picking up the large wooden needle, which he loaded with twine, he began to work.

Bel raised her eyebrows at Isa. 'Ye'll be sleeping in the parlour. Ye'll mind where to go.'

'Aye, like yesterday.'

The parlour. The best room. Everything was almost the same as when Davie had first brought her to Raumsey, but sadder. Damp streaks stained the once-fresh, lime-washed walls. A rag rug lay between a pair of winged chairs of cracked brown leather.

Two windows graced the room, the floral curtains faded to almost white. In front of one sat a Singer sewing machine, a plain wooden dresser with china cups hanging on hooks almost covered the back wall, and in the fireplace, kindling sticks crackled as young flames licked along their sides. By the other window was a table, on which a potted geranium once sat. Now, a large jug of warm water, an enamel basin, a threadbare towel, a well-used bar of carbolic soap and a newish face-flannel was in its place. Realising Jimmie must have brought them in and lit the fire, she thought of her own boy, Dan. How she wished the two lads could have met. Slowly, she stripped and began to wash away the grime of the journey.

'Come on now, sit down,' called Bel from the other room.

Newspapers lay over the table, and a pan of potatoes, still in their skins, was emptied into the middle.

'I'm sorry we've no better fare to offer ye. The larder's all but bare,' Bel said quietly. 'Since the war it's difficult to get food.'

'Sometimes we snare a rabbit, or shoot some auks, but nothing seemed to go right the day,' said Jimmy.

Bel dumped two fish for each person onto the newspaper and set the pan down on the hearth.

'Don't you use plates?' Annie's eyes opened wide.

'This way we can wrap up the bones and skin when we've finished; there's little use in dirtying plates when we'd have to go to the well for water to wash them,' replied Bel. 'And, anyway, when a plate breaks, we've no the means to replace it.'

Jimmy looked at her. 'The only way to eat salt herring is with yer fingers,' he said.

'Annie's never eaten salt herring,' explained Isa.

Annie stared at the meal before her. Her hands remained on her lap. Bel waited until everyone was seated, heads bowed, before she spoke. 'For what we are about to receive may the Lord make us thankful,'

A murmur of amens trickled through the kitchen.

'Oh my goodness, this brings back memories,' said Isa into the ensuing silence.

'Ye may have been used to better things in Canada,' said Jimmy, apologetically.

'In the beginning we had nothing. And Scartongarth is a palace compared to the shack where we first lived.'

Isa's breath caught. Davie should be here now. Being here was his dream. In her mind's eye she could see him, leaning over the table, shovelling herring into his mouth, contented at last. She shook her head, banishing the vision.

Until now, Isa had not fully realised the toll the war had taken on an already impoverished people. 'The fish is fine. Salt herring is one of the things I missed. But us being here – we're bound to make it harder for you.'

'We'll make do. Chrissie used to swear the good Lord got his story of the loaves and fishes from the women of Raumsey,' said Bel.

Isa tore a lump of flesh from the herring and put it in her mouth. It had been so long since she had eaten fish like this. She looked at Annie who was delicately picking the fine hair-like bones from between her teeth.

For the next few minutes, the only sounds were the chewing of food; the ticking of the clock, the crackle of the fire, the purring of the cat lying on the armchair and the crying of seabirds outside.

'Did ye manage to get all the lambs marked, Jimmy?' asked Bel, wiping her hands on her apron.

'Aye. They're good and fat an' all.' Jimmy sucked his fingers. 'Another six ewes are ready to give birth. Ye should get a fine price for them this year. The horse needs gelding though. He's daft.'

'I'd like to ride him.' Annie gazed across the table, straight into Jimmy's eyes.

Isa noticed the gaze and the way Jimmy's face flushed.

'We don't ride him. He's a work horse,' he mumbled.

'Surely I can sometimes? I'm good with horses – tell them, Mam.'

'Aye, she's too good with horses for a girl. Nothing ladylike about our Annie. I hope Bel can teach her some feminine ways.'

At this Jimmy laughed out loud, jumped and yelped. 'Dare

kick me again and …' He punched Bel's arm, but not too hard.

'I'll clean up and make the tea.' Bel sprung to her feet, the smile still on her face.

'We'll go round the croft later.' She bent close to her cousin's ear.

'I'll wash my hands.' Annie held her food-stained fingers away from her clothes.

After the remains of the herring were thrown outside to the cats and the fire banked up, Annie turned to Bel. 'Can you show me round now?'

'Bel'll be tired and it's dark,' Isa answered for her.

'I'm no' tired at all,' said Bel, 'and the moon's full.'

Isa yawned and stretched. The heat from the stove and the comfort of finally being home made her mellow. 'So you plan to run Scartongarth yourself, Bel?' she asked.

Bel's face pinked. 'I can manage. I'll no give it up. Aren't ye staying?'

'Probably,' said Isa. Canada was so far away, another life, and Dan was the only reason she might want to return.

'I hope ye do stay. Come on, Annie,' said Bel. 'We'll go and explore.'

Once at the shore, Bel and Annie gazed across a road of moon-cast silver stretching to the skerries and beyond. The slow beam of the lighthouse intermittently swept across the water and over the land to disappear on the far side of the island. Long rollers of blue white surf rattled over the shingle. The mourning of the seals filled the air.

'What is that weird noise?' asked Annie.

'Only the selkies.'

'Selkies. My dad told me about them.'

With her arms above her head, Annie lay back. 'Let's sleep here. Get a blanket and sleep under the stars.' She wondered whether Muraco was looking up at those same stars, if he was sorry now she'd gone. Maybe she should have stayed in Canada. Tried harder to win his love.

'It'll probably rain before morning.' Bel settled beside her and stared up at the sky – a navy dome pierced with glittering pinpricks of light. 'I sometimes do this. Lie here under the stars and listen to the sea. Makes me feel closer to my mam. I used to open the window in her room on a moonlit night. She liked that.'

'Do you think they'll meet up, your mam and my dad?' asked Annie. 'Do you believe there's a heaven? I don't know.'

'Of course,' said Bel. 'Don't blaspheme!'

'I feel closer to my dad here than I did back in Canada.' And she did. This was the place he longed to come back to, the place his spirit would fly to if it could.

The girls lay in silence for a while, absorbing the smells and sounds around them.

'We'd better go home.' Bel sat up. 'Or I will fall asleep.'

They scrambled to their feet and Annie grasped Bel's hand in hers. 'Your brother is nice looking,' she said. 'He looks like my dad.'

'Like mine too, I'm told. I don't remember him and they never found his body. His boat sank, you see. Ye're lucky, ye knew yer dad and ye've still got yer ma.'

Annie stared at her. She had not felt lucky. Her dad lost in the war, the boy she was in love with rejecting her. And yet Bel had less, and she was facing the work and responsibility of running a farm alone. She suddenly felt humble, a new sensation. Her throat tightened making it difficult to swallow.

'Just a minute.' Bel stepped onto the beach and walked along staring at the ground. Now and again she bent down and picked something up, dropping it in her pinny which she held up using it like a sack.

'What are you doing?' shouted Annie.

'Coal. It falls from ships and sometimes gets washed up on the beach. Burns longer than the peat.' When the moon disappeared behind a cloud, she returned to Annie's side. 'Let's go,' she said.

In the silent house they found Isa snoring in the winged chair, head back, mouth open. With a start she sat upright and for a moment gawped wildly around. 'Ach, I had a dream. I was away in the past.' Her voice trembled. Hands smoothed back rumpled hair and she took a deep breath.

'Ye get away to bed, ye look done in,' said Bel as she dumped her apron full of coal in the scuttle. She lifted a sieve full of the day's tea leaves and dampened down the fire.

'Good night, Mam.' Annie bent to plant a kiss on her mother's cheek, smiling at Isa's expression of surprise.

Chapter Thirty-Six

Isa

The following day, rays of early sunshine danced through the small-paned window of Scartongarth, highlighting dust motes and waking Isa from a deep slumber. With the chaff mattress moulded comfortably around her body, she stretched and yawned. Outside, a cockerel crowed, a cow lowed softly, and the smell of frying ham floated from the room next door. She sat up and swung her legs over the wooden sides of the box bed, jumping slightly when her feet hit the cold solidity of the flagstone floor.

In the kitchen she found Bel leaning over the stove. 'Ah, there ye are,' she said. 'I've made porridge and brought in some smoked ham. There's not much left of last year's pig, and when it's gone we'll only have salt herring and porridge. We've often got nothing else for weeks. But the day, ye'll have a good breakfast.'

'Is Annie still asleep?' asked Isa.

'No. She got up early and went to the mainland with Jimmy. He had something to do, he said. They won't be back till night.'

'How are you all faring, really?' asked Isa, pleased. She saw this spark between Annie and her cousin as a positive thing. Anything that would help her get over Muraco.

'Doing a lot better than folk in the towns, if ye can believe the papers.' Bel slapped another slice of ham in the pan where it sizzled and spat. 'We're lucky. We can take fish from the sea when the weather is fair enough, and once the crops grow we'll have vegetables, and we cut our fuel from the hill.' She shrugged. 'True there's things we need that we can't get, but we don't have the money anyway. Jimmy sends back what he can, but if he weds he'll need every penny. There's jobs with the herring, but the wages are poor, and the workers have to follow the shoals, up to

Shetland, down to Yarmouth.' She stopped and cleared her throat. 'Somehow I don't think he'll be marrying Bessie MacGuire.' She smiled, a mere stretching of the mouth but her eyes laughed. 'Things'll get better now the war's over.' Her limp hair was tied back with a piece of rag, her skin pallid, her body painfully thin, yet there was a calmness about the girl, a quiet optimism, an acceptance, even gratitude, for what she saw as her greater fortune.

Isa ate porridge without milk followed by the slice of ham and a wedge of bread washed down by weak tea. So Bel had sensed it too, something developing between Annie and Jimmy. She rose and collected the plates. She would bring in water and wash up, while she took stock of how best to help Bel and Scartongarth. Then there were a few visits she had to make, starting with the most important.

Outside, in the weak morning sunshine, she picked a bunch of daffodils, still wet with dew. Sounds of the island flowed around her as she adjusted her shawl across her shoulders, and set out.

***

Standing before an overgrown grave, a small numbered iron marker the only indication that her best friend and child lay beneath, Isa raised her face to the sky. Above her head the seagulls shrieked and circled. Beyond the cemetery wall, the sea sucked and dashed against the shore. A sun with little heat fought its way through the mists. Somewhere in the distance a foghorn moaned.

She spoke with her heart to Jessie and her baby, her child who had never seen the light of day, hoping that, in some other dimension, they would hear her. 'I've come back. I've never forgotten you.' She knelt down and began to pull the weeds from the grave. That done, she laid the bunch of flowers on the slight mound and stepped away, blinking at tears. A collared dove circled her head, then landed on the marker, seemingly unafraid. The sun glinted on the bird's pale plumage. He spread his wings and rose, slowly, Isa thought, as if sending her the message that her words had been acknowledged. And as she watched the dove climb higher and ride the thermals, she sensed the burn of another's eyes upon her.

Turning, she raised her head and she saw him. Dressed in black, he stood inside the gate, silent and still, the shape, the stance, the wide-brimmed hat that only he wore. She swallowed and there was nothing in her mouth to swallow.

'Isa.' He stepped towards her until they were no more than a few feet apart. His eyes were as dark and soft as she remembered, distant memories shifting within them. She became aware of a gaunt face, deep trenches from nose to mouth. He held out a hand and she moved forward to grasp it.

'Donald,' she said. 'I heard you were back.' The hand was dry and smooth and warm.

'I returned after the war.' His eyes never left hers. 'I hope you are well.'

'Yes, thank you. Very well.' She swallowed again. 'I heard you married. I'm happy for you.' Realising her hand was still in his, she pulled it away and closed her fingers around the warmth.

He cleared his throat. 'I met her in France. I thought we had a life together.'

'What happened?'

He shifted his position. 'Shall I escort you home?'

She nodded and as one they turned, not touching but not too far apart, and walked to the gate. He reached out easing it back on its rusty hinges, and she passed through, carefully, holding up her skirt a little, watching her feet on the tufts of grass. Nevertheless, she stumbled and he caught her arm.

'Come back to the manse. Have some tea.' His grip was firm and the warmth of his hand, his long, strong fingers, pressed through her clothes.

'Yes,' she said, wanting to recapture the old closeness, yet knowing the dangers of it, for in the last few moments her heart had begun to speed up and forgotten sensations had prickled her skin. There was a time when she could have loved this man.

Maybe she should have loved this man. If she had, her life would have been very different. Now an unexpected awkwardness that stiffened her tongue came from nowhere.

'She died.' He answered the question she'd been scared to pursue and his voice was dry and broken. A darkness passed across his face, like the ghost of a memory too painful to acknowledge. 'They called it Spanish Flu.'

'I'm so sorry.' She had heard of this lethal flu. Many young Canadians had also succumbed to it. 'I understand the pain of losing someone you love.'

They walked in silence for a while.

The manse had not changed since she had seen it last. A large iron kettle vibrated on the range, steam billowing from its spout, the wall behind, once white, was now smoke-stained. The mahogany table with four chairs still sat by the far wall, a dresser with blue and white china against the other. The green and yellow linoleum, the pattern now missing in places, still covered the floor, the rag rug, faded and sad on top. No curtains covered the window. Donald removed his hat. His hair was no longer as black as a raven's wing. He took the tea-caddy from where it sat on the mantelpiece next to the pendulum clock with the carved wood. 'Have a seat, Isa,' he said.

'I didn't think you'd return after the war and all.'

'The islands called me back. Do you still take milk? I'm afraid there's no sugar. Impossible to get.'

'That's fine.'

He poured the tea, not speaking until he sat across from her. Then, studying his cup, he took a deep breath. 'Margaret was from Paisley. She went home before me. I was offered a parish in Glasgow. We were going to make a life there.' He stared into his cup. 'By the time I returned she had gone. Damn bug killed as many as the Boche. After that, I no longer wanted to remain in the city. There's something about this place … it draws a body back.'

'It does.'

He turned his cup slowly around with his long sensitive fingers, smooth and uncallused, a few black hairs sprouting along the backs of them, clean, short nails. 'And you?' he asked, raising his eyes.

'It's not been easy, Canada. But then life never has been.'

'You're glad you went?'

'Yes. I've seen so many new things.'

'Are you happy?' His words dropped into the ensuing silence.

'Have you heard about Davie?' she said, to the dark liquid in her cup. A scattering of white bubbles clung to surface.

'I have. I'm sorry. I know how much you loved him.'

'For a long time I didn't believe it, thought he'd come back, like he did before,' she said. 'Was it bad, in France?'

'I was behind the lines, but the things I saw… these images never leave a man. I've questioned my faith ever since.'

'But you're still a minister.'

'I'm trained for nothing else.' He rose and walked to the window then turned and looked at her. 'You look well, Isa. Are you home for good?'

Home? Was this island still home or was her heart in the rolling prairies of Canada? She wasn't sure. She rose to her feet. 'I need to rest, to find myself again.' She shrugged. 'Who knows what the future'll bring.'

'Who indeed.' Donald sat down again.

'I still dream about him, that he'll come back, even after all this time. It's funny, you hang onto the impossible hope that somehow… that they'd made a mistake, that he might be here.' She spoke hurriedly, as if the spectre of Davie would dispel the quickening of her heart brought about by the Reverend.

'I know, I know what you mean.' He reached over and set a hand on her arm.

She covered his hand with hers and raised her eyes to meet his soft brown ones and in that instant she felt the pull of the old attraction and it scared her. Davie was still there in her heart, in her mind, and a wave of guilt rose and threatened. She rose abruptly. 'I'd better go,' she said. 'It's been good… seeing you again. There's somewhere else I have to be. A walk Davie and I promised ourselves we'd take again one day. Now I've got to do it for both of us.' She lowered her head, afraid to look at him, needing to get away lest she met those eyes again and read in them the same battle she fought within herself.

He reached the door before she did and held it open. She smiled and thanked him, stepping out into the misty air. She would walk the road to nowhere alone, but in her mind, Davie, the old Davie, the one she had fallen in love with, would be holding her hand. And she had to do it now, today, to somehow banish the self-reproach she felt over the pull of another man.

Chapter Thirty-Seven

Isa

Isa stood on the edge of the moor listening to the mournful call of the foghorn. Since she had left the manse, clouds had rolled from the north and lay over Orkney in a heavy, grey blanket. From the gathering mist, the sun slanted through, giving it an eerie brightness. She stepped onto the road of clay and stone. 'I'm here Davie,' she said. 'Back on the road to nowhere.' She closed her eyes and imagined his hand in hers and tried to speak to him with her soul. As she walked forward, the cries of the birds became muted and a haze fell against her skin with a prickly coldness. When she looked again, the fog was a thick, angry grey enfolding her like a damp, odourless smoke. There was no way of knowing how far she had walked or whether she was anywhere near the edge of the cliff.

Turning around, she tried to get her bearings, but it had only resulted in her losing all sense of direction. The sea sounded louder, nearer, and she realised how foolish she had been to try to walk the road on a day like this. Should she wait here until the air was clear again? But sometimes fogs could last for days. She called out for help, but her voice faded among the muffled calls of the seabirds and the waves that exploded against the shore, ever closer. It was unlikely anyone would come this way where it was all moor and heather, especially today. The cawing of the seabirds, the cry of the curlew, the twittering of smaller birds, the sigh of the wind, the thunder of the ocean, were hushed and for a time she seemed trapped in a place she didn't recognise. Even the strange, silent ribbons of mist that folded around her, the rutted road beneath her feet, the purple heather, moss- covered rocks to the sides of the road and the green of the few straggling blades of grass that fought for purchase through the untrodden clay, pastel shades through the veil of softness, were detached and unreal. She thought she heard her name, subdued in the distance, disembodied by the fog. Turning around she was about to step towards the sound, when out of the mist, directly to her left a figure took shape. Thank God, someone was here. She recognised the outline and the tilt of his head. 'Jimmy?' she said, partly relieved, partly disturbed.

Because it couldn't be Jimmy, he had left on the boat at the first light of day. 'Who are you,' she called. The figure didn't speak but stretched out his hand.

As she grabbed the hand, felt the solidity of it, a warmth filled her body, blotting out the chill in the air. She stepped towards him no longer apprehensive. Her breath stilled and as she stood face to face with him, she knew who it was. The mist blurred his features, but there was no mistaking the mole on the right cheek, the lop-sided grin, the chipped tooth.

'Davie,' she whispered. 'I knew I'd find you here.' She followed his lead, happy to go with him, wherever he took her. Then he stopped and turned her around. The hand slipped from hers. She felt a soft breath on her cheek. The shape began to fade.

'No.' She reached for a hand that was no longer solid. And she heard his voice in her head, as clear as if he had spoken aloud. 'Let me go now, Isa. Set me free. Get on with your life.' The warmth receded. The chill returned to the air. 'Davie,' she cried. The cool breeze hit her cheeks, dried the ribbons of tears she had not been aware she had been crying. The mist cleared, drifting away like spent smoke. The sounds, seabirds, waves crashing on the rocks below, the distant drone of a foghorn all returned. As the haze lifted, she realised how near she had been to the edge. Another step forward and she would have hurtled into oblivion.

She sank to her knees and touched the rough heather where there was a depression, a place still bearing the mark of another's feet. Shaken by what had just happened, she couldn't walk away, not yet.

'Isa, Isa.' She heard the distant voice. By now the sun had fought its way back to supremacy, but it was low in the sky. She stood up. Donald was striding towards her, Bel behind him. 'For God's sake, we were so worried. You were last seen going towards the lost cove and then the fog came in. Didn't you hear us shouting? It'll be dark soon.'

'No. I didn't hear.' She still hadn't fully come back to herself. Further words wouldn't form.

He grabbed her hands. 'You're frozen. Come on, I'll take you home.'

'How long have I been gone?'

'You left the manse four hours ago. Bel came looking for you.'

Wordlessly they walked together. Down the road to nowhere. She looked back once and fancied she saw a form in the remaining mist, lifting his arm in a wave before disappearing forever.

'Yes, Donald, please take me home,' she whispered, filled with the sudden acceptance that this was where she was meant to be.